SECRET
BROTHER

Virginia Andrews® Books

The Dollanganger Family Series
Flowers in the Attic
Petals on the Wind
If There Be Thorns
Seeds of Yesterday
Garden of Shadows
Christopher's Diary: Secrets of
        Foxworth
Christopher's Diary: Echoes of
        Dollanganger
Secret Brother

The Casteel Family Series
Heaven
Dark Angel
Fallen Hearts
Gates of Paradise
Web of Dreams

The Cutler Family Series
Dawn
Secrets of the Morning
Twilight's Child
Midnight Whispers
Darkest Hour

The Landry Family Series
Ruby
Pearl in the Mist
All That Glitters
Hidden Jewel
Tarnished Gold

The Logan Family Series
Melody
Heart Song
Unfinished Symphony
Music in the Night
Olivia

The Orphans Miniseries
Butterfly
Crystal
Brooke
Raven
Runaways

The Wildflowers Miniseries
Misty
Star
Jade
Cat
Into the Garden

The Hudson Family Series
Rain
Lightning Strikes
Eye of the Storm
The End of the Rainbow

The Shooting Stars Series
Cinnamon
Ice
Rose
Honey
Falling Stars

Virginia ANDREWS

SECRET BROTHER

**SIMON &
SCHUSTER**

London · New York · Sydney · Toronto · New Delhi

A CBS COMPANY

First published in Great Britain by Simon & Schuster UK Ltd, 2015
This paperback published, 2016
A CBS COMPANY

1 3 5 7 9 10 8 6 4 2

Simon & Schuster UK Ltd
1st Floor
222 Gray's Inn Road
London WC1X 8HB

www.simonandschuster.co.uk

Simon & Schuster Australia, Sydney
Simon & Schuster India, New Delhi

A CIP catalogue record for this book
is available from the British Library

Paperback ISBN: 978-1-4711-4270-3
eBook ISBN: 978-1-4711-4271-0

Printed and bound by CPI Group (UK) Ltd, Croydon, CR0 4YY

MIX
Paper from
responsible sources
FSC
www.fsc.org   FSC® C020471

Simon & Schuster UK Ltd are committed to sourcing paper that
is made from wood grown in sustainable forests and support the Forest
Stewardship Council, the leading international forest certification organisation.
Our books displaying the FSC logo are printed on FSC certified paper.

For Gene Andrews,
who so wanted to keep his sister's work alive

SECRET BROTHER

Prologue

I don't think I shall ever forget the exact time and what I was doing that second Saturday in October. It wasn't unusual for us to have an Indian summer in Virginia, but this one promised to linger longer than the others we had enjoyed. Six days before, we'd had an early frost, so no one had expected this change in weather. Of course, I was only sixteen years old then and hadn't experienced many weather surprises compared with someone like my grandfather, who was fifty-eight, or our nanny, Myra Potter, who was sixty-three. The lush green leaves on the trees and bushes on our property and other estates nearby hadn't even begun to show a hint of the brown and yellow to come. People, especially young people like me, returned to wearing short skirts, short-sleeved blouses, and shorts on weekends and after school. The day before, our grandfather had decided to reheat our pool for us to use on the weekend.

I remember the weather that day so well because it seemed out of place for what was to come. There should have been more clouds, even an overcast, dreary sky. If it had rained, what happened wouldn't have happened, because my nine-year-old brother, Willie, wouldn't have been out there. That day, the nice weather was our bad luck.

I was up in my room, sitting at my desk and gazing out the windows that faced the front of my grandfather's estate. It was one of those lazy mornings when, instead of flying about, birds would rather sit on branches and doze to the point where they looked stuffed. Even clouds were reluctant to move. As usual by ten thirty on a Saturday, I was on the phone with my newest best friend, Lila Stewart, planning what we would do with our afternoon and evening. I was thinking of having a pool party.

The Stewarts had recently bought the property next to my grandfather's on the north side. Because our property and theirs were at least ten acres each, their house wasn't exactly close by. If either of us walked to the other's front gate, it would take about fifteen minutes. Lila's house, like ours, had a long driveway with gates, so you had to buzz the house to get in and start up the drive. If we rode our bikes, we could do it in about five minutes.

Willie was very anxious to master riding his new bike on the street outside our grandfather's estate. Grandpa Arnold had bought it for him on his last birthday, but he had been permitted to ride it off the property only twice before, both times short rides accompanied by me. There was an immaculately kept sidewalk outside our property on both sides of the street. Nevertheless, people hardly ever walked there, which made it all right for Willie to ride his bike safely. At least, that was what we all believed.

I had my bedroom windows open to catch any cool breeze. Myra demanded that the maids air out the house at least twice a week even in cooler weather, and her orders were followed as if my grandfather himself had issued them. Lila was running through a list of boys and girls I should invite to a pool party when, suddenly, I heard what was clearly a man screaming for help. Jimmy Wilson, who was the head of Grandpa's maintenance staff, came out of nowhere and ran down the driveway to the front gate, where I could now see a man in a dark blue suit and tie grasping the bars like someone locked in a prison cell, shaking them as he screamed. I remember he had cotton-white hair, the strands of which looked like they were dancing every time he shook the gate.

Jimmy opened the gate. The man spoke to him, gesturing wildly, and Jimmy turned and shouted to one of his staff to call an ambulance. Then he charged out with the stranger and turned right, disappearing behind the tall, thick evergreen hedges that lined Grandpa's estate. They were so thick they seemed as impenetrable as the Berlin Wall.

"Something's wrong," I told Lila, interrupting her ramble. "Something bad just happened."

"Where?"

"Right in front of our property. I'll call you back," I said. I hung up before she could utter a syllable, threw on my sneakers, and rushed out of my room and down the stairs. I had no reason to suspect something involving any of us, but my heart was thumping so hard it felt like it might burst out of my chest. Grandpa was outside the house, charging down the driveway, too. I shouted to him, but if he heard me, he didn't want to pause to turn, so I started after him.

When I stepped out of the front door and turned right, I saw the red pickup truck on the sidewalk. The driver was bent over the steering wheel, his head down. And lying on the sidewalk was my brother, Willie. Beside him, barely able to sit up, was Myra. Only a short while ago, she had agreed to let Willie ride his bike slowly beside her while she walked up to the Qwik Shop. Grandpa, Jimmy, and the stranger, whose car was stopped on the street, were beside Myra and my brother. I saw his new bicycle against the fence and the hedge, bent into an L shape.

"Grandpa! Is Willie all right?" I called.

He was kneeling beside Willie. "Stay back, Clara Sue," he said, putting his right palm up like a traffic cop. "Just stay back."

I stopped and stood there, frozen by the uncharacteristic hysteria in his voice. Grandpa was talking to Jimmy, who was holding Willie's head off the sidewalk. The stranger was kneeling down now and talking to Myra. Then he rose and went to the truck and started yelling at the driver, who didn't so much as lift his head from the steering wheel. A siren sounded, and I looked behind me as paramedics leaped out of a truck and hurried to Willie's side. Carefully, they lifted him and put him on a stretcher.

There was blood running down the left side of his face, and his eyes were shut. I gasped. My throat closed so quickly I couldn't swallow. My whole body was shaking now.

"Grandpa!" I shouted, unable to contain myself any longer. He didn't turn to me. He just held up his hand again and watched as they brought out a second stretcher and helped Myra onto it. She glanced back at me and closed her eyes; she was obviously in great pain. Moments later, they had both been loaded into the ambulance, and the doors were being closed. Grandpa and Jimmy Wilson hurried past me.

"Come on, Clara Sue," Grandpa called, and I ran behind them. All the maids and grounds people were out front looking at us. As Jimmy started to explain to them what had happened, I got into Grandpa's car. He drove away so quickly I was still struggling to close my door. We sped down the driveway, turned, and shot off after the ambulance, neither of us speaking. By now, there were two police cars at the scene of the accident, and the pickup driver was sitting up and talking to the officers. I looked back and then looked forward again as we made the turn, the tires squealing. I had never seen my grandfather drive like this.

"Is Willie going to be all right, Grandpa?"

"I don't know," he said.

All my life, when something bad happened or seemed about to happen, adults would tell me everything would be all right. Grandpa Arnold was never someone who would lie to me or to Willie, but he certainly would do and say everything he could to make us less afraid and less sad. He tried to do this after our parents were killed in a boating accident off Naples, Italy, four years ago while we were staying with him and Grandma Arnold. It was supposed to be a very special holiday for our parents.

"That man was drunk," Grandpa suddenly muttered, his teeth clenched. I never knew any other man who had a face as strong and as hard as Grandpa Arnold's. It looked chiseled in granite. Anger didn't make him redden; it made him gray. When he turned his hazel eyes on people, they could feel the rage so quickly that it would start them stuttering.

"Drunk?"

"Drunk! This early in the day. Drunk!"

"What did he do?"

"Do? He lost control and hit the sidewalk, and instead of pressing down on his brakes, he apparently pressed down on his accelerator and smashed right into them. He couldn't have done worse if he had done it on purpose," he said.

"Who is he?" I asked. I just wanted to keep on talking and keep my grandfather talking. My heart was still beating so hard I was sure that if we were silent, he would hear it, too.

"Some rover. Jimmy says he works for Mackingberry's Plumbing Supply," he said, and took a breath. "He'll never work again if I have any say about it," he added. "And that company won't do another thing in any home around here if he isn't immediately fired."

Grandpa drove so fast that we were only about a

minute behind the ambulance. The paramedics and hospital personnel had just carried Willie and Myra into the emergency room. Grandpa pulled into a no-parking zone and bolted out, barely closing his door. I ran to keep up with him. He looked like he would walk right through the emergency room's glass door rather than take a second to open it. In fact, when he did open it, he nearly ripped it off its hinges. The sight of him, his face flushed, his eyes still burning with rage, stopped people talking.

There were many other adults in the lobby, mostly patients waiting to be seen because of minor accidents or illnesses and some of their relatives or friends. We could see there was a great deal of commotion in the hallways. My grandfather was never one to stand and wait for someone to ask if he needed help. He marched in past the admittance nurse despite her protests, and I followed in his wake.

When one of the doctors stepped out of an examination room and looked at us, Grandpa simply said, "It's my grandson."

"Which one?" the doctor replied.

"What?"

"We have two little boys just brought here. One brought by ambulance and one left here by some idi—" He sucked in what he was going to say when he saw me standing there, too. "Someone who left without giving any information."

"My grandson was in the ambulance. He was hit by a drunk driver, and his nanny was also brought in."

"Okay. Just give me a minute to check on your

grandson. The nanny is in the far right exam room," he said, and went down the hallway to a room where some doctors and nurses had gathered.

When a fancy-looking machine was wheeled into that room, Grandpa looked at me gravely. "Stay here," he ordered, and walked ahead, even though the doctor had told him to wait. He looked into the busy room and then took a step in.

I waited, holding my breath. No one seemed to notice me. I think everyone was simply too busy to waste time inquiring about my presence. Nurses rushed by. Another doctor appeared, this one in a suit and tie but with a stethoscope around his neck. He went quickly into the room Grandpa had entered. I had no idea how much time had passed; to me, every second was a minute, and every minute was an hour. When I finally saw my grandpa emerge, he had his head down, and the doctor in the suit was standing beside him, talking to him softly, his hand on Grandpa's shoulder. The doctor stepped away, but Grandpa remained there, looking down.

I know anyone would think I made it up, but there was the same high whistle I'd heard when I was told our parents had been killed in a freak boating accident thousands of miles away on a blue sea with the sun shining and excitement and laughter whirling about them. It was as if all the air was being sucked away from me. I could hear it seeping off—the whistling sound. I heard the same sound years later, when Grandpa returned from the hospital to tell me Grandma Arnold had died from a massive stroke. I didn't think I was breathing either time, and I didn't think I was breathing now.

When Grandpa Arnold finally lifted his head and looked at me, I knew: Willie was gone.

But I would soon learn in a strange way that he would not be gone forever.

1

Just like when I heard the terrible news about our parents and the news years later about Grandma Arnold, I didn't cry immediately. Something inside me wouldn't let me understand what I was being told. The words kept floating away like tiny bubbles caught in a breeze and bursting before I could bring them back. Nevertheless, I knew. Deep inside, where I went to find love and hope, where my best dreams were on shelves waiting to be plucked like books and opened during sleep, a cold, dark realization boiled and threatened to spill over and into every part of me. I fought it back, but it was oozing in everywhere. Despite my effort, I knew I would be soaked in the dark sadness in moments and be unable to deny it.

We had retreated to the lobby in silence, Grandpa resting his large right hand over the back of my neck and me clutching his shirt with my left hand. We needed to keep touching each other, comforting each other.

We sat on a pair of chairs facing the exam rooms. He held my hand and stared ahead; his face had never been more stone-cold. Somehow all the noise around us seemed to disappear. It was as if I had lost my hearing. We were waiting now to learn about Myra. She was having an X-ray. Would she die, too? Suddenly, my grandfather looked up. The doctor he had first spoken to was out in the hallway again, this time talking to a nurse. Grandpa rose and walked over to him. I couldn't imagine what he was asking, but whatever he said interested the doctor. Moments later, he was leading my grandfather back toward the exam rooms. I saw them disappear around a turn. Maybe Grandpa was finding out about Myra, I thought.

I certainly didn't move. I didn't know if I could even stand. My legs were still trembling. I was afraid to look at anyone, even though I could feel people staring at me. Had they heard about Willie? Were they waiting to see me crumple up in uncontrollable sobs? Some looked terrified themselves.

For some reason, I began to wonder what my friends were doing at that moment. Were they planning lunch, watching television, talking on the phone and giggling about silly things? What were Willie's teachers doing? Was anyone else anywhere thinking about him? How tense was the atmosphere around my grandfather's estate? Was anyone laughing or smiling? Were they all holding their breath, waiting for a phone call? Did someone call the hospital?

I looked at a little boy who was holding his mother's hand and had the thumb of his other hand in his mouth while he bounced against her. Most people avoided looking at one another. A look might bring bad news. Everyone's eyes appeared shut down, as if they had turned to glass.

Finally, my grandfather came back around the corner, obviously having realized he had left me sitting there. He beckoned to me, and I hurried to join him. Maybe what we were told was untrue. Maybe Willie didn't die after all.

"They're putting a cast on Myra's left arm. It was broken, and she has three fractured ribs, a few bruises, and a slight concussion. It'll be a while," he said.

Our concern was no surprise. Myra was part of our family now. Grandpa Arnold and Grandma Arnold's housekeeper of many, many years, Myra Potter became our nanny the day the terrible news arrived from Italy. She had also been a nanny for my mother and her younger brother, Uncle Bobby. A business associate of my grandpa had recommended Myra, who had been working for a Lord and Lady Willowsby in London. She came to America to work for my grandparents after Lady Willowsby died and Lord Willowsby moved to Cornwall to live with his son and daughter-in-law. Neither Grandpa nor I could imagine the house without Myra. She treated everything in it like her personal possessions and was, according to my grandmother, "more protective of it and your grandfather than I am."

Myra was barely five feet four but had gray-black eyes that seemed to double in size when something annoyed or angered her. She had a habitually stern, lean face on which smiles seemed to bubble up from some hidden place whenever she permitted them. I knew the maids my grandparents had were terrified of her, most not lasting more than six months; the grounds people, the gardeners, the pool man, and anyone who came onto the property to do any work made sure she was happy with what they were doing, even before my grandpa had a look at it.

"But what about Willie?" I asked now, hoping to hear a different answer.

He shook his head. His face was still ashen gray. When my grandfather was deeply upset about something, he seemed to close up every part of himself through which rage or emotion could escape. The steam built up inside him and made him look like he might explode. The only indication came in the way his hands and lips trembled slightly. Anyone who didn't know him well would probably not notice or would notice when it was already too late, especially if he was angry. And then, as Grandma Arnold used to say, "Pity the fool who got his engine started!"

Grandpa Arnold was always the biggest and strongest man ever in my eyes. He was six feet three and at least two hundred twenty pounds of mostly muscle. He owned one of the country's biggest trucking companies. He had been a truck driver himself, and because he hated the long days and weeks of separation from his family, he had put together his own company and built it to where it was today. It was even on the stock market now. I had no idea how rich my grandfather was, but to most people who knew us, he seemed to be the richest man in the country. Wherever he went, people practically leaped out of their skin to please him.

He put his hand on my shoulder and then brought me into a hug. We stood while nurses and doctors went around us as if we weren't there, which made it feel more like a dream.

"Come on," he said when he stopped hugging me. He took my hand and led me down the hallway to another room, where a nurse and a doctor were working around a very small boy. Despite the scary-looking equipment and the wires and tubes attached to him, the boy didn't even whimper. He didn't cry, and unlike any other child his age, he didn't call for his mother. He was lying there with his cerulean-blue eyes wide open but looking as glassy and frozen as the eyes of the worried people in the lobby. His pale face seemed to be fading into the milk-white pillow, making his flaxen hair more golden. I thought he looked like a fallen cherub, an angel who had floated onto the hospital bed and was still too stunned to speak.

"What happened to him?" I asked, sniffing back my tears.

"They say he was poisoned."

"Poisoned?"

"With arsenic. They don't know if it was done deliberately or if he was eating something meant for rats."

I grimaced. I was close to heaving up everything I had eaten all day as it was.

I looked up at my grandfather and saw something

different in his face. The terror, anger, and horrible sadness that had been there from the moment we had driven off to the hospital suddenly were gone, replaced with this look of awe and interest I had seen in him only occasionally since my parents' deaths and especially since Grandma Arnold's death. He always seemed impervious. It was as if he had a new limit to how deeply he would smile or laugh and how tightly he would hold on to the reins of his curiosity, especially about people. He did what he had to do for Willie and me, but I couldn't help feeling that he was moving about robotically most of the time and that we were very dependent on Myra to care for us.

I waited a moment to see what my grandfather wanted to do now. Why were we looking in on this little boy, anyway? How would this make what happened to Willie different? There was nothing that could make it any better.

"He was dumped off here," my grandfather said, his eyes still fixed on the doctor's and nurse's actions around the boy.

"Dumped?"

He looked down at me. "Like the doctor told us when we first arrived, someone brought him to the hospital and left him without giving any names or telling what had happened. They said it all happened so quickly that no one could do anything about it."

"But what does this have to do with Willie and Myra, Grandpa?" I asked.

He looked at me but didn't answer. He just looked

back at the boy and nodded as if he heard someone else speaking.

"Where is Willie?" I asked, sounding annoyed. Why didn't my grandfather take us to Willie's room instead of this little boy's room? Was he already too terrible to look at, his face distorted by death? I wanted so much to look at him, to touch him. Maybe if he knew I was there beside him, he would come back to life. I still believed in miracles.

"They're taking him to a place in the hospital where he'll be until the funeral director comes for him," he said. Now his voice was thinner, his throat closing up. His lips and hands had that tremble again.

The word "funeral" brought an intense rush of heat to my face. I felt like a blowup of myself losing air quickly. My body seemed to be sinking in on me, collapsing.

"No," I said, very softly at first, so softly that Grandpa Arnold didn't hear it. It was all taking a firmer grip on me. "No," I repeated, much louder. He turned and looked down at me. He was still holding my hand. "No!" I screamed, squatting and pounding my hands against the sides of my body. "No! Willie can't be dead! No!" The nurse and the doctor stopped working on the little boy and looked at us.

Grandpa reached down and lifted me up. I realized immediately how silly that looked, a sixteen-year-old girl picked up like a child half her age. To him, it was just the natural thing to do, I guess. For a moment, that took my breath away.

"Shh," Grandpa said, stroking my hair. He lowered me and then he turned with me, and we headed back to the lobby to wait for more news about Myra.

I slumped over in the chair, my head resting against my grandfather's shoulder. My emotional outburst had drained me of so much energy that I didn't think I'd be able to get up on my own when the nurse came to tell us Myra was ready and we could take her home.

I felt Grandpa's strong arm around my waist. He literally lifted me to my feet. Then he took my hand. The nurse, a woman who reminded me a little of my mother, put her hand on my shoulder and stroked my hair.

"I'm so sorry about your brother," she said. "You have to be strong for everyone now," she added.

Strong for everyone? What language was she speaking? How could I be strong for anyone now?

Tears were frozen in my eyes. I thought I probably looked as comatose as that little boy with the flaxen hair. We walked back toward the exam rooms, where the nurse led us to another exit. Myra was in a wheelchair. An attendant was waiting to wheel her out to Grandpa's car.

"She's under some pain sedation," the nurse told Grandpa.

Myra looked terrible. Her eyes were mostly closed, there was a bad bruise on her left cheekbone, and her mouth hung open as if her jaw had been broken, too. The cast looked twice as big as her arm. Looking like this, a way I had never seen her, she seemed much older to me and quite small. I wondered if she knew about Willie. As the attendant wheeled her out with the nurse accompanying them, I tugged on my grandfather's hand.

"Does she know about Willie?" I asked.

"Not yet. Wait," he said. He rushed forward to help get her into the backseat.

The nurse gave my grandfather a prescription for Myra's pain medication. He took it and then nodded for me to get into the backseat with her.

"Don't let her fall over or anything, Clara Sue," he said. "She's very unsteady."

Myra groaned and opened her eyes more. "Where's Willie?" she asked me.

I didn't have to say anything. My tears did all the talking.

She uttered a horrible moan, and I put my arm around her and buried my forehead against her shoulder. Grandpa drove off silently. I lifted my head quickly and looked back at the hospital.

We're leaving Willie, I thought. *We're leaving Willie*.

Myra cried softly in my arms as we rode back to Grandpa's estate. Everyone came out when we drove through the opened gate. Jimmy Wilson practically lunged at the car, and when Myra was helped out, he lifted her in his arms like a baby to carry her into the house. I could see that everyone had heard the news and had been crying. The person who would take it almost worse than me was our cook, Faith Richards. No one spoiled or loved Willie more than she did.

Myra was becoming more alert. "Put me down. I can walk!" she cried. "Don't be ridiculous."

Jimmy paused in the doorway and let her down gently. She glared at him, trying to be angry about it, but anyone could see she was putting it on.

"Got your bed all ready, Myra," My Faith said. My grandmother used to refer to her as "My Faith," and Willie and I did, too.

"I don't need to go to bed."

"You need to go to bed and rest," Grandpa said sternly. "No back talk," he added.

It was the first thing he had said since we left the hospital. Myra took one look at him and started to head to her room, which was next to My Faith's at the rear of the estate. Then she paused and looked at me. I knew she didn't want to be alone, and neither did I. I hurried to her side, and we walked through the wide hallway, past the kitchen and into the corridor that led to her and My Faith's rooms, all the while not looking at anyone. I was afraid that if I looked at any of them, I would burst into hysterical sobs.

I was in that place between a nightmare and just waking up, this time fighting against waking up but also pushing away the nightmare. How could all of this be happening to us? How could any of it be?

We lived in Prescott, Virginia, a community thirty-five miles northeast of Charlottesville that seemed to have been created for millionaires. If you were a resident, it was easy to believe you lived in a protective bubble, which made any misfortune happening to you or your neighbors seem impossible to imagine and even more impossible to accept.

"Fires don't kill rich people, you know, love," I heard Myra tell My Faith one day. "Rich people don't go to jail. Rich people always get saved in the best hospitals by the most expensive and brilliant doctors. Maybe rich people go to a higher class of heaven when they die, and they're always supposed to die in their sleep without pain, don't you know. That's how Lady Willowsby died. She closed her eyes, began dreaming of biscuits and tea, and never woke up."

Myra concluded, "That's in the English Constitution, passed in the House of Lords."

"Ain't that the truth, I bet," My Faith said. They both laughed about it. I was always intrigued by how easily My Faith could get Myra to laugh. Except for Grandma Arnold and Willie, she was the only one who could.

It didn't surprise me that I recalled that conversation so vividly at this moment. I had heard this before my parents died, and I believed we were all so special that nothing bad would ever happen to us. Everything seemed to tell us so.

Before our parents' fatal boat accident, whenever Willie and I visited our grandparents, we went to bed soaking in security and comfort. New toys and bedding with images of our favorite cartoon characters were always in the immaculately kept rooms reserved for us. There were children's movie characters on the wallpaper. There were dressers and mirrors so shiny and clean that they looked just bought, carpets as soft as marshmallow, and curtains on the windows that looked like the curtains that opened and closed on theater stages. When Myra opened our curtains in the morning, we half-expected to hear music and see a puppet show.

Willie and I imagined we were sleeping in a castle surrounded by high walls and moats, a place that evil creatures and nightmares could only glance at from the outside and then move on from, never daring to enter and certainly never daring to touch us while we were here. Maybe it was all my doing. I wove stories of knights and dragons, always ending with us being protected. It was important to me to be sure my little brother was safe and unafraid, especially after our parents died.

But it was easy to create such a fairy-tale view of the world when you lived in Prescott. Almost every house was a custom-built estate with a minimum of five acres, walled in with elaborate stonework, tall hedges, or high scrolled gates. When we drove by one, I would tell Willie it belonged to this prince or that princess. Some estates had small ponds on the property, and all had foliage and fountains, flowers and bushes designed by well-known landscape artists.

In late spring, there was a competition to determine who had the most beautiful grounds, and the prize was awarded at the public park. People dressed up as if they were going to the Kentucky Derby, and there were musicians and singers, and a few dignitaries made speeches that Myra said were so full of soap that if we looked closely, we'd see bubbles coming out of their mouths. It helped keep us interested.

Willie loved attending, even when he was barely three. There were balloons and ice cream, and circulating among the attendees were magicians, jugglers, and clowns. Myra said it was Prescott's version of Covent Garden in London. People came from everywhere, even those who lived outside of Prescott. There was always an impressive trophy for the winner. Grandpa had won twice in the last seven years. We did have the most impressive estate.

Because of the restrictive zoning, there were no apartment buildings in Prescott, no middle-class people, and especially no low-income people sleeping here unless they were in-house employees. All the residents were influential business and political people who had, through those zoning ordinances, made it almost impossible for anyone of more moderate means to build a home and settle in this small community. They were also able to keep all fast-food restaurants out. The only businesses approved within Prescott's borders were convenience stores attached to gas stations. The restaurants in Prescott that "didn't raise the king's eyebrows," as Myra put it—and there were only six—were all gourmet places with chefs who graduated from prestigious culinary institutes. Some Prescott residents were investors in these restaurants.

Rich people and people splurging on dinners for special occasions came from miles away to the restaurants in Prescott. All of them were in beautiful buildings. The moment you walked into one, you knew you were going to spend a lot of money. They all had immaculately dressed waiters, waitresses, and busboys and maître d's who knew most of the customers by name.

What *wasn't* perfect in Prescott?

However, I had heard a joke about Prescott that a newspaper reporter told my grandpa at the landscape competition. The reporter joked that the nondenominational cemetery should be entered in the contest, too, because it truly was the most beautiful property within its boundaries.

"You do more for the dead here than you do for the living, Mr. Arnold," he said, "and you don't get paid for it until you join them."

He wasn't wrong. The burial sites and the monuments were as carefully designed and as full of restrictions as the houses of the living. Myra said that the trees and the landscaping, the fountains, and the chapel looked like they were all part of a property owned by the British royals or something: "You'd think you had entered Buckingham Palace." Graves were dug only at night so it appeared as if the ground simply had opened up with perfect proportions to gently accept the newly departed the following day. I even heard Myra tell My Faith that you practically needed an invitation from the Queen of England to get in.

But, as my grandpa and I now too painfully understood, being rich, even as rich as we were, really didn't bring us immunity from tragedy. Everyone knew that was true, but here in Prescott, there was an attempt to get back at death by creating a cemetery so elaborate and attractive that a popular joke outsiders supposedly cracked was "Prescott residents are dying to get in there."

Well, Willie hadn't been, I thought, *and neither were my parents or Grandma Arnold.*

My Faith and I sat with Myra until she fell asleep, and then My Faith rose quickly and said she had better get into the kitchen and start to prepare food.

"I'm not hungry. I'll never eat again," I said.

She smiled and stroked my hair. "You will, darlin'," she said. "But we'll need food 'cause all your grandpa's friends will be comin' to pay their respects as soon as . . . as they know," she said, and walked off, mumbling about how quickly bad news can travel.

I sat there. Of course, she was right. I remembered how it had been after the news about my parents spread and especially after Grandma Arnold died.

Our house, a Greek Revival mansion, had already been indelibly stained with the weight of those tragedies. Willie's death was just going to make it all darker, heavier. Already, to me, there were shadows now where once there had never been. I sat fixed and afraid to leave Myra's side, because I was sure the vast rooms would seem terribly empty to me, despite the elaborate and expensive furniture and large classical paintings on the walls. From now on, voices would always echo, footsteps would hang longer in the air, and in a few hours, people would be whispering. Maybe they would never stop whispering.

Myra moaned in her sleep. I looked at her, afraid to touch her because she had been so broken. Maybe she hurt all over now. I certainly did. I rose slowly, confused about where I should go and what I should do. I really was afraid of the house, afraid of how much smaller I would feel in it now that Willie was no longer to be with me. No matter how annoying he could be sometimes or how demanding of attention, he was still like the other half of me.

I left Myra's room and walked slowly back to the kitchen to look in on My Faith. She and one of the maids were working quickly to prepare dishes, sobbing and dabbing their eyes as they worked. They paused when they saw me, but I walked away. I didn't want to be any part of that or even admit to myself that it was going on.

I thought about calling Lila, but just the idea of doing something I would normally do sickened me. The world should have stopped. Clocks shouldn't be ticking. No one should be working or playing. Certainly, no one should be laughing, anywhere. I walked past the living room and paused at the doorway of Grandpa's office. He was behind his desk, his big, strong hands pressed against his temples, and he was leaning over and staring down at what I knew was his favorite picture of my mother. I couldn't speak. I just stood there. Finally, he looked up and realized I was there.

"How's Myra?" he asked.

"She's asleep."

"Good. I had Jimmy go for her medicine." He sat back. "I called your other grandmother," he said. He always called my father's mother my "other" grandmother. He never used her name, which was my name,

Sanders. She was Patricia Sanders. "She'll be coming with her sister Sally to the funeral. Seems that's the only time we ever see her, eh? Funerals," he said bitterly. "Death has had a feast here."

He had his hands clenched into fists. I didn't know what to say. He looked like he would spring up out of his chair and start swinging at anything and everything. I supposed the expression on my face softened him. He unclenched his fists and stood.

"My secretary, Mrs. Mallen, is on her way here. She'll oversee what has to be done. Your uncle Bobby is on his way, too," he said, but not with much enthusiasm.

I looked up with more interest. Both Willie and I loved Uncle Bobby, but Uncle Bobby and Grandpa had never really gotten along as well as a father and a son should, and I don't think it was only because Uncle Bobby didn't want anything to do with the business Grandpa had created.

In looks, he resembled my grandmother more than my grandfather. He was tall and lean, with much more diminutive facial features. He had my grandmother's sea-blue eyes and her more feminine high cheekbones. My grandfather was burly, muscular, someone who would be cast faster as a bartender or a bouncer than as the owner of a multimillion-dollar business, often wearing a suit and tie.

From what I knew, Uncle Bobby was always more interested in music and dramatics than in running a trucking company. His goal was to become a Broadway choreographer. Currently, he was on the road with a new production, a revival of *Anything Goes*. My grandfather had attended some of his performances in high school but never any in college and only went to a Broadway show my uncle was in because the whole family went. Grandma Arnold and my mother followed Uncle Bobby's career but were careful not to talk about it too much in front of Grandpa. Most of the time, he would simply get up and walk out of the room.

"You'd better go upstairs and rest a bit, Clara Sue," he said now, and started around his desk. "I'll look in on you later when I return."

"Where are you going, Grandpa?"

He paused. I could see he was debating what to say. "I have to go to the funeral parlor," he began. "Then I have to go back to the hospital."

"The hospital? Why, Grandpa? Are you going to see Willie? I want to go, too."

"I'm not going to see Willie," he said. "There's nothing more I can do for Willie."

"Then why are you going to the hospital? To pay a bill?"

He almost smiled. "No," he said. He pressed his lips together for a moment like someone who was trying to keep words locked in, and then he said the strangest thing. "Your grandmother wants me to go back."

"What?"

"For that other little boy," he said. He had the strangest expression on his face, stranger than I had ever seen. "She was with me the whole time. She comforted me about Willie, but she practically whispered in my ear when I looked in at that other little boy."

"The poisoned boy?"

"Yes, the poisoned boy."

"Why?"

"No one can be more traumatized than that little boy."

I could feel my eyelids narrow. Rage that had been subdued under wave after wave of heavier grief was rising up. Grandma Arnold used to say that Willie and I were the most traumatized that children could be because we had lost both our parents in a terrible accident.

"He has no one, Clara Sue," Grandpa said, seeing the confusion and anger in my face. "You remember how your grandmother felt about grief-stricken children. There's no one here for him—or anywhere, it seems. I'm going to make sure he gets the best medical treatment."

I knew in my heart of hearts that this act of kindness was something to be proud of my grandfather for doing, but it just didn't seem like the right time to be doing anything for anyone else. Everyone should be doing things for us now.

Suddenly, I hated this strange little boy. Why would anyone blame me? I wanted to devote all my energy and strength, and I wanted Grandpa to devote all of his, to mourning my brother. I didn't want anyone else stepping onto his stage, his final place in our lives. Willie deserved every moment of our attention. Worrying about someone else's child, especially that of someone who didn't care about his or her own child, denied my brother what he deserved. But I could see that Grandpa was determined to do this—and all because he believed my grandmother had appeared like a ghost and whispered in his ear?

Where did this come from? My grandfather wasn't a particularly spiritual man. He wasn't one to believe in miracles of any kind. It was my grandma Lucy who had persuaded him to go to church occasionally, and after she died, he wouldn't go to any church except for funerals and weddings. If anything, the tragedies in our lives had made him more cynical. He was always impatient with the minister's "stock talk," as he called it. "They don't know any more than we do about why this world is the way it is," he often mumbled, maybe more out of pain than anger.

I shook my head. Tears began to well up in my eyes. I thought I might start screaming again.

Suddenly, he put his hands on my shoulders and looked firmly into my tearful eyes. Then he took my right hand firmly into his left hand. He was gripping so tightly that he was on the verge of hurting me, but I was afraid to move.

"Do you realize, Clara Sue," Grandpa whispered, "that the same hour your brother passed, this little boy was brought to the emergency room to fight for his life? That means something." He repeated it in a whisper, looking past me as if he was talking about it with my dead grandmother. "That means something."

It would be a long time before it would mean anything remotely close to what he was suggesting to me.

The truth be told . . .

I never wanted it to.

2

I wasn't sure whether My Faith had told Grandpa what happened to me that first night after the accident. I had awoken and thought I couldn't breathe. It was like the room had closed in on me, all the walls had moved, and I was trapped inside a very small space. What had happened to Willie was truly more like a nightmare now. Who could blame me for hoping that was all it had been?

I got out of bed and walked softly out of my room, moving like someone walking in her sleep, and was actually surprised to find myself outside Willie's room. The door was closed, but I opened it and tiptoed in, hoping not to wake him. I saw that his bed was still unslept in, and I stood there staring at it for I don't know how long before I began to cry, the pain in my stomach so fierce that I had to squat and hold myself. Apparently, no one had heard me leave my room. I lay down on my right side and kept my body folded tightly, my hand over my mouth, and I fell asleep again right there on the floor.

My Faith discovered me much later. She had come up to my room because Myra had told her to see how I was. When she saw I wasn't there, she came immediately to Willie's room.

"Oh, you poor child," she said, kneeling down to embrace me when I opened my eyes. "You poor, poor child."

It had been a long time since I had cried in anyone else's arms, my head snugly against anyone's breast except my mother's and my grandmother's, but I couldn't help it. My Faith helped me up and back to my room. She tucked me in, and I fell asleep again. I remained in bed all the following morning, anticipating Grandpa Arnold coming in to see me, but he never did. My Faith told me he had gone to see about Willie's funeral and then to the hospital. I could see she didn't know why he would return to the hospital, but I knew. It was surely about that boy.

However, I had no idea what Grandpa Arnold was doing or planning for the poisoned boy. Apparently, because he had been brought in and left and was in a coma-like state, no one knew his name. I didn't want to think about him anymore. I didn't want to remember anything about him or the hospital. Despite my not finding Willie in his bed, my mind was still trying to reject reality. How many times can you survive your whole life being turned inside out and upside down? It had happened with my parents dying, it had happened when Grandma Arnold died, and now it was happening because of Willie's death. I was afraid to look at myself in the mirror, thinking I might see Death hovering over my shoulder and smiling gleefully, especially after what Grandpa had said in his office, and there were mirrors everywhere in this house, on almost every wall, most of them antiques. It didn't help to avoid looking left or right. You'd have to keep your eyes closed to escape your reflected image when you walked through the Arnold mansion.

Myra came up to see me, despite how hard it was for her to navigate the stairs. She was upset that I hadn't eaten any of my breakfast. I thought she might say something about my grandfather returning to the hospital, but all she talked about was how she and I had to be strong for him. I promised to eat something, mostly to please her, and then she went back down to her room to rest, but before she left, she assured me she wasn't going to take any more of those dreadful pain pills: "They should call them 'fog pills,' because that's where they put you."

When I had dressed and gone down, Myra was still trying to move about and see after the things that had to be done, despite her pain. I didn't want to trouble her with any more of my questions about Grandpa. She looked like just the mention of something related to what had happened would drop her to her knees. I couldn't stand watching all the preparation in anticipation of mourners. I returned to my room and finally decided to answer my phone when it rang. I knew it was Lila.

"Everyone I speak to is devastated," she began.

"I started out for your house twice and broke down twice and had to go back. I wouldn't have been any good to you."

"I understand."

"I can't believe Willie will not be there when I do come."

For a moment, I couldn't speak. I thought she knew it, knew the words were crashing together somewhere in the base of my throat.

"I want to be there for you," she said. "I really do!"

"Come this afternoon," I managed. "My uncle is arriving any moment."

"How is your grandfather?"

"I don't know. I haven't seen him yet today."

Now she was the one who was silent.

"He's doing what he has to do," I added, just to kill the silence.

"Everyone, especially my parents, feels terrible for him to have suffered so many losses. And for you, too, of course."

"Thank them," I said. I heard Uncle Bobby's footsteps on the stairway. "I've got to go. I think my uncle has arrived."

"I'll be there later," she said.

A few moments after I hung up, Uncle Bobby knocked on my door and then stepped in. I was sitting on my bed, my back against the pillows. He didn't say hello first. He just embraced me and held me for a long time. I laid my head on his shoulder and cried, and I could hear him fighting back his own tears.

"Hey, Clair de Lune," he said. Because my name was Clara Sue, he said he always thought of me when he heard that song and told me that thinking of me was like remembering the most beautiful moonlight.

"Hi," I managed in a voice so small and unrecognizable that I thought it came from someone else.

"Pretty unreal. All of it," he said. I nodded. "You're sure getting older. You look more and more like your mother," he continued.

"Do I?"

"Your dad was a handsome guy, but I think you're lucking out looking like my sister, with your auburn hair and those hazel eyes. You have her button nose. You're her height, too. What are you, five-six, seven?"

"Seven," I said.

"You should be on the cover of teen magazines. Of course, I'm a little biased about it."

He tried a smile, but he couldn't hold it long, and I couldn't help him by smiling back. He held on to my left foot and stared down at the bed. I thought Uncle Bobby had the kind of face that would never look old. He hadn't gained an ounce since I had last seen him. He still had that soft-looking light brown hair, always a little too long for Grandpa's taste, and those striking sea-blue eyes with eyelashes that I knew women envied. I was aware of how much he loved Willie, who, despite Grandpa's attitude about the career he was pursuing, enjoyed Uncle Bobby's singing and demonstrations of new dance steps. He even tried to imitate him. Uncle Bobby always brought interesting things to us whenever he did visit—dolls from countries he had gone to for shows, toys that were handmade, simple things like magic boxes and puzzles and hand-painted yo-yos.

"Is Grandpa back yet?" I asked.

"No."

"You know where he is and what he's doing?" I said. From the way he stared at me and from how his eyes were darkening, I realized he knew.

"I don't think he's himself right now. Who could blame him?"

"Do you know about the poisoned boy? Do you know all he's doing for this strange little boy?"

"Yes. He told me when I called him before I left St. Louis," he said.

"He told you? I don't understand, Uncle Bobby. Why is he so concerned about him? Why isn't he thinking more about Willie?"

"He's thinking about him, too. He's just . . . afraid," Uncle Bobby said. I couldn't imagine a stranger thing for him to have said.

"Afraid? Grandpa Arnold? Of what?"

"Of dying of sadness. You're the only one left whom he really loves."

"He loves you!"

"Only because he has to, because I'm his son, but it was really only you and Willie after my sister and my mother died. Now he's lost Willie, and he's like a ship that's taken on too much water. I think he's lost and confused, too, but today I realized he thinks that saving the little boy will help him save himself and continue to give him the strength he needs to be here for you, too."

I smirked. How could a stranger's future make any difference for me now?

"It's true, Clara Sue. He's mostly angry right now, and he wants to strike back at something. I know my dad. He doesn't accept defeat, even when it's staring him right in the face. He wants revenge."

"What do you mean? What revenge? On whom? The truck driver?"

"That, too, I'm sure, but mostly on death," he said. He looked away.

"I don't care. He should be here, with us, not at a hospital worrying about a boy he knows nothing about. You know he told me that Grandma told him to take care of the boy?"

Uncle Bobby looked up quickly. "He said that? He didn't tell me that."

"He said he could hear her whisper in his ear at the hospital."

He thought a moment, and then his lips did relax into a small smile. "Maybe my old man is softening up," he said. He didn't look upset about it anymore.

"People are calling and starting to come over, and he's not even here yet. His secretary, Mrs. Mallen, is here in his office handling Willie's funeral like it's a truck delivery. Myra won't tell Grandpa, but she told me she heard Mrs. Mallen arguing about prices with the funeral director."

"We'll take over for him and hold down the fort until he gets here," he said, rising. "Let's go down and have something to eat. I see My Faith has whipped up her wonderful fried chicken."

"Willie loved it the most."

"Well, we'll eat it for him, then. Come on, Clara Sue. Let's be together. I need you by my side," he said, holding out his hand. I knew he was saying that to make me feel better. The truth was, I needed him by my side and not vice versa.

I couldn't say no to him for anything anyway. I put on my shoes again and took his hand, and we walked out of my room and down the hallway, both of us deliberately avoiding looking into Willie's room. Some of Grandpa's friends and business associates had begun to arrive to comfort him. Uncle Bobby greeted them and simply told them Grandpa was out making the arrangements for Willie and would be back very soon. He did not mention the poisoned boy. We looked at each other after he spoke. He didn't have to tell me not to say anything about it. I wouldn't if I could.

Grandpa arrived a little while later and began to talk to people. He tried ordering Myra back to her room, but by now, she was almost herself again. With my brother killed and her arm in a cast and a sling, people were even more frightened of seeing those eyes turned in their direction. Both Grandpa and I knew she was far too stubborn to stay in her room recuperating. Despite what Grandpa had told her, it was easy to see that she still carried some guilt for what had happened to Willie. It was written across her wrinkled brow: if only she had not taken him with her. She would think about that all her life, even though no one would blame her.

When Lila arrived, I had never been so happy to see her. I wanted to get away from the older people, who were all looking at me with such pity in their eyes that I had to take deep breaths to keep from crying hysterically. Uncle Bobby tried to console me as much as possible, but people were pulling him away with their questions about his musical career and talking about anything they could that would avoid mentioning the horrible tragedy. It was almost as if they would stop when someone said something and then raise their eyebrows with curiosity, as if they were thinking, *Oh? Little Willie was killed?*

No wonder I took Lila's hand quickly and led her to the stairway so we could rush up to my room and close the door. I felt like I was rising out of a bigger and wider grave than the one Willie would be laid in tomorrow. The first thing we did in my room was hug each other.

"Don't cry," I warned her, pointing at her. "If you start, I won't stop."

She swallowed back her tears and nodded. Then, as we often did, we lay beside each other on my bed and looked up at the embossed circles swirling on my ceiling. She reached for my hand. I closed my eyes because I was getting dizzy.

"I can't imagine what you went through at the hospital," she began. "I thought about it all night and couldn't sleep. How hard it must have been to look at him."

"I never did," I said. "My grandfather did. He was in the room when they were trying to save Willie, but he didn't take me there to look at him." I paused, then opened my eyes and added, "He took me to see another little boy."

"What? What other boy?"

"The poisoned boy," I said, and then I told her some of what my grandfather had said and what I knew he was doing for the boy.

She was silent, thinking. "He probably doesn't know which way to turn or what to do," she finally concluded.

"That's what my uncle Bobby thinks, but my grandfather has always been in control of everything. He always knows what to do."

"Well, you can't be angry at him for trying to help someone."

"Now? Now he tries?"

"What else can he do for—" She stopped herself and turned away, but she didn't have to finish her sentence. It was one of those sentences that finish themselves, like a launched rocket you couldn't turn back.

"For Willie," I muttered. "What else could he do for him? He could think of nothing and no one else but him, just like me."

"I know. Did the boy say anything to him?"

"What difference does that make?" I snapped back at her.

She bit her upper lip as if to keep herself from saying another word.

"No. He didn't speak to anyone. He was in something they called a semicoma. He looked awake, but he also looked like he didn't see or hear a thing."

"Who poisoned him?"

"I don't care!" I got up and went to the window to look down at people coming and going. "My brother is dead," I said. As I looked down at the wide driveway and the area for cars to park, I could envision Willie down there trying so hard to master riding his bike. He had wanted to feel older and independent. He had wanted to be able to ride his bike to the convenience store, buy something, and come back. And he had wanted to go on longer rides with me as soon as Grandpa decided he was good enough.

"Everyone in our class is calling me to ask if they should come over to see you. Some said they'll come over with their parents today," Lila said. "Whoever can will come to the funeral."

When I didn't speak or turn from the window, she continued, "Everyone really likes you, Clara Sue. We know Aaron Podwell really does," she added, hoping to somehow slip back into one of our secret talks about the boys we thought were good-looking. No matter what homework we were doing together, our attention always rushed to the subject of boys now, boys in the twelfth grade, too, and the dreams we had about them. We hadn't been friends that long, but we were growing increasingly comfortable talking about our own sexual fantasies.

Lila was a little more physically mature than I was, with bigger breasts and a more dramatic rear end. She had started getting her period just after she was eleven. I didn't get mine until I was almost thirteen. For her, all this interest in sex and boys was much easier. She still had a mother who would talk to her about these things and an older sister, now a freshman in college. I really had only Myra, who, even though I loved her like a grandmother, was someone I felt embarrassed talking to about such things. She had described her own mother as "queen of the prudes." She said she wouldn't be caught dead buying herself sanitary pads. Myra's older sister, Kate, had to take care of it. I certainly wouldn't run to Myra with questions about boys and how far you should go or, more important, how you could stop.

"Aaron?" I said now. The moment I uttered his name, I felt guilty about even thinking of him. How could I care about anything as unimportant as good-looking boys? Tomorrow was my brother's funeral. Again, it irked me that if I felt this way, how could Grandpa be spending so much time on a stranger right now?

"Yes, he called me asking about you," Lila said, eager to get me on the topic. I couldn't blame her.

"That's nice, but I can't think about him. I should be talking to my grandfather about Willie's funeral," I said. "He probably is wondering why I'm not."

"Oh."

"Let's go back down. I can't run away from anything, even though I want to so much that it makes my head spin."

"I'm so sorry, Clara Sue. I'll be right beside you all the time. I told my parents I would stay home from school if you needed me the rest of the week."

"Thanks," I said.

She rose, and we hugged. Then I took her hand, and we returned to the living room, where people had gathered. Grandpa was sitting in his favorite chair and talking softly with some people. Uncle Bobby saw us and immediately crossed the room.

"Your other grandmother is arriving in an hour. I'm going to pick her and her sister up at the airport. Do you want to go along?" He looked at Lila. "Your friend could come with us if she would like."

I glanced at Lila. We were good friends now, but I could see that this was going to be a little too much sharing, asking her to be there to greet another grieving grandparent.

"That's all right," I replied for her. "Lila will come back later or see us tomorrow. Her parents are coming to the funeral."

"Oh, yes, for sure," she said eagerly.

"Has Grandpa given you any details about . . . ?" I asked Uncle Bobby. I couldn't finish the question, but it was obvious what it was.

"He said he would talk to us after I bring—"

"My other grandmother back, I know," I said, and he finally did smile. I turned to Lila. "Her name is Patricia Sanders, and her older sister's name is Sally. My grandfather likes to call them two peas in a pod."

Lila nodded. She still had both sets of grandparents. Her Thanksgivings and Christmases and birthdays would always be better than mine. A family was like a fortress, I thought. When one important member died, there was a big hole through which everything bad could have an easier time getting to you.

"Okay, let's go," Uncle Bobby said. "You want a ride home?" he asked Lila.

She looked at me. "No, I . . . rode my bike here," she said, as if riding a bike was forbidden not only to do but also to mention since Willie's accident.

"Okay. Clara Sue?"

I looked toward Grandpa to see if I should let him know I was going with Uncle Bobby, but he was too involved in a conversation to notice anyway. We all walked out together. Lila got onto her bike and started away. Uncle Bobby and I got into Grandpa's car, and we started for the airport.

"I guess there is one thing I should tell you, Clara Sue. My father just told me. Maybe it will make you feel better."

"What?" I asked, like anything could possibly make me feel better. The only thing would be his saying it was all a mistake. They were looking at the wrong boy in the hospital. Willie was fine.

"My father's hired a private detective to find out who the boy is, who dropped him off, and where his family is. Once that's known, he'll be returned to his family, I'm sure. Maybe he had been kidnapped or something."

I really tried not to be interested in him, but the idea that he had been kidnapped and then poisoned was enough to divert my attention for a while.

"He said that was why he went to the hospital, to meet with his detective and make sure all was being done medically for the boy."

"Oh."

"So I wouldn't think about it much anymore," he added, and smiled at me. "My father likes to take charge of everything around him. Believe me, I know. I bet you know that, too."

"Yes." I didn't want to admit it, but what he was telling me was making me feel better. Maybe now all we would think about was Willie.

My grandmother Sanders was crying as she got off the plane. Her sister dabbed at her eyes the same way. When they saw me, they only started to cry harder.

Uncle Bobby put his arm around my grandmother, and then both she and my great-aunt Sally hugged me to them.

It occurred to me that I was really the one they wanted to comfort the most. My parents weren't here to comfort me, and neither was Grandma Arnold. I was sure they couldn't envision themselves doing much to comfort my grandfather. He was never very close to either of them. If anything, I thought they were afraid of him.

Uncle Bobby took their overnight bags, and the four of us walked out to Grandpa's car. They sat in the back, and although I could tell they didn't want to, they asked questions about the accident. Then my grandmother said what I thought was an odd thing. She said, "I bet Myra wishes it was her instead."

"No," Uncle Bobby said softly. "She wishes it was no one."

Neither my grandmother nor my great-aunt said anything else about it. My great-aunt started asking me questions about school as if nothing terrible had happened. My answers were short, almost impolite. I was actually happy to get home, even though the house was full of people paying their respects and offering their sympathy, some bringing their sons and daughters, who looked even more uncomfortable than I did.

My grandmother Sanders and her sister went directly to speak with my grandfather and hug him. He looked very stiff about it, and moments later, Myra was taking up all their attention.

"I hope they're not making her relive the accident," Uncle Bobby told me.

We watched her lead them off to the guest bedrooms. I thought I might return to my own room, but my grandfather caught my attention.

He said something to Uncle Bobby, who came to me and said, "We're going to my father's office to talk about tomorrow."

He put his arm around me quickly, and we left the living room. Moments after we sat on the dark brown leather settee, Grandpa and Mrs. Mallen came into the office. My grandmother Sanders and my great-aunt Sally had been summoned. Grandpa went behind his desk, and Mrs. Mallen began to rattle off the details from a clipboard. I had my head down the whole time.

Mrs. Mallen was saying that my brother's little body was in a coffin in a funeral parlor. She described the coffin and how Willie was dressed. Dressed? I hadn't seen anyone go to his room to get his clothes. She mentioned that a story about the accident was in the *Prescott Gazette* and that the article also included details about the funeral. I looked up once at the door, imagining Willie popping his head in and laughing about the trick he had pulled on everyone. But that didn't happen. That or anything like it would never happen again.

We all did look up when Myra entered. I could see she was upset about not being included. Before she could say anything, my grandfather said, "I was hoping you went to take a bit of a rest, Myra."

"There'll be plenty of time to rest, unfortunately, Mr. Arnold," she replied. "Right now, I'm sure Clara Sue needs to know what to wear tomorrow." She looked at me.

I hadn't even given a thought to that. I was too afraid to let myself think about it. Of course, I needed Myra to help me decide. What if I wore the wrong thing and brought embarrassment to the family? I could have asked my grandmother Sanders to help, but I was actually closer to Myra. As Grandpa Arnold said, I'd seen my grandmother Sanders mostly only at funerals these past years. When she had realized that Willie and I would be brought up here, she seemed to drift away from us.

Right now, she sat quietly, dabbing her eyes and shaking her head. She held her sister's hand. Seeing them like that brought tears to my eyes.

"Okay," Grandpa said.

"We'll work on it after dinner, Clara Sue," Myra told me.

I didn't say anything, but I felt Uncle Bobby's

hand on my arm. We looked at each other, and he gave me a small, soft smile.

Mrs. Mallen recited the schedule for us all, and then she left to talk with Myra and My Faith about arrangements for tomorrow's after-the-funeral party, as she called it. Grandpa Arnold sat back. He was looking at us, but it was more like he was looking through us.

"Is there anything else you need done, Dad?" Uncle Bobby asked him.

"No, I don't think so, Bobby, thanks."

"Okay. I think I'll just go up to take a shower and get some rest."

"Sure."

"You should, too, Dad."

"I know."

Uncle Bobby rose and looked at me. "And so should you," he said.

"Yes," my other grandmother followed. "It's harder on young people than they think."

"I will," I promised, and watched Uncle Bobby leave. I always liked watching him move, even if it was only to cross a room. He seemed to float. Grandma Arnold used to call him her Fred Astaire. I had to watch some old movies to see exactly who that was, but once I did, I was fascinated. Even Willie would sit still and watch the dancing, both of us thinking about Uncle Bobby.

My grandmother Sanders and her sister followed him out, claiming they also needed a good rest, after the trip and all.

"If you need us to do anything . . ." my grandmother Sanders told my grandfather.

"Thank you, Patricia. Go rest," he told them. After they left, he turned to me. "Sorry I haven't been able to spend more time with you, Clara Sue," he said. "I'm glad Bobby's here. He's very fond of you."

"And I'm fond of him. Willie loved him."

Grandpa nodded. "The poisoned boy," he said.

"What about him?"

"I'm working on finding out where he came from and who's responsible for what happened to him."

"Hasn't he said anything?"

"No. I've had them bring in a neurologist to examine him. The boy seems unable to speak right now."

"Just like Willie," I said, my eyes burning. "Just like Willie. Only . . . unless you're Jesus, you can't do anything for him."

I left quickly and didn't look back.

3

Maybe my grandfather had said something about me to everyone, but as soon as I woke up in the morning, I was the center of attention. I could see it in the way everyone was looking at me, catering to me. It was more important for me to have something in my stomach than it seemed to be for everyone else. As far as I could tell, except for my grandmother Sanders and my great-aunt Sally, no one had more than a cup of coffee. The night before, Myra had lingered over every item of clothing I was to wear, as if choosing the right socks was as critical as any decision the president would make. I knew she was just trying to distract me from thinking about what this all meant, but I couldn't help feeling that all eyes would be on me for the whole funeral.

I sat between Grandpa and Uncle Bobby in the limousine. My grandmother Sanders and my great-aunt sat across from us, both sobbing softly, sighing, and looking away from me. Uncle Bobby held my hand all the way to the church, but Grandpa sat stone still. I hadn't said much to anyone, even Myra. At the moment, I hated the sound of my own voice. Every time I spoke, my throat ached.

It was still very warm for this time of the year. At least there were clouds to interrupt the sunlight; today the sun felt more like a spotlight in one of Uncle Bobby's stage shows. We passed the small park near the school, and I saw about a dozen mothers with their children, all screaming and laughing around the swings and seesaws. I wanted to lean out and shout, "How dare you have fun today?"

It wasn't until we entered the crowded church and I set eyes on the coffin that I felt as if my body was disappearing. I was shrinking inside myself. I tried not to look back at anyone who was looking at us. I was holding on to both Grandpa's and Uncle Bobby's hands, but Uncle Bobby seemed to sense what was happening to me faster than my grandfather did, maybe because Uncle Bobby was so in tune with how people moved. He let go of my hand and quickly put his arm around my shoulders. No one knew it, I think, but he was actually holding me up until we got to our seats.

My grandpa sat with his head down most of the time, clasping his hands so tightly that his knuckles turned white. When he did raise his head, he looked at Willie's coffin and then looked down again, shaking his head slightly. The only part of the sermon and the eulogy that I heard was Willie's name. Otherwise the words just flowed past my ears. I wouldn't let any of them in. As I sat there, I knew the worst part was yet to come. This part seemed more like a show with a coffin for a prop, and the church choir and the minister were more like actors. We were simply all part of the performance.

But at the most beautiful cemetery in the whole state of Virginia, it was like a sledgehammer struck me in the heart and broke the dam that held back my tears. I cried so hard and continuously that Grandpa nodded at Uncle Bobby, who then hugged me closer in his arms and finally practically carried me back to the limousine. I think the sight of me crying hysterically did more to raise the sobs and moans of everyone else than the sight of Willie's coffin hovering over a perfectly shaped grave.

I collapsed in the car and fell asleep for a few minutes against Uncle Bobby's shoulder. I kept thinking about Grandma Arnold saying that Uncle Bobby had "angel feet." Now Willie did, too. I dreamed instead of arriving at the house and seeing Willie out front, smiling impishly as he often did and saying, "Ha-ha, joke's on you."

After we arrived at the house, Lila and some of my other classmates came up to my room to be with me. No one really wanted to be there. I didn't want to be there, but they all tried to help me. Finally, with no more tears left in my well of sorrow, I suggested we go downstairs and have something to eat.

"Before some of my grandfather's friends gobble it all up," I added, which finally brought smiles.

It was My Faith who said that the week after such

a sad funeral was "like the days after a tornado." My grandmother Sanders and her sister left the morning after, inviting me to visit whenever I liked. I had never done it when Willie was alive. I couldn't imagine doing it now. They hugged and kissed me and then left quickly, like two people fleeing a fire. I couldn't blame them. Everyone remaining moved about as if they were still stunned, poised to see more suffering. People did not raise their voices very much. Looks and gestures replaced words. Silence seemed soothing.

That was with the exception of Grandpa Arnold. Getting back to work and working even harder was his way of dealing with our tragedy. He was out of the house before I had even risen to get dressed. Uncle Bobby stayed another day and a half. Before he left, he came to see me. I knew, of course, that he couldn't stay with us long. He wasn't being selfish by thinking of his work and his career. He was, like everyone else, trying to survive in a flood of sorrow.

"Hey, Clair de Lune," he said as he came into my bedroom. I was beginning something that I didn't know whether I could finish or continue. I was writing my first letter to my brother, Willie, in heaven. I think I was terrified of the possibility that I would soon forget him or stop thinking about him. I knew Grandpa didn't stop thinking about my mother or my grandmother, but he very rarely mentioned their names. That was why I had been so surprised to hear him say that Grandma Arnold had told him to take care of the poisoned boy.

"Hi," I said. From the way Uncle Bobby was

dressed, I knew he was minutes away from leaving. "Going?"

"Yes, but I'll be calling you and writing to you. I'll send you a playbill from the show I'm in now. You know what that is, right? I mean, it's not really a bill, it's—"

"I know what it is," I said, smiling. It felt good to smile. I knew it was part of what would bring me back, even though a bigger part of me wanted never to come back. That part wanted to stay with Willie.

"Good. So . . . you'll return to school on Monday?"

"I guess so. My friend Lila has been helping me keep up with the classwork."

"Best thing you can do, although I know it won't be easy, maybe not for a long, long time. Whenever I saw you two together, you were more like a mother to him than an older sister." He paused and shook his head. "Of course, you would be, having lost your mother, but other girls might have withdrawn completely into themselves. You're a great kid, Clara Sue."

I nodded. I knew Uncle Bobby meant it all as a nice thing to say and not to get me crying again. I could see, however, that he had something else on his mind. He had the look of someone debating with himself whether he should speak. He looked away and pressed his lips in and out.

"How's Grandpa?" I asked, as a way to help get him to talk. "I didn't see him this morning."

"He's Grandpa," he said, smiling. "He won't show it, but I know he's struggling. You have to wonder how I could be his son. There I was when I was your age, bawling like a baby at the sight of a dead butterfly. It still makes my eyes tear to see beautiful things die. Your grandfather is just one of those guys who cry on the inside and not on the outside. He's also one of those guys who use anger to overcome sorrow."

"Getting his revenge," I said, nodding.

"Right."

"Has he said any more about the poisoned boy?" I could sense that this was really what he was holding back.

He nodded. "Thing is, he received a report from the private detective concerning him."

"He's going home?" I asked quickly, hoping this was the end of it.

"No. The detective has apparently run into a dead end."

"What's that mean?"

"My father's exact words were 'Whoever the man was, he had dropped the boy off like a bag of plague and then hightailed it into the shadows like a ghost.' There wasn't even a decent description of him. He wore some kind of hat and kept his collar up. His height and all that were too vague to draw a picture. Not much to go by. The boy had nothing on him that would identify him. Basically, my father's given up on the private detective for now. Of course, the police are still involved."

"But he's still visiting him every day, isn't he? That's probably why he leaves so early."

Uncle Bobby nodded.

I thought about it. "Isn't there some kind of child protection service that takes over?" I didn't want to tell him that I had asked Lila to ask her father about it. Her father was a corporate attorney for a company that had something to do with supplying the Navy with things, but I thought an attorney was an attorney and should know something about other legal things. He didn't know all that much, but he had mentioned a government agency.

"That's just it. Dad doesn't want this little boy to get 'lost in the system,' as he puts it. I waited to see if he would tell me that my mother had whispered in his ear, just what he had told you, but he didn't mention it. Shows how he trusts you, cares about what you think, more than he does me."

"Well, what's he going to do now?"

"He's still looking after the boy's medical needs. He's even hired a psychiatrist to work with him. The boy remains in serious condition, something to do with his motor skills."

"Motor skills?"

"His legs, mainly. Your grandpa says he's improving, but he has a ways to go yet. I'm just telling you all this so that you'll know he's still deeply involved," he added quickly. "As I said, I think it helps him to care about someone that helpless."

I wanted to say that I was helpless, too, and that Willie was beyond helpless, but I didn't. I just nodded.

"You know your grandfather," Uncle Bobby continued. "When he gets on something with any determination . . ."

I nodded again. I remembered my grandmother saying that when Grandpa made his mind up about something, he looked like a bulldozer couldn't move him. "I swear," she had told me, "sometimes I believe he has tree roots growing out of his soles." She would get angry about it and tell him he was as stubborn as a corpse, but I remembered that most of the time, she was proud of how determined he could be whenever he decided to do something he thought was right, especially something good for the family. She said he made her feel safer and more secure than anyone she had ever known, even her own father and mother.

"Whatever strength this family has now," Grandma Arnold had told me sometime after my parents had died, "comes from those roots coming out of his soles. Don't tell him I said so," she'd whispered afterward. "He doesn't need to have his ego blown up any more, or he'll be even more impossible to live with."

She had laughed just the way someone who declared she would swear off chocolate would, knowing in her heart that she would violate her own pledge. No one could brag about or compliment my grandpa as much as she did, and she knew it. Later she would confess, "You don't stop eating chocolate, no matter what oath you swore."

"Anyway, don't spend any time worrying about it, Clara Sue," Uncle Bobby said now. "Everyone has his or her own way of grieving. Let it play itself out. I know I'm going to dance harder, work harder. What I mean is, don't let the grieving overtake you and prevent you from being who you are. I know you take pride in everything you accomplish in and out of school. Now you can tell yourself you're doing it all for Willie, too."

"Okay." Those all-too-familiar tears were returning. Would they always be there, just appearing willy-nilly? Who would want to be around me?

Uncle Bobby came over to hug me and kiss my cheek. "Maybe you can come see me in one of my shows," he said. "There's a good chance I'll be back on Broadway this coming year. You'll be able to stay with me, and I'll show you around New York. How's that?"

"If Grandpa lets me. Sometimes I can even hear the chains rattling."

He laughed. "I know. We'll get Myra to agree first, and if necessary, we'll invite her along," he said.

He started out but stopped, thinking for a moment in the doorway. Then he turned back to me.

"Look after him, Clara Sue. He's more lost than you think," he said, and left.

Was he right? I could only think back to how my grandfather had acted after my parents were killed and then after Grandma Arnold's passing. Both times, he was the one taking care of everyone and everything with such authority. I did feel safer. Was the loss of Willie greater to him than I thought it was? Perhaps he'd had high hopes for Willie and even envisioned the day when he would begin to work in the business, something Uncle Bobby never did. Now that was gone. What did he have left? Millions of dollars? A beautiful estate? A thriving big business?

And memories captured and locked away in pictures. How often must he look up at Grandma Arnold's portrait in his office and ache? How empty were his nights? Nowadays, I was tempted each morning to stay in bed forever. How did he manage to get himself up? Where did he find the energy and the desire?

I decided to be less intolerant of the attention he was giving the poisoned boy. I didn't like it any more than I had yesterday, but perhaps once he saw to it that the boy was restored to health, he would surely move on to other things. He'd probably help find a new home for him. I was used to the idea of my grand father having influence on many things besides his own business interests. He knew so many politicians. There was once talk of him running for mayor of Prescott. He could even call the governor if he wanted.

I sat at my desk again and continued my letter to Willie.

Uncle Bobby just left. I miss him already. I love everyone here, but Uncle Bobby is special. You know that, too.

I still can't believe you're gone, Willie. Even after all we've gone through and all the people who've tried to comfort us, I still expect you to come barging into my room and annoy me when I'm on the phone or trying to get some homework done and study for a test. I know you hate to be alone and want me to watch television with you or play one of your games.

I'm sorry now for every time I snapped

*back at you. You know I ended up being with
you anyway. People always say Myra and My
Faith spoil you, but you and I know that I spoil
you the most. Or did.*

*I have to tell myself that you're not alone
now, that you're with Mommy and Daddy, and
the truth is that you feel sorrier for me than I
do for you.*

*When I die, will you still be a little boy
when I see you again, or do people grow older
in heaven? You have to be in heaven. You
didn't get a chance to do anything very bad,
not that you would have.*

*Uncle Bobby was right about my getting
back to myself, but I can't help being afraid
of going to school again, seeing the faces of my
classmates, who I know will all be thinking
about what happened and waiting for me to
break out in tears at any moment.*

*People are afraid of people who are in
mourning. They don't know how to talk
to them, and they worry that they will say
something that will get the person crying or
running off. They'll feel just terrible about it, so
the best thing to do is avoid them.*

*I'm so afraid that will happen to me,
especially next week when I return to school.*

*I even think that might be why Grandpa
is leaving the house so early these mornings.
He's hoping I'll get all my crying done before
he comes home. One look at him told me not to*

*cry in front of him anymore. He would just call
for Myra and rush away to his office, closing
the door behind him. Then I'd feel even worse.*

*I didn't want to put this in a letter to you,
Willie, especially not one of the first ones I
wrote, but I think there's going to be more
and more about him over the next few days.
I'm talking about the poisoned boy. If you
were here and had seen him, I know you'd
be as interested in him as Grandpa is, and I
would be, too. But if I was to count the minutes
Grandpa has spent thinking about you and
the minutes he is spending thinking about the
poisoned boy, I think I'd find that he's spent
more on him than on you.*

*Maybe Uncle Bobby is right. Maybe
Grandpa is afraid to think about you and
thinking about this strange boy helps him avoid
it, but I don't have to like that.*

*Sometime next week, after school, I'm
going to ride my bike to the cemetery and talk
to you, Willie. I promise.*

Mostly, I promise I will never forget you.

*I'm going to write to you all the time,
because I believe as soon as I finish a letter,
Mommy will read it aloud to you and Daddy.*

Forever.

I put my pen down, folded the paper, and stuck it into
one of my personalized envelopes. Then I put it in the

bottom left drawer of my desk and went downstairs to see what My Faith was going to make us for dinner. Actually, I just wanted to talk to someone. I didn't want to play my radio or watch television. It seemed wrong to do any of that so soon after Willie's funeral, but I was having trouble with my loneliness.

Lila had wanted to stay home from school and be with me every day, but her mother didn't think she should, and besides, how could I get the schoolwork if she was home, too? At least I had something to look forward to in the afternoon, and although I didn't want to ask or admit it to her, I was interested in what the others in our class were doing. It bothered me when I thought about these things, because I thought I shouldn't, not yet, but I couldn't help it just as much as I couldn't help taking another breath.

Maybe Lila can stay for dinner tonight, I thought. With Uncle Bobby gone, the table would seem so empty, and I was actually afraid of my grandfather talking about the poisoned boy, afraid that neither of us would mention Willie's name, either now or ever, just the way Grandpa avoided talking about my parents.

Unfortunately, Lila couldn't stay. She hadn't told me, but her parents were taking her and her older sister out to celebrate her father getting a major promotion at his company. I could see it was something she had known about for a few days, but she had been reluctant to mention good news. Like most people right now, she didn't want to make it seem like everything was just hunky-dory for them while everything was horrible for me.

"Everyone asks about you every day, especially Mr. Leshner," she said to make me feel a little better.

Mr. Leshner was our social studies teacher. Everyone agreed that he made the subject interesting. I had never gotten anything less than an A in his class, and he kept predicting I would be the valedictorian when I was a senior.

"And, of course, Aaron," she added.

As hard as I tried, I couldn't push him or the things we had all planned to do during the upcoming Christmas break out of my mind. Lila and I had been toying with the idea of having our own New Year's Eve party and sneaking in some alcoholic drinks. Her parents were considering letting us use their house. Some of our other girlfriends would stay over, too, maybe even one or two of the boys.

But that was all before.

This afternoon, as we did some homework together, she made a few comments about people in school, but not once did she mention Willie, nor did I.

Grandpa came home just before she left. He looked in on us. It was the first time he had done so this week.

"Hello, girls," he said.

"Hi, Mr. Arnold."

"Joining us for dinner, Lila?"

"Not tonight."

"Her parents are taking them out to celebrate her father's promotion," I explained for her quickly.

"Oh, great. I think I heard something about that. Congratulate your dad for me."

"I will."

He nodded, glanced at me, and walked on to his room.

"Everyone wonders if your grandfather will ever remarry," Lila said. It took me by complete surprise. "Do you?" she asked.

"No," I said. The whole idea seemed foreign, even a little terrifying to me.

"I heard my mother talking to some of her friends about him. They all think he's very handsome but also the most eligible bachelor because he's so rich and successful."

"He's not a bachelor. He's a widower," I said.

"He's not old," she said, with an insistence that annoyed me.

"He can't love anyone like he loved my grandmother. Any other woman would be quite disappointed."

She shrugged. "Maybe he can't, but he can love someone enough to marry her, can't he?"

I didn't reply. I looked at my math book instead.

"I guess I'd better start home," she said.

"Have a good time," I told her. I tried not to sound bitter.

"Thanks. I'll call you if it's not too late when I get home." She paused in the doorway. "Do you think you might want to do something this weekend?"

"No," I said sharply and quickly. She nodded. I knew she was bored with just coming over to spend time mostly in my room. "But you do something. Don't worry about me."

"We'll see. 'Bye," she said.

I tried to go back to the math homework, but I couldn't concentrate. I slammed the book shut, went to the window, and watched Lila get onto her bike and start off. As she sailed down the driveway and out the gate, I realized that I felt like a prisoner, a prisoner of grief.

The dining-room table was barren and bleak without Lila, Willie, Uncle Bobby, or my grandmother Sanders and my great-aunt Sally joining us. These past few nights were all difficult. I know Grandpa was trying to look as comfortable and happy as he could. This evening, My Faith had made something we both loved, her special meat loaf and incredibly delicious mashed potatoes. They were practically the only potatoes Willie would finish. Usually, Grandpa drank wine with his dinner, but he wasn't drinking any tonight. We had yet to have a private conversation about our tragedy. Usually, Lila was here or he was at work right after dinner in his house office, but tonight I could feel it coming, the way you could feel an impending thunderstorm. My whole body tensed up, and even the little appetite I had was threatened.

He didn't start talking until we had been served our meal. He complimented My Faith, as he always did. Myra was having her dinner in her room. She was finally admitting to her aches and pains, and I imagined she was more exhausted than any of us, with the combination of grief and injuries.

"I have survived our terrible share of sorrow, Clara Sue," he began, "by making myself work harder and do what I could to avoid thinking about it all. We're never going to stop hurting over Willie, but we've got to do the best we can so that everyone we've lost would be proud of us. Right?"

"Yes, Grandpa."

"So, you're going back to school on Monday?"

"Yes."

He ate and thought, and I ate, avoiding looking at the chair where Willie would sit. I knew I was eating faster than usual just to get it over with and hurry out. Would I avoid every place in this house where I could envision Willie?

"You don't know," my grandfather began again, "but one of your grandmother's and my favorite charities is something called Angel View. It's an organization dedicated to providing assistance to handicapped children. I mean, we do our share of charity contributions, but that one was at the top of your grandmother's list. She even volunteered to work at their center in Charlottesville occasionally. I don't think you knew that."

I shook my head.

"She wasn't one to talk about what she did for others. Unlike a lot of people I know, here especially, she just did it and didn't ask anyone for any thanks or recognition. If anything, that embarrassed her and took away from the main goal—helping someone in need."

I paused. I could feel it. He was leading up to something, something to do with the poisoned boy.

"It's good to think of people other than yourself, especially when you're suffering some disappointment or tragedy."

"I don't want to ever stop thinking about Willie," I said firmly.

"Of course, you shouldn't, and neither should I. We should cherish his memory, and I plan to create an endowment in his name," he said. "You'll be with me when we establish it."

"What sort of endowment, Grandpa?"

"I'm not sure yet. Maybe a grant or an award. Maybe a scholarship at your school. I tell you what. You'll be just as important to the decision, okay?"

I nodded. That sounded good. Uncle Bobby was right, I thought. I shouldn't be so intolerant of how Grandpa was acting and what he was trying to do.

I could see that he was hesitating. He finished his meal, drank some water, and sat back. "I was thinking that you might like to go with me tonight to the hospital. I'm meeting with the neurologist about that little boy. He's rather sad and I'm sure still very frightened. I have him in a private room, which is the most comfortable place he could be there, but there are no other young people. He sees only nurses and doctors," he said.

I didn't say anything.

"It would be nice if you spoke to him. He has yet to say anything to anyone," he added.

I looked up. "What would I say, Grandpa?"

"It doesn't matter. You can ask him how he is. Anything."

"Why would he talk to me?"

"I don't know. You're a young person, too. Maybe he has a sister."

"Well, where is she? Why doesn't someone come to ask about him and take him home?" I demanded. I couldn't contain my anger. "How do you just deposit your own child like some . . . garbage?"

He shook his head. "I'm trying to find out."

"But you've run into a dead end."

"Right now," he said. "I'm still on it."

"Someone could have a little boy, and they don't want him, and we lost Willie. It's not fair."

"No, it's not fair. That's a lesson you have to learn in life. Things don't happen just because they should or because it's fair. You have to make things happen, even the right things, Clara Sue. So what about it? You should get out of the house, and I could use your help with the boy."

"I don't know," I said.

"Whatever. I'll be going in about . . ." He looked at his watch. "A half hour."

My Faith appeared. She looked at my plate.

"I ate all I could," I said sullenly. She nodded. "It wasn't any less delicious than ever."

"No, that's for sure," Grandpa told her. "How's Myra?"

"She fell asleep eating," My Faith said.

"I'll check on her later," Grandpa said.

"I'll check on her now," I snapped, and got up before he could say anything.

"You want some of that peach pie you love?" My Faith called after me.

"I don't love it," I replied. "Willie loves it."

The silence fell like thunder behind me.

4

When I looked at myself in the hallway mirror, I thought I looked more mean than mournful. I didn't like that. It seemed a wrong feeling to have right now. My sorrow over Willie should make every other feeling do what my grandfather often said about things he didn't think were as important: "take a backseat."

I obviously had an expression on my face that drew Myra's attention. The moment I opened her door, even though I did it softly and slightly, she looked at me, her eyes taking on that familiar curiosity, this time when she correctly suspected that something was bothering me more than what was to be expected following Willie's funeral. I wasn't surprised. Who, after all, knew me better than Myra? Even before my parents died, she had become like another grandmother to me. Having been my mother's nanny for so long, she was as familiar as my grandmother Lucy had been with the gestures, expressions, and quirks I had inherited from my mother. Both of them often said, "You're just like your mother."

Myra lifted her good arm, and I ran to her bedside to let her take my hand.

"Someone said something that bothered you?" she asked. "One of your grandfather's friends?"

"No. There's no one here now but Grandpa. How are you?" I asked.

"I think I can now tell My Faith how Lazarus felt the moment he was awakened," she replied, and struggled into a sitting position. "Let's not talk about me, love. I'll mend. I've had plenty of practice with sadness, as, unfortunately, you've had in so short a time. So? What is it? You look ready to take on the House of Commons." She brushed strands of my hair away from my eyes.

"Grandpa wants me to go with him to the hospital to visit that poisoned boy tonight. He thinks I might get him to talk."

She nodded. "Thought it might have something to do with that." She sat back against her pillow but held on to my hand. "May I tell you something I've learned, love? There's an abundance of mean, selfish, and uncharitable activity in this world. We'll never lack for it, so we should always embrace the opposite wherever we find it. You're not ready to care about anyone else. That's understandable, but maybe you should think about it more for your grandfather than the little boy, as sad and horrible as his life is now."

"That's what Uncle Bobby was telling me."

"My mum used to say you can spend your life

coping with the unhappiness and disappointment you'll experience, or you can spend more on the happiness and successes. Dad would tell her that was nothing more than seeing the glass half full and not half empty. Then they'd squabble about who said it better. They'd disagree over whether to put the milk in first or the tea, both quoting this king or that queen, but they loved each other to beat the band."

I smiled. Being in Myra's company was like walking out to a cloudy day and suddenly entering a burst of sunshine. I hoped she would always be here to cheer me up. "So you think I should go?"

"We'll never forget our Willie, but it's important now to get your mind on other things, too. I can't say I'm not curious. Aren't you? Where'd this boy come from? Did the man who brought him just find him lying about somewhere? Why was he afraid to tell anyone anything? Who'd want to poison a little boy, anyway? Unless it was by accident and they were afraid of getting blamed, of course, but why was he so thin and small?"

"Okay," I said. "I'll go with him and let you know what I've learned."

"I'll be up and about when you come home. I just need a bit more of a rest. But I'm not taking those fog pills," she added firmly.

I hugged her and went looking for Grandpa. He was on the phone in his office. When he saw me in the doorway, he put up his right forefinger.

"I'm heading there now in a little while," he said into the phone, "but I don't have much more to tell you. Suit yourself," he added, and hung up.

"Some police detective. He called my office to ask me more questions about the boy today, too, but I didn't have time to speak to him. Don't know why the police are hounding me about it. You go and do something for someone, and suddenly you're the one with all the answers," he muttered. "Like I can hand them all over, neatly tied with a ribbon on a silver platter. Everyone wants their work made easier."

"I decided I will go with you," I said.

"Good. We'll leave in ten," he said.

I nodded and hurried up to my room. I never thought of my mother as a conceited person or even a little too much concerned about her looks, but one thing that impressed me about her was that she wouldn't leave the house without looking her best, no matter where she went, even if it was just to the supermarket.

"Looking messy in public says a lot about how you live your life, Clara Sue," she told me. Myra either agreed or wanted to be sure she always pleased my mother, even now. She always made sure I didn't leave the house with my hair disheveled, or wearing something torn or missing a button, or certainly wearing anything with a stain on it.

I chose a prettier blouse than the one I was wearing, changed my shoes to a newer pair, and then brushed my hair, pinning it back with hair clips. I couldn't throw off my sense of guilt for caring about my looks so soon after Willie's funeral, but it wasn't that easy to push aside what I knew had pleased my mother.

Grandpa certainly looked pleased when he saw me.

He smiled, put his hand on my shoulder, and then held my hand as we walked out to his car. Jimmy Wilson and two of the grounds workers paused to look our way. They were replacing bulbs in the driveway and landscape lights. Jimmy smiled and waved, obviously happy to see me out and about. I waved back and got into Grandpa's sedan, immediately feeling funny about it.

There hadn't been all that many times in my life when I had gone somewhere with Grandpa and not had Willie along, too. Sometimes Grandpa took me to a friend's home, but even if we went shopping for something I needed, Willie would be with us, because he knew that Grandpa would find something to buy for him, too. I usually sat in the front, and Willie sat in the rear. He would talk from the moment we drove out of the estate to wherever we were going. Grandpa called him "Motor Mouth" and said he could get more words to the mile than anyone he knew. He also said he would have been a good passenger for him to take along when he used to drive trucks long distances. "I wouldn't ever fall asleep with Willie in the truck," he'd say. That didn't discourage Willie. If anything, it got him to say more.

Perhaps it was the quiet. Maybe Grandpa was thinking about Willie talking a blue streak, too, but we rode for quite a while before either of us spoke.

"The poisoned boy really hasn't spoken yet, Grandpa?" I began.

"He doesn't even cry. He doesn't call for his mother. First they thought he might be deaf, because he wouldn't even turn toward the person speaking to him, but they know he's not. My guess is he doesn't trust anyone."

"Why not?"

"Someone he should have trusted disappointed him. That's one theory Dr. Patrick expressed. She hasn't had any luck getting him to talk to her, either."

"Who is she?"

"The psychiatrist I asked to look in on him," he said.

I didn't know anyone who went to a psychiatrist, much less a young person. It seemed so strange. Weren't his physical injuries more important? "Uncle Bobby said he can't move his legs."

Grandpa nodded. "Dr. Friedman, the neurologist, told me it's like the boy's neurological systems have shut down. He said he has seen similar cases. The arsenic did some damage to his nerves and affected his muscles. It could take a long time for him to recuperate. Some patients don't. He's stopping in tonight and will tell me more about it."

"What's that all mean? He'll die, too?"

"No, not now. He could have, almost did. They said another hour or so might have made all the difference. He'll be in a wheelchair for a while . . . maybe forever."

"Oh. Then he'll have to go to a special place, right?" I said quickly. Even though I had agreed to go to see him and even to speak to him—mainly because of the things Myra had told me—I was still hoping he would be out of our lives soon and forever.

"We'll see," Grandpa said.

When we arrived at the hospital, the police detective who had been looking for Grandpa earlier greeted us in the lobby. He introduced himself as Lieutenant Bronson. Grandpa wasn't happy he was there and didn't hide it. He approached us the moment we entered.

"I told you everything I knew on the phone," Grandpa snapped before the man could even say hello. He had shown us his identification. "I don't know why you're coming to me to ask these questions. I never saw him before," Grandpa said. Before the detective could ask anything else, he added, his voice sharp, "And neither has my granddaughter. I don't know anything more about him than you do."

"So you don't know anything about the man who brought him here, either?" Lieutenant Bronson asked, as if Grandpa hadn't said a word yet. Either he couldn't see how annoyed my grandfather was or he didn't care. "You did hire a private detective, I understand."

Grandpa looked surprised that the police detective knew, and then he shook his head. "He didn't find out anything, and I didn't learn anything about the man on my own, either. We weren't exactly watching and listening to other patients' problems at the time we brought my grandson here, you know."

Grandpa Arnold wasn't usually this irritable when it came to police or anyone else who didn't have anything to do with his business. He was a very easy-going, gentle man, despite his size. If anyone accused him of being that way, he usually blamed it on my grandma, who he claimed softened him up. I was

puzzled about why he was so antagonistic with the
police. Did he blame them somehow for what had
happened to Willie?

"I know. I'm sorry about your loss. Terrible
thing," Lieutenant Bronson said. "I just thought that
with the interest you were showing and the money
you were spending, you might know a little more by
now that would help us get to the bottom of this."

"There is no bottom for something this bad,"
Grandpa said. "All we know right now is what we were
told by the nurses in the emergency room and what the
doctors are telling me. I'd have no reason to hold back.
I'd like to see whoever did this punished, too."

Lieutenant Bronson nodded, glanced at me, and
stood there staring for a few dead moments, moments
when he looked like he couldn't squeeze a thought out
of his brain or a word off his tongue. It was as if he
had gone off somewhere for a few seconds and left his
body behind.

I supposed everyone got like that sometimes, but
it reminded me of a time when I was playing with my
food at breakfast instead of eating it, and my grandma
told me not to be wasteful of my time and especially
to avoid what she called "dead time." Those were the
moments when you were in a sort of daze, not thinking or talking. She said seconds were like bubbles,
and just like you couldn't keep them from popping,
you couldn't keep time stored up in your pocket.
There was no piggy bank for minutes. Time wasted
was time lost forever: "Even blessed Jesus couldn't
resurrect it."

"Amen to that," My Faith had said. She knew all about Jesus and often quoted the Bible. She traveled thirty-five miles every Sunday to attend her church in Charlottesville and volunteered to cook church dinners regularly.

"Well," Lieutenant Bronson finally said, "as of today, we still don't have a missing-child report that would fit him. It's really weird."

Grandpa grunted. I had the feeling his private detective had at least told him that much.

Lieutenant Bronson produced a card and gave it to my grandpa. "If you learn anything that will help get the people who did this . . ."

Grandpa took it and shoved it quickly into his pocket.

"We'll follow up on what we have and see what's what," Lieutenant Bronson added.

"You do that. In the meantime, I'll look after him," Grandpa told him, with such firmness in his voice that I couldn't help but imagine steel doors slamming shut. There wasn't even a hint of *temporary* when he used the word "meantime." He seemed to know instinctively that whoever had done this to the little boy would avoid detection and especially avoid having to care for him. The poisoned boy was disowned, cast out to either die or disappear, and my grandfather was determined to make it impossible for him to suffer a moment more than he already had.

Lieutenant Bronson smiled at me and then hurried away.

"C'mon," Grandpa said, taking my hand. We went

to the elevator and rode up to the floor where the boy was being treated in a private room.

When we got there, I paused in the doorway, even though Grandpa marched right in. The boy didn't look much different from the way he had that day Willie was brought to the hospital. He still looked withered and tiny, way too small for all the equipment that surrounded him. After a moment, I followed Grandpa in. The boy's eyes were on us, and I thought he almost smiled at the sight of Grandpa.

"Hey, champ," Grandpa said. "How you doin'?"

The boy didn't answer. He looked from Grandpa to me and just stared at me. Grandpa noticed.

"This is my granddaughter, Clara Sue," he told him. The boy seemed to show more interest in me. Grandpa urged me on with his eyes. I stepped closer.

"Hi," I said. "What's your name? What grade are you in?"

We waited, holding our breath, because his lips parted, and he looked like he might speak, but they closed again, and this time, he looked away, turning his head away. I looked at Grandpa. His eyes urged me to continue.

"I'm in the tenth grade," I said. "Do you like school?"

We waited, but he didn't turn back.

"How do they know he's not deaf?" I asked.

"They know. Keep trying," Grandpa said. "I just saw the neurologist arrive. I have to speak with him."

He walked out, and I stood there. The boy was so thin. His wrists looked tiny, certainly tinier than

Willie's. His eyebrows were very fine, almost invisible. All of his features were small but perfect. I imagined every one of his nurses had a broken heart over him and couldn't keep their hands off him. He looked as fragile as one of my mother's special collectible dolls given to her as a child. Despite what he had gone through, his skin looked as smooth as glass. How could his mother or father not want to cherish him? How could anyone want to kill someone so dainty and precious?

Standing here beside him, I was losing my anger. I didn't expect that, and I didn't like it. I kept telling myself that I should be home thinking about Willie, writing another letter to him, and not standing here caring about this . . . strange bird. My rage once again began to rise to the surface.

"Someone brought you here the same time my brother, Willie, was brought here in an ambulance," I began. "A drunk driver hit him on his bike, even though he was riding on the sidewalk."

The word "bike" seemed to attract his attention. He looked at me, waiting to hear more.

"He died," I said. "He really died in the ambulance, and they couldn't do anything wonderful for him here."

The boy didn't show any surprise or sympathy. He just stared blankly.

"He was only nine. He was so excited about riding his bike outside our property," I continued, but still, the boy showed no reaction. "Did you hear what I said? My little brother is dead, killed, and the man who did it was drunk."

He barely blinked.

"Do you know why you're here, at least? Do you know you were poisoned? Did you eat something you shouldn't? You almost died, too, but the hospital saved you, and my grandfather is helping you."

He looked away. *How infuriating*, I thought.

"They couldn't save my brother," I continued, raising my voice. He turned back to me. "Willie couldn't speak now even if he wanted to, or smile or thank anyone for anything, especially my grandfather. You know, he's paying for everything that's being done for you. He even hired a private detective to find out who you are and who did this to you."

He turned to me. His eyes blinked, but he still didn't speak.

"Why don't you at least say thank you? Didn't your parents teach you any manners? Who are they? Where do they live? Why aren't they looking for you? Why isn't anyone looking for you? Don't you want to go home?"

His lips trembled a bit, but he didn't speak. Instead, he looked away again.

"You're going to have to talk someday. It's stupid now to pretend you can't. People want to know what happened to you and how they can help you and how to get the people who did this to you and put them in jail."

He looked at me again, this time his eyes a bit wider. Was I finally getting him to talk?

"Yes, jail, if they deliberately poisoned you. Who would do such a thing to you? Was it someone you knew? It was someone you trusted, right? Or were you kidnapped, and no one would pay your ransom? That's it, isn't it?" I asked harder. It seemed right, seemed like I might have solved the mystery. I had read stories about things like this. I couldn't wait to suggest it to my grandfather. Then he might return to the police and get it all solved, and the boy would be on his way back to his family.

His lips moved like he was tasting something, and then he turned away again quickly, as if someone was talking to him on the other side of the bed, too.

"What's your name? Tell us! Who did this to you?" I demanded, raising my voice even more. "This is stupid! No one can help you if you don't talk! I know you can talk. You need to trust us. We'll get you home! *Talk!*"

A nurse appeared in the doorway and came rushing over to me. "Why are you shouting at him?" she asked.

"He's just being a stubborn little brat," I said. "My grandfather is helping him, and he won't even say thank you."

"Maybe you should step out," she said.

"Gladly," I said, and walked out into the hallway. I could see my grandfather talking with a doctor near the nurse's desk. I folded my arms across my chest and leaned against the wall.

When she emerged from the poisoned boy's room, the nurse glared at me and then walked to the desk. She said something to the doctor and my grandfather. They both looked my way and then continued talking. I shuddered a little. Grandpa did look annoyed.

Suddenly, the nurse behind the desk called to him and handed him a telephone. I watched him talk and listen. He handed back the phone and turned to walk toward me.

"I wasn't really shouting at him, Grandpa," I said. "I just think he could talk if he wants to. I tried."

"Oh, he could talk," he said. "But you gotta wonder why he doesn't want to."

I hung back when Grandpa went to the boy's bedside. I couldn't hear what he was saying, but I knew he was talking to him. The boy seemed to be paying attention, too, more than he had to me. Grandpa reached down and touched his hand. Then he turned and walked toward me.

"I have to get to the office," he said.

"Now?"

"That was Mrs. Mallen calling me here. One of our trucks was in a bad accident about an hour ago."

"Oh, no. Was the driver hurt?" I knew some of the drivers by first name now. My favorite was a man they called Curly, but it wasn't because he had curly hair. Grandpa explained that everyone teased him and called him that because he could curl up anywhere and fall asleep. Even though he was a little more than six feet tall, he could twist his body so that he could put two chairs together and take a nap. He called me Starlight, because he said I had two eyes that could be stars.

"Some broken bones," he said as we walked to the elevator.

"Was it Curly?"

"No," he said, smiling. He knew how fond I was

of Curly. "It was a new guy. He'll be all right. We just have a delivery problem. I'll take you home first."

"What did the doctor tell you just now?" I asked after the elevator doors closed.

"That as he first thought, it was going to take a while, maybe quite a while, for the boy to get well," he replied. "He'll need physical therapy. He's still evaluating the extent of the damage caused by the poison. He said it looks to him like a slow but steady ingestion of arsenic. Most likely, then, not an accident."

Accident? I thought. The word brought Willie back to mind instantly.

"He'll need lots of tender loving care," Grandpa said as the doors opened for us.

"Who doesn't?" I muttered, mostly to myself.

He was very quiet after that. I could see that he was in deep thought. I imagined it was because of the truck accident, but later I would find out that it wasn't, and I wouldn't be happy about it.

By the time he took me home, before he went on to his company, Myra had come out of her room and was having coffee with My Faith. They hadn't heard about the truck accident. I sat with them, had a cup of cocoa, and described the poisoned boy and how I was unable to make any difference.

"It was stupid for me to go. The nurse even asked me to leave his room."

"Why?" Myra asked.

"I guess I got a little impatient and annoyed and raised my voice."

"Oh. Well, let's give it time," she said.

"I don't want to give it time. No one's giving Willie any more time," I snapped back. I immediately felt bad about yelling at Myra. "I'm sorry," I said.

"It's all right, love. It's very hard right now," she said, and then told us about a little boy who had been hit by a lorry on her street in London when she was fifteen. I knew from some of her other stories that a lorry was a truck. She said she used to babysit for him and that it was like losing a little brother. "Those parents were devastated and were never the same. Surely this little boy's parents are desperate to know about him," she added.

My Faith agreed. "Children are a blessing and a gift from the Lord," she said. In my way of thinking, someone was returning the gift or trying to. "Your grandfather will get it solved," My Faith said.

Afterward, I went up to my room. Some of my friends had big brothers or big sisters. Some had both. I wished right now that I had one. I wished Uncle Bobby had stayed longer. Despite Myra and My Faith, I hadn't felt this alone since my parents died and then even more when Grandma Arnold died. Grandpa Arnold was just too busy to keep me company, and now it looked like whatever spare time he had he was devoting to this boy wilting like an undernourished flower.

I couldn't deny that he had a nearly perfect doll-like face with hair more golden than that of any blond boy or girl I knew. Again, I wondered how anyone could want to hurt someone like that or not care about him. He looked huggable and precious and now so helpless. When I was calmed a bit—even though I refused to acknowledge it—it wasn't hard to believe that someone, my grandfather, would want to help him.

Don't think about it anymore, I told myself. Grandpa would pay for the doctors, and then they'd send him somewhere to get therapy and recuperate. If his parents never appeared, someone would surely adopt him, and that would be that.

I began to think about Monday and returning to school. My teachers would all feel sorry for me, but I didn't want to linger in sorrow at school. I couldn't help Willie anymore, and it certainly wasn't going to do me any good. The truth was, I had to stop feeling guilty for being alive. It seemed so cruel to even think it, but what else could I do?

I sat at the desk and began another letter to Willie.

Dear Willie,

I made Grandpa happy tonight by going with him to the hospital to see that poisoned boy I described to you. It was a worthless visit. I couldn't help him. All I could do was think of how lucky he was to have our grandfather care about him and how ungrateful he was.

I suppose that was unfair. Something is seriously wrong with him, and maybe he can't help being ungrateful. I'm going to tell Grandpa I don't mind him helping the boy and paying for him to go to some institution or something. Then I'll put him out of my mind.

*I have to return to school on Monday.
I know how hard it's going to be. I'll keep
looking for you, keep wishing that all this is a
nightmare and that it will be over soon.*

*Sometimes I think you're the lucky one.
You're back in our parents' arms. I know
everyone would be angry with me for thinking
that, so I'll never say it aloud.*

*I'll go to sleep thinking about you and push
all thoughts about that boy out of my mind. I
promise.*

*I'm still planning on riding my bike to
the cemetery. I'll visit you as much as I can,
forever.*

Clara Sue

I put the letter in another envelope and put that in the same drawer. I was thinking about doing some more of the homework Lila had brought me, but I heard footsteps in the hallway and peeked out. It was Grandpa. He was back from the office. He was standing outside of Willie's room and thinking so deeply that, as Grandma Arnold used to say, "you'd need a microscope to see his thoughts."

As quietly as I could, I stepped out of my room and walked up to him, expecting to see tears streaming down his face, just like mine every time I looked in on Willie's room. I even had seen Uncle Bobby do that and wipe away tears. But Grandpa was firm and dry-eyed. Uncle Bobby was right about him. He cried only on the inside. I didn't think he realized I was there, but he surprised me. He did.

He started to speak without turning to me. "I think I'll leave everything as it is, Clara Sue," he began. "What little boy wouldn't want all that your brother had?"

My heart stopped, and my blood froze. "What do you mean, Grandpa? Leave what as it is?"

"The room," he said, nodding.

"Little boy? You don't mean the poisoned boy? You don't mean you're bringing him here?"

"Yes, that's exactly what I mean," he said, still staring into the room.

"But . . . he can't come here! He has to go back to his own family someday."

"I doubt that, Clara Sue. I doubt that very much." He looked at me and smiled. "I'm confident that he'll end up here with us."

"End up? For how long?"

"Forever, I think."

I felt an electric shock go through my body. I looked into Willie's room and shook my head. I couldn't be hearing right. I couldn't. Give this strange boy Willie's things? It was as if Grandpa was sweeping away our memories of my brother as easily as erasing a blackboard. *No!* I screamed inside myself. This room should be locked away, especially from strangers. It should be kept as a shrine. I wanted to come in here often and think about Willie and cry about Willie. I didn't want to see another boy's face, see any other boy, especially a stranger, in Willie's bed. My heart would do flip-flops, and my stomach would shrink into a thimble.

"He's so tiny, being so undernourished and all," Grandpa continued, nodding as he spoke. "You saw that, but we'll get him up to speed. No sense throwing away Willie's clothes, either. He'll grow into them. He might even fit into his shoes. Some of the things in his closet are practically brand new."

"You shouldn't do that, Grandpa," I said, the words practically choking off my breathing as my throat tightened.

He looked at me as if he had been talking to himself and just realized I was there beside him. "What else would we do with it all, Clara Sue? We don't want to throw it out. That would be stupid, a waste. We'd only have to go out and buy lots of new things for him. Not that we won't, of course, but . . ." He looked back into Willie's room. "It would be a shame not to use what we have."

"But they're Willie's things," I whined.

It was just a little while ago, not even a full week ago, that Willie was in that bed having dreams or sitting up and playing with his toy soldiers and little cars. He recuperated from colds and coughs in that bed, had nightmares there that brought Grandma Arnold to him and, later, Myra and even me sometimes. No matter how many times those sheets and pillowcases were washed, they probably still had Willie's scent, that of his soaps, his shampoos, and all the things he played with, the flowers he touched, and the grass he stained his hands and knees with. Somewhere on the bed, I was sure I could still find a strand of his hair, no matter how the bed had been remade. That bed was a holy place. *No!*

"No!" I shouted. "You can't do that. I won't let you. I'll hate him, and I'll hate you." I raised my arms, my hands clenched into fists. I wanted to pound him.

He looked at me with more disapproval than I could ever remember. It frightened me, and I turned and ran back to my room, slamming the door shut behind me, and then I fell forward on my bed and cried almost as strongly as I had at Willie's funeral, maybe because this felt like he was being buried again.

I heard my door open and turned.

My grandfather was standing in the doorway. With the light behind him, his face was in a mask of shadows. For a few moments, he didn't say anything. I sucked back my sniffles and wiped my cheeks, flicking off the tears.

"I'm going to forget what you said," he began. His voice seemed deeper, making him appear even bigger. "You are not a mean, selfish girl. I know you would never hurt someone who is so helpless and alone. It would especially dishonor your brother's memory. Life is like a relay race. When good people die, they pass something important of themselves on to those who continue. Think of it that way, and you'll never stop being a big sister. And I . . . I will never stop being a grandfather," he concluded, and then he backed up, closing the door softly. It was like someone bringing down a curtain on Act One.

I couldn't help it.

No matter what he had said.

I was still very much afraid of Act Two.

5

My reasons for dreading my return to school proved true. As I moved through the building from class to class, I kept my gaze down as much as I could, because every time I met someone else's eyes, I saw the discomfort of having to greet someone dressed in such sorrow. Not that I wore black. I deliberately avoided it and chose a blue blouse and a light blue skirt. I could feel the dark veil over me, however. It was as if shadows born at the foot of Willie's grave were following me and always would.

The principal, Mrs. Greene, her secretary, and my teachers, especially Mr. Leshner, made it a point to take me aside and express their sympathy. Even the school's head custodian, Henry Hull, paused in what he was doing and came over to me to express his condolences. I think I said "thank you" more times during my first day back than I had said my whole life.

Lila was practically glued to my side from the moment I arrived. She was there ahead of me and

waited at the front entrance to escort me to homeroom. She started babbling immediately, but I kept
my face forward and sank into my seat like someone
settling on a life raft. After that, Lila leaped up at the
sound of every bell ending a class to walk step by step
beside me until I was safely wrapped in another seat
and desk. I feared that somehow she saw herself as
imperative—my protector, my personal secret service
agent, through whom everyone had to go to speak
with me. At one point, I looked at her and thought
she was wearing my grief like a ribbon of distinction
over her breast. I overheard her whispering to Ellie
Patterson and Cora Burns, with Aaron Podwell beside
her, describing how devastated I had been and how
difficult it had been for anyone, including her, to get
me to eat a morsel of food. *Oh, what a burden she has
endured*, I thought, and hurried away.

She came looking for me with her favorite question
of the day: "Are you all right?"

"Are you?" I asked, spinning around on her. I
could feel my eyes blazing. Suddenly, I had found a
target at which to aim all my discomfort. The shocked
look on her face only encouraged me.

"Me? What do you mean?"

"This is so difficult for you, this burden of having
to explain my state of mind," I said very matter-of-
factly. "I'm sorry about that."

Her eyes blinked, but she had missed my sarcasm
entirely. "Oh. No, no. As your closest friend now, I
shouldn't run away from helping you."

I nodded. "I'll tell you what. Do me a favor, Lila.

Run away," I said, and hurried ahead to our last class of the day, leaving her stunned behind me.

If there was one good outcome from the pressure I felt the first day back, it was not having much time to think about what Grandpa was planning to do with the poisoned boy. In fact, I didn't think about it until the car service that Grandpa had hired to take Willie and me to school brought me back to the estate. It was a mostly cloudy day, and the Indian summer we had been experiencing was in fast retreat. Fall was rushing in, angry that it had been held back. Leaves were already beginning to turn golden brown. Winter would be on its heels, equally eager to strip the woods and leave us surrounded by skeletons. Everything about the future looked glum. No holiday, no birthday, and no party loomed with any promise. I feared I would never dream nice dreams again.

As we passed through the entrance gate, I avoided looking at the house. I had this dark foreboding, this apprehension, that kept me from looking up at the windows I knew to be the windows of Willie's room. I had no idea yet when my grandfather intended to bring the poisoned boy here, but I was afraid that if I did look up at the windows, I would see him peering out from between the curtains, watching and waiting for me, his tiny face the color of bone.

When the vehicle stopped, I practically lunged out, ran up the short stone stairway, and burst through the front door. I did not, however, head for the kitchen to see My Faith or Myra, who usually took her cup of tea at this hour. Before Willie's death, he would rush in there with me, because he knew My Faith would have some special homemade cookies waiting for him with his glass of milk. I enjoyed them, too. Most of the time, there was an aroma spiraling out of the kitchen, hooking us both like fish the moment we set foot in the house.

Instead, I kept my urgent pace and took the stairway two steps at a time, rushing to get into my room and close the door behind me. Anyone would think I was being pursued by goblins or ghouls. The truth was that there were creatures after me, creatures born out of my own dark thoughts, thoughts that haunted me. How was I supposed to do what I had done for years and years with Willie and not continually think about him and look for him in the places I had always seen him? It had even been weird sitting in the car that took us back and forth to school.

Our current driver, Mr. Beal, a man who looked like he was seventy but was probably only in his fifties, had said only one thing during the entire round trip: "Sorry about Willie." When I didn't respond, he just drove. I avoided looking at him when I got into the car after school. Would he say "Sorry about Willie" tomorrow morning, too? Or was Willie already forgotten, better forgotten? Who wants to have a sick, empty feeling in your stomach every day, especially if all you had to do to avoid it was forget?

Lila was so shocked at my response just before the last period of the day that she didn't say anything in class and didn't hurry to walk me out to the pickup area when class ended. I didn't wait for her, anyway.

Maybe I was being unfair, but I couldn't help it. All I could think about was being back in my room and away from sad eyes and helpless smiles, all on faces that were like balloons caught in a dreadful gust of cold wind, the wind that hovered around graveyards and waited eagerly for funerals so it could toy with tears streaming down cheeks.

I sprawled on my bed, burying my face in my pillow. I couldn't remember feeling lonelier. Seeing my classmates and hearing them talk about their happy, everyday lives just sharpened the pain. Like someone afraid of drowning, I had avoided even dipping into a conversation. When would it be any different?

I heard the knock on my door, but I didn't respond. She knocked again and then opened it. If I needed any reminder that everything really had happened, it was the sight of Myra in that cast, the bruises healing on her forehead and cheek. She was still slightly bent over, her eyes registering some ache or pain, because she probably had kept her word and avoided any pills.

"Hello, love," she said, and came to my bedside. I turned completely to look up at her.

"It was dreadful," I said. "I hated every minute."

She nodded and sat on my bed. "I would have been surprised to hear otherwise. All I can tell you is it will get better."

"Time," I said disdainfully. I practically sneered. "I hate hearing that."

She shrugged. "What's true is true. All the king's horses and all the king's men . . ."

I looked at her and then, unable to prevent it, smiled. "My Faith has the Bible, and you have English nursery rhymes."

"Together we know it all," she said, smiling now, too. With her good hand, she brushed back strands of hair from my forehead just the way my grandma Arnold used to and my mother before her.

I sat up. "Did he tell you?"

"Who?"

"My grandfather. Did he tell you about that boy, what he plans on doing?"

"He did this morning. He told My Faith and me before he left for work."

"When is he bringing him here?"

"He didn't say exactly. He doesn't know yet. It's up to the doctors. He did tell us there would be a live-in private-duty nurse, too, and he would be bringing her around soon to get her settled in."

"A nurse? Living here, too?"

"The boy will need special attention and care, at least in the beginning, I'm sure."

"Why bring someone like that to a house? He belongs in some special clinic."

"People do recuperate better at home than they do in the hospital," she said.

"This isn't his home!"

She looked away a moment and nodded. "Well, your grandfather would like us to do what we can to help him feel like it is," she said, and stood up. "Don't you want one of My Faith's oatmeal raisin cookies? She made them today because they are your favorite."

"I'm not hungry," I said.

"Did you eat your lunch?"

"What I could."

"Well," she said, sighing as she walked toward the door, "if you get yourself sick, I suppose we'll be happy that we have a nurse in the house."

"I don't want a nurse in the house. I don't even want to see her."

"Then if you get yourself sick, you'll have to take care of yourself, Clara Sue. I can't be running up and down the stairs for a while, and My Faith will be busier than ever."

I turned away from her and pouted.

"It's all right to be angry, but don't punish yourself," she added. "Are you listening?"

I sucked in my breath and nodded. Of course she was right. It was also like a door had been opened in my mind. I understood now what Uncle Bobby meant when he had told me my grandfather was full of rage and wanted revenge. Grandpa was running on anger. It was helping him survive the grief. Maybe it would do the same for me. "I'll be down in a little while," I said, just as the phone rang.

Myra left when I picked up the receiver.

"What was it exactly that I did to you?" Lila asked.

"Nothing. It wasn't your fault. I was just frustrated and angry at everything and everyone. I'm sorry," I said. "I shouldn't have taken it out on you."

I could almost hear her sigh of relief. "All I was doing was trying to get everyone to understand."

"If they don't, that's their problem. If something horrible happens to them, they will for sure."

"I know. You're right, and I'm sorry. Should I come over? You didn't look like you were listening too well to anything we did in classes today."

I laughed to myself. That was an understatement. "Yes, you're right. Come over and enjoy some of My Faith's cookies, too," I told her.

"Good. I have a story for you. Ellie Patterson's parents might be getting a divorce. Her mother caught her father cheating with his secretary. Wait until I tell you how she let him know she had found out."

"I'm holding my breath," I said, and hung up.

Would I ever care about gossip anymore, delicious or otherwise?

As usual, I hurried to get out of my school clothes, tearing them off as if they were on fire. Our school had a boring dress code. At least we didn't have to wear uniforms like students in other private schools, but the restrictions for ours were strictly enforced. More than one girl and boy in my class had been sent home to change and warned that if it happened continually, they could be expelled, and their parents wouldn't get a tuition refund.

Our school required that we not dress in anything that revealed underwear or bare skin between the upper chest and mid-thigh. No spaghetti straps, strapless tops, or halter tops and especially no see-through mesh garments. No one could wear shorts, and girls could be sent home if their clothes looked too tight.

Girls could not wear skirts shorter than knee length. The only makeup tolerated was some lipstick if it wasn't put on thickly. If it was, you were sent to the girls' room to wipe it off entirely. Everyone hated the rules, and every girl I knew couldn't wait to get home and change into something else.

I put on the sloppiest-looking sweatshirt I had and a pair of jeans that were way too tight on me to "pass muster" at school, as Myra put it. I slipped into a pair of sandals without socks and, after unpinning my hair and shaking it around so it hung loose and wild, hurried downstairs. Even though I hated to admit it to myself, I was looking forward to seeing Lila now. Being alone only sharpened the pain and sorrow.

It was obvious that she had rushed to get here, because she was at our front door almost the exact moment I stepped off the stairway. Myra could be heard bawling out one of our two maids about the poor job she had done polishing furniture in the living room. The look on Lila's face at the sound of Myra's voice almost made me laugh. I shrugged to indicate that it was no big deal and led Lila to the kitchen, where My Faith eagerly piled up a plate full of her cookies. We grabbed some sodas and headed up to my room. As we passed Willie's room, I saw Lila pause to look at it. The door was open. The words wanted to come pouring out, describing what my grandfather intended, but I bit down on my lower lip, and we went to my room.

"So," Lila immediately began when we sat in lotus position on my rug, "I was in the girls' room after school when I heard someone crying in one of the toilets. I listened for a moment and then realized it was Ellie Patterson. I called to her, and she was quiet, and then she threw open the door and, still sitting on the toilet, began to tell me about her parents. She had been holding it in all day, and you want to know one reason?"

"I think I know."

"Yes, because of you. She thought her problem was . . ."

"Meaningless compared to it," I finished. "It is."

"Anyway . . . these cookies are fantastic. Anyway, her mother must have had a spy or something in her father's law offices. Somehow she knew to be at this motel outside of Prescott at lunchtime. She was waiting right outside the motel-room door when he came out with his secretary. How's that for being caught with your pants down?"

"They'll all live," I said dryly. I turned over to lie on my stomach and braced myself on my elbows. I couldn't keep it in any longer. I was thinking about it even when she was revealing her hot gossip. "He's coming here," I said after a few moments.

"Who's coming here?"

I turned over and looked up at the ceiling. "The poisoned boy."

"Why?"

"My grandfather has decided he should stay here to recuperate. He's hired a private-duty nurse for him, and she'll move in to live with us, too."

"Oh."

I looked at her. *She thinks Grandpa Arnold is*

simply being charitable, I thought. *She doesn't get it.*
"He's putting him in Willie's room."

Now her eyes widened. "Why? You have guest rooms. This house is bigger than ours."

"And giving him Willie's things, Willie's clothes, Willie's toys, everything."

She was silent, her mouth slightly open. Lila was far from beautiful. However, she had what Myra called a comely face, a face that could be called pretty but not extraordinarily so. To me, that sounded unflattering, and I hoped nobody ever thought of me that way. If there was one word I had learned to hate, it was "average." It sounded like everything you enjoyed that was exciting would be through someone else or because you tagged along with someone who truly enjoyed it, someone beyond average.

Did that make me snobby?

"Can he fit into Willie's clothes?" she asked.

"That's not the point! I don't care if he can or can't. Those are Willie's things."

She nodded, trying to look as outraged and disturbed as I was but so obvious about it that I had to turn away.

"Well," she offered, "if he's just borrowing them for a while . . ."

"Oh, Lila," I moaned, "once he uses any of it, it's his forever."

"That's terrible. I have an idea," she said after a moment.

"What?"

"If there are some things you don't want him to

have, why don't you go in there now and get them and keep them hidden in your room?"

I thought for a moment. There were many things of Willie's that I wouldn't want anyone else to have, but going in there to retrieve them suddenly seemed intimidating. Would I just start crying uncontrollably? Would I feel guilty taking them? Would it be another way to convince myself of Willie's death, not that I needed much more to do that? What would Grandpa think? How angry would he get?

"I suppose if I chose carefully, I wouldn't need to take that much," I said, working on convincing myself.

"Were you in there . . . since . . . ?"

"Just the first night."

She nodded. "I'll go in there with you," she said. I could see she was a little scared of the idea but was willing to do it for me. She was a good friend after all.

"Thanks. Let's do it," I said firmly, and got up. She nodded, and we walked out together, suddenly moving slyly, like burglars or something. I certainly didn't want Myra or My Faith catching me doing this.

At Willie's doorway, I paused to make a list of what I would retrieve. It began with the windup train set that our parents had given him when he was only five. Even though Grandpa had replaced it with an electric train set we would bring out every Christmas and set up around the tree, Willie cherished his simple train set.

There was his favorite winter hat, the one with the built-in earmuffs. It was hard to think of him on a sled or playing in the snow without it on. He never seemed to outgrow it. He wasn't the sort of boy who would ever play with dolls, but he had a Superman doll that he kept on the shelf built into his bed headboard. Although I hadn't heard him doing it lately, I could clearly recall overhearing him talk to Superman about some imaginary villain they were both going to get. And, of course, there was his copy of *The Complete Fairy Tales* by Hans Christian Andersen that our mother read to him and that I read to him after she was gone.

I feared that once I was in his room, however, I would be like someone told to evacuate their home because a terrible fire was bearing down on it. In a panic, what would they grab to save? Surely, I was in a very similar place. I looked at Lila, nodded, and went in. I went directly to the things I had listed in my mind, piled them on his bed, and paused to look around. There were other toys and books that I knew he treasured. Of course, the Slinky, I thought, and went for it. And what about the paddle ball with the target on it? Yes, and his bag of marbles. There was his baseball bat and the glove Grandpa had bought him last Christmas. He and I had played with it in the snow, which made everyone laugh. I knew I could go on and on, but I didn't have room in my closet for much more.

"Okay," I said. "For now."

Lila and I gathered it all and brought it to my room. I put as much as I could in my closet but decided to keep the Superman doll on my desk with his winter hat beside it.

"If you want to go get more, I'll go back with you," Lila said.

"No, this is enough for now. There's a lot downstairs that belongs to him, but I can't imagine the poisoned boy ever getting his hands on any of it."

"Sure. He'll probably be out of here once he gets well enough, anyway," she said.

"Maybe," I said.

"His family has to be looking for him, right?"

"His family?" I laughed. "All this time, no one calling the police or getting it into the papers?"

"You told me there was the possibility that he was kidnapped and the ransom wasn't paid."

"So? Wouldn't you still be looking for him?" I asked.

She nodded. "Weird."

"Let's not talk about it anymore," I said, as if that was the secret to making it all go away. "Homework."

"Right," she said, relieved. "Math first."

When we went at it, I realized just how much I hadn't absorbed. I must have been in a daze all day, I thought, and quietly told myself that I would do better tomorrow. We worked for hours and didn't talk about anything else. After Lila left, I looked at all of Willie's things that we had gathered. It gave me some satisfaction. I had told Lila not to talk about it, any of it. She took an oath. I had wanted to invite her to stay for dinner, but I could see she thought she should go home to be with her parents. What was happening to Ellie Patterson, the destruction of her family, frightened Lila. Who could blame her for wanting to cling harder to her loved ones? She knew I had lost most of my family in tragedies.

When you're young, even a teenager, you just don't believe in the possible end of some things. Divorces weren't as common as they would become. Sickness and tragedy always seemed to happen to someone else. We were gliding on naivete, seemingly just a few days away from the innocence and gullibility we left behind in preadolescence. You didn't have to live in our privileged world to drift about in a refusal to accept reality. There would be time for that years from now, right?

Go home, Lila, I thought enviously. *Cherish every moment as if it will be your last. Somewhere above or around us, God is turning a page, and you might not like what is written on it.*

Grandpa didn't come to see me as soon as he arrived. I was half-hoping he would, but he went to his room and then to his office before I went down to dinner.

When Willie was at the dinner table, Grandpa always seemed to have a lot to say. Whatever Willie said about his day or something special he had done, Grandpa had a story to tell about himself when he was Willie's age. He told it as if he was telling it to both of us, but I knew he was really telling it to Willie. Boys needed fathers and grandfathers; girls needed mothers and grandmothers. I had become more and more of an orphan as I grew older and needed them more.

Of course, Grandpa asked me about school. I tried to make it seem as if it had gone all right. I assured him that I had caught up with my work. I kept waiting for him to say something about the poisoned boy, but he didn't talk about him. Instead, he told me things about his business, things he never really talked about. I thought he was just trying to fill the silence. I tried to pay attention and be interested, but it was like listening to someone speaking in another language.

The following evening, he talked about his business less, and the evening after that, he stopped altogether. Our meals grew quieter and shorter. Myra and My Faith did their best to make them festive, but as that first week drew to a close, Grandpa missed the last two dinners entirely. Myra sat with me, and one night, Lila did come to dinner. We worked on homework and talked about boys again.

The grip that sadness had on me weakened. I could feel myself moving with more energy in school, and I was paying attention to the work again. I did well on my first tests and quizzes since returning. However, I still refused to do anything social on the weekend, and I regretted it. I insisted that Lila go to a party without me, promising her I would do something with her the following weekend. But in the middle of the following week, Grandpa introduced me to the private-duty nurse, Dorian Camden, and I couldn't think about much else.

He had finally decided to tell me directly of his specific plans to bring the boy to our house, how he would accommodate him and provide what was necessary for his recuperation. He went on and on about his medical treatments, the diagnosis, the horrible impact the slow arsenic poisoning had on his body, filling his descriptions with terms the doctors had used. He emphasized how important it still was for him to have private nursing care.

I sat and listened, sullen and quiet, but if he noticed, he either didn't care or thought that the more he talked, the better the chance would be that I would relent and be more cooperative, even happy about it.

"I introduced her to him at the hospital," he said.

"Did he talk to her?" I asked sharply.

"No. He still hasn't said anything to anyone."

"Then maybe she's not a good nurse," I said petulantly. "Nurses are supposed to be trained for that, aren't they?"

"Oh, no, no. Dr. Friedman recommended her. She was the first one who came to his mind."

I didn't say anything more. There was no way I could discourage him.

When he brought Dorian Camden to our house and introduced her to everyone, I saw that she was an attractive woman, with intelligent light blue eyes and short but stylish hair the color of a ripe lemon. I wondered if my grandfather had gone searching for a nurse who bore some resemblance to the poisoned boy, with his cerulean-blue eyes and flaxen hair. Nothing seemed too ridiculous when I thought of how determined my grandpa was to provide for this boy's needs. Although he didn't tell me how old she was, I concluded from her description of places she had worked that she was easily in her mid-forties.

"I hope I can count on you for some help," Dorian

Camden told me. I didn't answer. She held her smile. It was a soft, warm smile. I wished it wasn't. I wanted her to be ugly and mean so I could have an easier time hating her being here, but she had a pleasant voice and a kind way about her. I supposed a nurse had to have all that in order to provide tender loving care.

Grandpa asked Myra to show her where her room would be. She was going to take the room upstairs that had always been my parents' room when we visited. It was close to Willie's room. Of course, it bothered me that she would stay in that room. No one had since the day we learned of their deaths, but Myra always made sure it was kept clean and polished, as if she expected their miraculous return.

I assumed that because she was moving in now, it wouldn't be too much longer before the boy was brought here. My grandpa still didn't come right out and say he would be here tomorrow or the next day or anything. I could see from the way My Faith and Myra were moving about that things were being rearranged in anticipation. I wasn't going to give anyone the satisfaction of asking about him. I wanted them all to believe I had little or no interest. I expected Myra at least would force me to know things, but suddenly, every mention of him was behind closed doors or well out of my hearing. To me, it felt like the house was full of whispers, new secrets that made me feel like more of a stranger than the boy who would be here.

Of course, Lila was asking me about him whenever we spoke. My answers were short and simple. "I don't know. I don't care. No one has said."

"Well, maybe he's not coming after all," she said the day after Dorian Camden moved in.

"Why would the nurse be there, then, Lila?"

"Maybe only just in case," she offered weakly.

"I don't want to talk about it," I told her, and she stopped. Meanwhile, despite my sour face, our friends tried to include me in everything when I was in school. But thoughts about the poisoned boy and my grandpa distracted me again, and on the ride home, I was no better emotionally than I was on the ride back the first day. My heart was beating faster as we approached the front gates. I could feel every muscle in my body getting tense. All eyes would be on me if that boy was here. Everyone would be waiting for my reactions, for sure.

The moment I saw that Grandpa was already home, I knew he was there. He was in Willie's room.

It was beginning. I had to face up to it. *Right now*, I thought. I would pretend that nothing was different, that he wasn't there. I wouldn't see him or hear anyone talking about him. The moment I entered the house, however, Grandpa turned from speaking with Dorian Camden and nodded at me.

"He's here," he said.

I looked down. For a moment, I didn't move, and then I started toward the stairway.

"Clara Sue!" he called firmly.

"What?"

"I'd like you to welcome him. I'll go up with you, and you can just welcome him, help make him comfortable."

"He didn't talk to me before, and he didn't even want to look at me. He won't now," I said. "I don't want to waste my breath," I added, and before he could say another word, I shot up the stairway. I heard him shout after me, but I kept going. I practically ran past Willie's room, not looking in, and when I got to my room, I shut the door quickly behind me.

My heart was pounding. I just stood there, anticipating my grandfather coming up after me.

But he didn't.

Silence was uncomfortable, but I was glad to have it.

Later, I heard the activity in the hallway, but I didn't look out to see. The walls in Grandpa's mansion were thick enough to prevent talking or almost any reasonable noise from being heard by the person in the next room. I did put my ear to the wall to see what I could hear, but the murmur of Dorian Camden's and my grandpa's conversation was so muffled and incoherent that I quickly gave up. And then I chastised myself for having any curiosity or interest at all. It wasn't good enough just to hide it from everyone else; I had to prevent myself from having it. Was that impossible? After all, he was here with all his mystery, his emotional and psychological problems, and my grandfather's determination to do something about it. Those weren't easy things to ignore.

At dinner, Dorian Camden declared that for the first few days or so, it would be wise for her to have her dinner with the boy. She explained to Myra and My Faith, who were obviously fascinated by all of it, that what she had to do was win his trust.

"All the patients I've had who were wounded or injured badly were angry at everyone and everything in the beginning. The first question that comes to mind is 'Why me? What did I do to deserve this?'"

"Even someone this young?" Myra asked her. I couldn't help listening. I tried to pretend I wasn't.

"Oh, especially so, because at this age, you are dependent on someone who is supposed to care for and protect you. Obviously, that didn't happen or was prevented from happening. I've spoken with Dr. Patrick, who has treated children who were taught to believe they were somehow unworthy."

"You mean evil?" My Faith asked.

"Possibly, so between her work and what I will try to do, we have to get him to believe more in himself."

She looked at me.

"We can all help," she added. I turned away, tempted to ask, "What if he really is evil?" That would widen My Faith's eyes for sure, but I didn't say a word.

Grandpa was obviously very angry with me and said little at dinner. The way we were behaving, it could have been only a day or so after Willie's funeral. The air around us was that heavy. A phone call drew him away, and I finished eating before he returned. Then I went up to do my homework. I walked quickly past Willie's room, tiptoeing, in fact, so Dorian wouldn't hear me approaching and try calling me in. Then I closed my door.

It was almost impossible to concentrate on my homework. Lila called. I told her the boy was here.

Her sympathy began to irritate me, and I told her I had to finish my homework because I had been too upset to start it. She apologized for not coming over, "especially tonight."

"Especially tonight, it's better that you didn't," I said, and said good night.

Hours later, after everyone seemed to have gone to bed, I opened my door and peered out. The light from Willie's room was spilling into the hallway. Would the boy always need a light on? I wondered. Was Dorian Camden still in there with him? Was he hooked up to the same sort of machinery he was hooked up to in the hospital? It was impossible not to be curious now. I relented and tiptoed down the hallway. Just before I reached the door, I heard Grandpa's voice clearly.

"You're in Willie's room. It will make it easier," I heard him say.

Make what easier? I drew closer and peered into the room.

The boy was in Willie's bed but without any machinery attached to him. He was just lying there, and Grandpa was sitting beside the bed. It looked like he was holding his hand.

"Lots of his stuff has the initials W.S.," he continued, "but there is one difference. You won't be Willie Sanders, which was my grandson's name, but I want you to be Willie Arnold . . . William Arnold. It will be more like you are another grandson. Yes, that's my name, too, but it's not uncommon for boys to be named after their fathers and grandfathers."

I tried to swallow when I realized I was holding my breath to the point where my throat and my chest ached. Grandpa was giving him Willie's name, too!

"Until you remember your own name," he added. "Okay?"

I waited to see if the boy would speak, but he didn't.

Grandpa acted as if he had, however. "Good," he said. "Good."

I felt everything I had eaten churn in my stomach. I covered my mouth and then moaned and rushed back to my room and into my bathroom, where I vomited and vomited until I sank to the floor by the toilet.

Which was where Myra found me in the morning.

6

Dorian Camden was at my bedside, looking as concerned as my mother would have. Myra had called her out of Willie's room. I imagined everyone expected I would be happy that we had a real nurse in the house when we needed one, but I still couldn't get used to the sight of her parading about in that nurse's uniform and all that it meant.

"How do you feel?" she asked.

"Sick," I said. I wanted to add, *What kind of a nurse are you? How am I supposed to feel after throwing up and falling asleep on the bathroom floor?* But I didn't. I didn't want to talk at all. I closed my eyes and then opened them when I felt her hand on my forehead.

She looked at Myra, who was gray with worry. Who could blame her? Willie was killed, and now I was sick. What was next? The very walls falling in?

"Are you going to the bathroom a lot?" Dorian asked.

"You mean, do I have diarrhea?" I wasn't the poisoned boy. She could talk to me like an adult.

"Yes."

"No."

"It still could be a touch of the stomach flu," she told Myra. "I don't think she has any fever. I'll check. You don't always have a fever with the flu."

"I'll get My Faith to put up some tea and honey," Myra said, and hurried out.

Dorian looked down at me, her eyes full of suspicion. "You haven't eaten or drunk anything you shouldn't have, have you, Clara Sue?"

"Of course not." Was she thinking I had been sneaking whiskey into my room? "You can search my room if you want," I snapped at her, and turned away, just the way the poisoned boy would turn away when someone spoke to him or asked him questions.

"But you threw up?"

I didn't respond. I could feel her gaze locked on me.

"Do you have any pains in your stomach?"

"No."

"Are you still nauseated?"

"No," I said, a little louder. I didn't want her asking me any more questions.

"People can make themselves sick, you know. They can get themselves so upset that they start to take on the symptoms of illnesses or just make themselves more vulnerable to diseases and such. Is that what's happening here?"

I spun around and glared up at her. "You're the nurse. Figure it out," I said.

She winced, turned, and walked out. I thought that was the end of her, but she returned with a thermometer and said, "Please open your mouth." She put it under my tongue. As soon as Myra arrived with the tea, she took out the thermometer, looked at it, and said, "Normal."

"That's good."

"I would keep her on a light diet today and make sure she has lots of liquids," she advised Myra. She looked at me, expecting me to say thank you, I was sure, but I just turned away until she started out.

Myra watched her go and then set my tea down. I saw she had brought along a piece of toast and jelly as well.

"She's a very good nurse, Clara Sue. I watched her with the boy. I could see he likes her."

"The boy? You mean William?" I said disdainfully.

"What?"

"Didn't Grandpa announce it today?"

"Announce what?"

"Drumroll, please. The poisoned boy has been baptized."

Myra shook her head. "I don't understand what you're saying, Clara Sue."

"Grandpa wants him to accept being called William Arnold," I said.

I sipped some tea and studied her reaction. She was in deep thought a moment. "He told you he wanted you to call the boy Willie?" she asked.

"No. I overheard him talking to the boy and giving him Willie's formal name, William, until he remembers his real name. He's sorta borrowing it, borrowing everything that was my brother's."

"I suppose it must be pretty frightening not to remember your own name," she offered. "Your grandfather is just trying to help."

"Why doesn't he call him something else, anything else? Jack? Mark? Tom? Or just keep calling him Boy. Tarzan called his son Boy, didn't he? Maybe if everyone called him Boy, he would finally get tired of it and remember his name."

She shook her head.

"He told him Willie's initials are on lots of things, W.S. But he wants him to accept William Arnold. He'll probably get the initials changed."

"You think your grandfather would change them?"

"Yes. Lucky boy, huh?"

"Well, I wouldn't say he's been too lucky up to now, would you, Clara Sue?"

"I don't care. Right now, he falls into a vat of good luck just when my brother Willie fell into a vat of very bad."

Myra pressed her lips together. Her eyes were filling with tears. I realized that I wasn't helping her feel less guilty about what had happened.

"None of it was your fault, Myra," I said, now struggling to keep back my own tears. "It was just bad luck to be there at the same time some horrible drunk man was driving along our street. This all just makes it . . . makes it worse!"

She patted my hand and stood up. "We'll see. In the meantime, try to hold down some toast and jam, and maybe you'll be able to have My Faith's mushy eggs for lunch." She started to turn away.

"Bad things can happen to good people, too, Myra. I know My Faith doesn't like to talk about it, why God lets that happen, but it's true. And it doesn't matter how rich you are or where you live."

I thought she would stay and argue with me about it, but all she said before she left was "Don't make yourself sicker over it. Stop having these thoughts. If you ever need strength in this life, it's when you have troubles like this."

I felt like pounding the bed and screaming. How could I stop having these thoughts? All these dark thoughts seemed to have seeped in under my door and through my closed windows. They were swirling around me. Nightmares would dance at the foot of my bed forever. What Grandpa was doing was only making everything more terrible. I wanted to scream louder, until Myra would call him and he would come rushing home from work and decide to put the boy into a clinic or something, but I choked it all back and fell asleep.

When Myra returned with another cup of tea, I felt guilty about her waiting on me like this. She wouldn't tell anyone else to bring it up to me, and I knew she was still having trouble getting about with that cast and her aches and pains. A little while before, I had heard some voices in the hallway. One of them was Dorian Camden's, but I didn't know who the other person was, except that it was another woman. I asked Myra about it. I was hoping it was someone from one of those government agencies here to arrange for the boy to be taken away. She would tell Grandpa that no matter how rich he was, he couldn't just scoop up some child and take care of him. There were rules.

"Oh, that's the psychiatrist," she said. "Her name is Dr. Patrick. They were very excited because the boy was speaking a little."

I was disappointed. "Really? What did he say?" On the other hand, maybe he was finally revealing his family name, and they could contact the police and get him home.

"He wasn't answering much about himself, but he was expressing how happy he was to be here."

"Who wouldn't be?" I said. "Look what he's been given."

"You don't want to sound uncharitable, Clara Sue. He's a helpless soul."

"Maybe we all are," I muttered, and she gave me one of her schoolteacher disapproving glances that could probably stop a charging bull in its tracks. "I'll get up for lunch."

"Mrs. Camden will be happy to hear it. She thought it was nothing more than an upset stomach."

"I'll bet," I said, and paused. "'Mrs.'? I don't remember Grandpa saying she was married. How can she be married and live here, anyway? What about her husband?"

"Her husband passed away a little more than three years ago. She said he was a severe diabetic, and that led to other complications."

"What about her children?"

"They never had any. She's really a very nice lady besides being a very good nurse," Myra said. "Your grandfather hired her to do a job, and that's what she'll do."

In other words, I shouldn't take my unhappiness out on her, I thought. That's what Myra was saying. I grunted and drank a little more tea. Dorian Camden had been right, of course. I was making myself sick, and who benefited from that? Not me.

"Please tell My Faith that I've been thinking about her scrambled mushy eggs," I told her.

She smiled. "Good."

"Is that Dr. Patrick still here?" I asked. I was thinking that I'd like to ask her some questions and maybe get at the truth.

"No, she just left, but your grandfather is coming home."

"You told him I was sick?"

For a moment, she looked confused or afraid to reply. She shook her head. "No. I didn't speak with him. He called to let Jimmy know he was bringing a contractor to do some work. He's arranging for a wheelchair for the little boy," she told me. "Mrs. Camden thinks they should be able to get him up and into it in a day or so."

"What did you mean by 'some work'?"

"Your grandfather is thinking about making some changes in the house to accommodate him," she replied.

"What sort of changes?"

"I don't know yet, Clara Sue. Changes. I'll tell

My Faith you're coming down, then," she said, and left.

Why would Grandpa be making changes in the house? How long was the boy going to be here? How long would he be in a wheelchair? Did I care? Was he turning this place into a hospital or something? Hospitals smelled like . . . hospitals. Was that what the hallways outside my room would soon be like? How could I bring any friends here?

I went to take a shower and get dressed. Curiosity about the things Myra had told me was motivating me to get up and about. By the time I descended, Grandpa was home, and there was a man talking to him about the stairway.

"We'll have two wheelchairs, then. One for upstairs and one for downstairs," I heard Grandpa say before he saw me. "Hey," he said. "I just heard you were home from school because you were sick this morning."

"Just an upset stomach. I'm all right now," I told him.

He nodded. I knew what he was thinking. Grandpa Arnold was never good about anything that could possibly be related to feminine problems. He fled from the mere suggestion. He returned to talking with the man, the back of whose shirt read, "TLC Healthcare Equipment." I lingered to hear more of what they were saying. Grandpa wanted the man to install a stair lift. The man was saying he'd been busy doing that work ever since the polio epidemic had created such a dramatic need for lifts, especially for young children who were teenagers or young adults by now.

He wanted to know if the child had not had the Salk vaccine and had contracted polio.

"From what little I know of the way the boy was treated, it wouldn't surprise me to learn that his parents never had him vaccinated, but no, that's not his problem," he said, and didn't say anything else.

Install a stair lift? I thought. On that stairway Grandma Arnold was so proud to show off because of its thick, embossed mahogany banisters and newel posts carved from a single block of wood? As soon as someone entered the house, it was the first thing they saw. It was like our centerpiece. Sometimes Grandma used to laugh and pretend she was some actress in a movie descending those steps. I remember how my mother laughed at her and called her Scarlett O'Hara. What would it look like with a lift?

After lunch, I would discover that Grandpa had also contracted with some construction workers to build a ramp in the front right beside the short stairway. They were already constructing it, in fact. What other changes would he make? Would he buy an ambulance and have it parked outside the front door?

I returned to my room. In a few hours, Lila was sure to be calling to see why I didn't go to school. I thought I would do some reading for English class. This time, as I approached Willie's bedroom, I paused and glanced in. The boy was sitting up in bed. He had what looked like a small pile of new comic books. Grandpa would always buy a bundle of them for Willie when he was home sick. The boy was wearing what I knew to be a newer pair of Willie's polka-dot yellow pajamas. When he glanced up at me, I hurried away.

As expected, Lila called the moment she came home from school to find out why I wasn't there. I told her I had woken up sick, but it was just an upset stomach.

"You know, I still get bad menstrual cramps occasionally," she said. "Sometimes so bad that I don't want to go to school, either, but my mother makes me." I could sense that she wanted my problem to be anything other than my sadness or my attitude about the boy taking over Willie's things.

"It wasn't that, but I'm okay," I told her.

She then informed me of our homework assignments, because she wasn't coming over. Her mother wanted her to go with her to buy some new clothes for the approaching winter.

"If you want, you could come along. Maybe you'll see something you want or need."

One of the things I liked about Lila was how casual she was about inviting me to do things with her family. My other girlfriends were tentative about it. I think they believed my participating in events with their mothers or mothers and fathers would be painful for me. It was reminding me that I didn't have parents, only grandparents. Even when Grandma Arnold was alive and well enough, we didn't do half as much as my girlfriends and their mothers did together. The truth was, I did feel different and a little uncomfortable doing things with my girlfriends and their parents. How could I not remember times I had gone places with my own parents or with just my mother? Lila either was indifferent to my feelings about it or never really noticed.

"Thanks, but I think I'll just stick to my homework and be sure I feel better for tomorrow."

"There's talk of a party next weekend," she said. "Audrey O'Brian's parents said she could use their basement, and you know how big that is. We could hold a school dance in it. They have that jukebox and pool table. It'll be lots of fun."

"Maybe I won't be invited."

"Oh, no. I already spoke to her," she followed too quickly, almost swallowing back her words.

"Spoke to her? What's that mean?"

She was quiet, knowing she had taken a step too far to pull back. "Oh, she was just worried you weren't ready yet," she finally revealed.

"So she thought I might spoil her party, depress everyone?"

"Oh, no, no."

"What did you do to convince her I was *ready*?" I added. *How can you think like that, anyway?* I wondered. Was getting over your little brother's death something you declared "done" at some point so that you could be "ready"?

Again, she was silent.

Another thought occurred to me. "Lila? You didn't say anything about the boy in Willie's room and what we did with my brother's toys?"

"Oh, no, no, no. I just told her you needed to get out and be with your friends now. It would be good for you."

"Good for me?" *Funny how fast you can become a charity case in this world*, I thought, now thinking of both myself and the boy.

"Yes. She agreed, and she was happy about your coming. Really. Everyone wants you . . ."

Don't say "to get better," I thought. Maybe she heard me think it.

"To be part of everything."

"I'll think about it," I added.

"Aaron is hoping you'll come," she sang.

"I said I'll think about it."

"Okay. I'll check on you later," Lila said.

"Right."

Check on me, I thought. *See if I'm still here.*

And what if I had really been sick last night and this morning? I wondered. What if I had died? Would Grandpa Arnold go looking for a poor girl my age who needed tender loving care and put her in my room, give her my clothes, my things, and call her Clara Sue?

After I hung up, I did get into my homework. I wanted to do whatever I could not to think about it all, even though it was nearly impossible. Right now, all my good memories of my parents, my grandma Arnold, our seemingly charmed lives, full of laughter and the wonderful surprises Daddy would bring home to my mother and Willie and me, seemed more like fiction. Was there really ever a time when I felt safe and protected, when the worst disappointment might be having to go to sleep too early or having it rain on the day we were going to the funfair? Could I say we lived a charmed life, never wanting for anything?

We didn't simply have expensive clothes and cars and homes. Our family was glued together with love. Kisses fell over us like warm raindrops. Not a day went by without warm hugs. We truly cherished one another and welcomed every chance to touch one another. Laughter was the music we heard daily. It got so that I never even contemplated real sadness and unhappiness.

Perhaps there was a part of me now, a part that was self-protective, that deliberately made my memories of good times distant and vague. Anyone who had gone through what I had could spend the rest of her life in a sulk, hating the sunshine, hating the smiles on other people's faces, and even hating the sound of her name, for no one said it as beautifully as my parents and Willie had. Not even my grandfather or Myra or My Faith. *Remember and suffer,* I told myself, *or get up and do everything you can to forget and live.*

Maybe that was the real reason I hated the idea of the boy in Willie's room. Every day, every time I saw him or passed by the room, I would see Willie dying on that sidewalk, his little body smashed. How could I look at another boy around his age wearing his clothes, playing with his toys, and sleeping in his bed and not mourn Willie? Why couldn't anyone else see how true that was? Why wasn't it as true for them?

Anger returned and ironically gave me the strength to get up and move about. I heard Grandpa come home. Because my door was partly opened, I knew he had gone directly into Willie's room. I could hear him and Dorian Camden talking. They were saying things

with a happy tone for the boy's benefit, compliment-
ing him on doing the simplest things like finishing
his breakfast and his lunch or brushing his teeth. The
sound of their laughter was as grating as fingernails on
a blackboard. Finally, it grew quiet. I waited to see if
Grandpa would come into my room to be sure I was
not still ill, but he didn't. He either went to his own
room or went back downstairs. My appetite had returned, so I was eager to go to dinner.

When I reached Willie's room and looked in, I saw
Mrs. Camden preparing the bed table for the boy to
have his dinner. She was describing the food and the
chocolate cake he would have for dessert. He did look
more alert and excited about it. I stood there for a few
moments and listened to how sweetly she spoke. I
wasn't jealous. I was actually happy she was so good at
her nursing, because it occurred to me that if she really
was a great nurse, she might get him well faster, and I
still harbored the hope that once he was well enough,
he would be gone.

Everyone seemed cheerier at dinner this evening.
Mrs. Camden joined us at the table. I was surprised at
that. I thought she would have to eat her meals with
the boy, if not for any other reason than to be sure he
ate his food and didn't choke on anything. Myra rarely
ate with us and only ate with me when my grandfather
couldn't be at dinner. There seemed to be this unspo-
ken rule that those who were employed were not dinner guests, but if that was a rule, Grandpa was happy
to break it for Dorian Camden. I could see clearly how
pleased he was to have her there. For a while, it was

almost as if I wasn't present, but I didn't mind, because Grandpa was getting her to tell more about herself, and despite everything, especially how I felt about her being here, I couldn't help but be interested, too.

"So how long were you at the veterans hospital?" he asked her.

"Nearly ten years. As you can imagine, especially for those who had been injured in some military exercise and had suffered the loss of limbs, there was a great deal of psychological counseling. Of course, we had veterans who had been seriously injured doing other things since they had left the service, but the end result was the same: lots of bitterness and depression. Who'd blame any of them for wanting to forget it all?"

"Probably takes more tender loving care than in other hospitals."

"A bit more, yes," she said. She looked at me. "I'm glad you're feeling better, Clara Sue."

"Thank you."

She glanced at my grandfather and then turned back to me. "I'm expecting to get our boy up and about in his new wheelchair this weekend. The stair lift should be installed by then, won't it, Mr. Arnold?"

"Please. Call me William. Yes, it should be done in one day."

"Good. We can show him more of the house and the grounds. Clara Sue, you can come along and describe things."

"Describe things? It's not a museum or something."

"Well, it's still your home, not mine. You can talk

about it more. It's a beautiful property. The landscaping is breathtaking."

"Won some prizes, eh, Clara Sue?" Grandpa said proudly.

"Yes."

"I'll have to show you the trophies," he told her.

"You have a lovely pool, William," Mrs. Camden said. "Next summer, he can use the pool for therapy, too."

"Next summer?" I looked sharply at Grandpa Arnold. "He'll be here until next summer?"

"I suspect he'll be here a long time, Clara Sue," he said. "There's been no progress in learning about his past. I've made a formal request to be his foster parent for the time being."

"Foster parent? But . . ." I looked at Mrs. Camden. "Won't he remember everything eventually?"

"Dr. Patrick thinks he will be selective about what he does and doesn't remember. It might not be enough to track back to what happened. Whatever it was, it was so emotionally traumatic that his mind is repressing it, and that might continue for some time yet. You understand?"

"Yes, I understand," I said sharply. "I understand that he can pretend to be unable to remember just so he can stay in my brother's room forever, too."

Neither she nor my grandfather said anything. They simply stared at me as if I were the weird child. I took a breath. What Myra had said upstairs was true, I thought. Every time I said something bitter, I looked like the bad one. I stared back at my grandfather nevertheless.

"I'm never, ever going to call him Willie," I said. "He's not Willie."

Grandpa didn't change his expression. "That's fine. I'd rather he simply went by William," he said.

"That doesn't make any difference. His name is not William, either."

"We don't know that for sure," Grandpa said. "Could be William."

"Not William Arnold," I countered. I could feel the muscles in my neck straining.

"Try not to upset yourself so much," Mrs. Camden said.

I looked down and then up, smiling. "You're right. I'm not going to upset myself about it. I'm just going to do what he's doing."

"What's that, dear?"

"Forget. Forget he's even here," I said, and put down my fork and got up.

"Clara Sue!" Grandpa said sharply. "It's impolite to leave in the middle of dinner."

"Oh. I'm as full as I can be, Grandpa. I don't want to eat too much on a sore stomach. That's right, isn't it, Mrs. Camden?" I asked her.

She nodded.

I turned and walked away slowly, and when I reached the stairway, I pounded my way up loudly enough for a boy who was as deaf as he was dumb to hear. I paused when I reached Willie's room. The boy was obviously waiting for me. He was simply sitting up and staring at the doorway.

Maybe, I thought, just maybe, I could get him to tell the truth. I looked back, listened, and then stepped into Willie's room. He eyed me with caution as I walked slowly toward him. This close, I could see how dainty he looked, so fragile. Could he have gotten this way just from the poison? His skin was so thin that I could see little blue veins in his temples and cheeks. He looked like he had the bones of a bird.

I waited to see if he would speak, but he just stared at me, those blue eyes looking so anxious. He wasn't as handsome as Willie had been. He looked more like a pretty boy, a doll, with his perfect nose and mouth and that golden hair. His hands were small, too, and his arms looked like they might snap if he raised them too fast or too hard.

"Did they hit you a lot, too?" I asked.

His eyes widened a bit, but he didn't speak.

"You know you were poisoned, right? They told you that, right?"

He nodded, barely.

"So you almost died and would have if my grand-father hadn't gotten you the best doctors and nurses."

He still didn't speak.

"How do you like living in my brother's room?" I asked.

He looked around as if what I said had made him aware of where he was for the first time.

"I bet it's a lot nicer than the room you had in your home, right?"

He stared at me.

"Did you have a bed this big?"

He looked like he was thinking.

I drew closer. "Well?"

"Bed?" he said. The sound of his voice surprised me but also encouraged me.

"Yes, bed. Bed. Where you sleep, remember?"

He shook his head.

"Oh, come on. You can't forget where you slept. I'll tell you what," I continued, now standing beside him. "I'll tell you a secret about this room if you tell me one of your secrets, like where did you live or what's your name or who you think put poison in your food. Okay?"

He widened his eyes and stared at me like he was trying to figure out if I was human or an alien from some distant planet.

"Okay. Here's the secret. My brother had a secret place in this room where he kept interesting bugs because he knew the maids would clean them up. He kept them for a while, and then he got rid of them himself after he studied them. In that closet, he has a microscope. It's not a toy. My grandfather got it for him two years ago. I'll show you how to use it, and you can look at a strand of your hair or something. It's amazing. Would you like that?"

He nodded.

"Good. So what's your name?" I asked.

He smiled. *He's going to tell me.* My heart started to race. I looked at the door. I would get him to say what they couldn't. I'd be the one to end this. I'd be the one who got the police to do something. My grandfather could stop changing the house immediately.

I waited a moment. "Your name? What's your name?" I demanded. "If you don't tell me, I won't tell you anything. There are more secrets, more fun things to find. I'll tell you everything, but you've got to tell me your name first. Okay?"

He nodded and smiled.

"Good. So what is it? What's your name?"

"William," he said. "William Arnold."

7

I turned and ran out of the room. I was actually trembling when I sat on my bed. I couldn't get out of my mind the look of glee on his face when he suddenly said, "William Arnold." It was weird. He looked like he believed he really had remembered that was his name. His eyes lit up as if it had just come back to him, and he smiled just the way someone who had been trying hard to remember something would smile. I was shivering. I sat there with my arms wrapped around myself, partly chastising myself for getting so foolishly frightened and acting like it. Maybe that was what he had wanted.

When I heard footsteps on the stairway and in the hall, I rose quickly and shut my door. I didn't want to talk to anybody or let anyone see how disturbed I was and ask why, not even Myra or My Faith, but when the phone rang, I leaped at it. My hello was a little over the top. I'm sure I sounded like someone stuck in a coal mine for days who finally had contact with the outside world.

"Clara Sue?"

"Yes, yes."

"It's Lila. Hi," she said.

"Hi, hi, hi."

"Are you all right?"

"Yes, yes, what's happening?"

"Nothing. I was just checking to be sure you're coming to school tomorrow."

"Yes, I'm coming. I'm fine, fine." I took a breath and added in a tone of defiance, "And I'm definitely going to Audrey's party."

I was determined now not to punish myself anymore. Fate had done enough on its own, and the boy next door was compounding it.

"Oh, good. And you know who will be happy about that."

"We'll see how happy he really is. I think his picture is next to 'flirt' in the dictionary," I added, feeling my body soften and calm as a flood of images returned. Boys, parties, music, and laughter. I flopped onto my bed. "Don't forget. You were the one who told me he had 'bedroom eyes.'"

She giggled. "You sound more like yourself," she said. I could almost see her biting down on her lip and holding her breath after uttering those words, and for the first time, I really did feel sorry for her.

When someone is emerging from the darkness of great sorrow like I was, it was natural to be timid about saying anything that seemed like you didn't share that sorrow or respect it any longer. But how long could I expect my friends to be sympathetic?

Who wants to walk continually in the shadows, tip-toeing and watching every word she spoke and checking first before she permitted herself to smile or laugh?

"I'm myself. I'm myself. Never more myself," I said. "I've got to finish the math. That last problem was a doozy. I put it off for a while because my head was spinning."

"I didn't even start math yet," she confessed.

"Well, get to it. I don't want to see you grounded for failing grades."

She laughed, more relaxed this time. I welcomed the sound of it, but it did seem strange to hear it. When was the last time I had laughed? When was the last time I had heard Willie's laugh? My Faith always claimed that laughter was "the gift of angels." It certainly beat crying.

"Okay," Lila said. "I'll get to work. Oh. All the girls in our class are wearing red tomorrow."

"Why?"

"The joke we pulled on Mr. Leshner. Oh, right. You wouldn't know. It was Rose Mosely's idea. She sent a note to him telling him she had a crush on him and couldn't stand it. She piled it on, claiming it was making her sick. She couldn't sleep; she couldn't eat. She got all the lines out of some romance novel about this schoolteacher who seduces a student, or vice versa. She sent a different note saying something similar for four days in a row, without signing them, and then yesterday in a note, she told him that tomorrow she would wear red so he would know who she was. And so we're all wearing red. Get it?"

"Yes. I'll think about that," I said.

"Everyone will understand if you don't want to do it."

"I didn't say I won't. I said I'll think about it," I snapped back. "I meant I would think about what to wear," I told her, even though that wasn't true.

"Oh. Great. See you in the morning," she added, and quickly hung up.

I guessed I had sounded like a ticking time bomb. My nerves felt like they were sparking. Any moment, I might just explode as if I was made of the same ceramic material used to make my old dolls. I swallowed back the urge to scream and scream but sat there until I realized I was still clutching the telephone receiver like someone desperate to keep in contact with the world outside. Finally, I took a deep breath and returned to my math. The solution to the problem was obvious to me this time around. I felt a sense of accomplishment, closed my books, and prepared for bed. As I was brushing my teeth, I heard a knock on my door. For a moment, I considered pretending I was asleep, but then I wondered if it was Grandpa coming to say some nicer things to me.

"Just a minute," I called, and put on my robe before opening the door. I was only in my bra and panties, and whenever Grandpa saw me that way now, he practically lunged out a window.

It was Dorian Camden, however. She could tell immediately that I was disappointed. Grandma Arnold had always accused me of failing to disguise my feelings. "Women, especially, are at a disadvantage when they do that," she told me. "Don't look so pleased so quickly, for example. Boys take an inch to mean a foot. You'll find that out quickly enough."

How much I missed her.

"Just checking to see how you are feeling after eating," Mrs. Camden said.

"I feel fine. It's over. Whatever it was."

"May I come in for a moment?" she asked. I was still holding the door, poised as though I might slam it in her face at any moment.

I nodded, relaxed, and retreated to my desk chair. She entered, closing the door softly behind her.

"I suppose this comes under the title of extracurricular activities," she began with a smile, obviously trying to establish a lighter mood with me.

She looked around the room when I didn't smile back or respond.

"This is a beautiful room. I didn't really look at it when I came in earlier today. You have very pretty furniture. I like that you have an eastern exposure. You wake up to sunshine."

"When there is any," I said dryly. "Every day looks cloudy to me, no matter what," I added, the bitterness so sharp I could taste it.

She ignored me and looked at the books I had on my bookshelf and the collection of small dolls from other countries. It was something my mother had subscribed to when I was five. We'd get one every two months for years.

"What are all these?"

"Dolls from other countries."

"Can you tell which country each is from just by looking at them?"

"Yes. The clothes give them away, don't you think?"

"Well . . ."

"If you know the colors in their countries' flags, that is."

"Oh." She nodded. "Very smart." She smiled. "I had a rag doll forever. I even took it to college," she said. "The other girls made fun of me, but I didn't care. As my mother used to say, accept me for who I am, warts and all, or don't accept me."

She waited for my response again, but I just stared at her, wondering what sort of wisdom I was missing now that my mother was gone and Grandma Arnold, too.

She turned back to the dolls. "Do you still get these international dolls?"

"They come, but they don't mean as much to me as they did when my mother was alive. She was the one who started my collection."

She nodded. Then she sat on the Chippendale side chair that matched the bed and dresser. She pressed the tips of her fingers together and looked like she was taking careful measurement of every word she was about to say. "He might not show it," she began, "but your grandfather is very worried about you."

"You're right. He doesn't show it," I said.

"He misses your brother terribly, I assure you. You have to realize he's a bit lost."

"Like the new William Arnold?"

She dropped her soft smile. I could almost hear it

shatter on her lap. "He doesn't know where to put his energy. This boy has helped him way more than he's helped this boy."

I was about to say, *What about me? He could put his energy in me*, but she anticipated it or saw it in my face.

"A man, especially a man like your grandfather, is more comfortable devoting himself to sons and grandsons."

"He's not either one. He's a stranger," I insisted.

"For now," she replied, which took me aback. What did that mean? "Look," she continued, "I don't know how much of a recuperation he's going to enjoy. I've spent time with the doctor, of course, the neurologist, and was given as full a diagnosis as he had, but . . ."

"When?"

"I went with your grandfather before I agreed to take on this position. It was important that I knew where the boy stood in relation to what's happened to him. There is some doubt that he will have a full recuperation. And I'm not even talking about the psychological and emotional wounds. Is he a big problem to take on? Yes, a very big problem. I can't say I'm not surprised at how determined your grandfather is to make a difference in his life, but rather than fight it, why not become part of it?"

"Part of it?"

"Really. You don't have to consider him your brother or anything. Just think of him as a child who needs comfort, support."

"Not love?" I asked.

She stared at me a moment. She knew I was being quite sarcastic. "Yes, Clara Sue, that, of course, but that's not something you just toss into the mix. It has to be something that develops. I know you're very bright. You're quite attractive, too. I'm sure you're popular in school. You're all that now, and I think you're quite mature for your age."

"How do you know that? You haven't been here that long, and we've hardly spoken to each other," I challenged. Both Grandma Arnold and my grandfather had by their example instilled in me an intolerance for false compliments.

"Let's just say you're more mature than I was at you age. I don't have to be around you long or talk to you long to realize and expect it. I've seen it too often. Tragedy makes you grow up faster."

"Who wants to?" I shot back. "Especially because of all that."

"We don't have much choice about it. I'm sure you were quite the big sister for your little brother, much more than other girls your age would be."

She was right, but I didn't feel like agreeing with her about anything, ever.

"Now, what I'm asking you to consider is how you were, too, when your parents were killed in that accident, how lost you were, even though you still had your grandparents, and just imagine it's the same for him. For him, it's like his whole family, whoever they were and how many there were, is gone. He doesn't even have a distant cousin at this point."

"No one knows any of that for sure yet."

"It's what we know right now, and you can deal only with what you do know, right?" she said, sounding more like she was pleading.

"It doesn't matter," I said. "I really don't want to think about it."

"Look. Maybe this will be a big disaster . . . the medical attention, the counseling, the expensive changes and machinery being brought into the house, but for now, why not contribute something toward the resolution?"

"What machinery?"

She sat back. "Your grandfather is turning the den into a therapy room. He has hired a professional therapist to design it and treat William. It will all be set up rather quickly."

"William," I said, as if the name had become profanity. I looked away.

"He's only trying to make him comfortable. Everyone agrees that if the boy feels safe and comfortable, he'll recuperate quicker."

"Make him comfortable, make him comfortable," I shot back. "When does he try to make *me* comfortable?"

"You know he does, he has," she said, with that comforting smile I was beginning to hate. I was sure she was now an expert at deflecting nasty remarks thrown at her by patients soaked in their own self-pity.

"You're just saying all this because you want to keep your job. He's probably paying you more than you usually get, right?"

"I have plenty of offers for work, Clara Sue. That's never been a problem for me."

"He's paying you more," I insisted, nodding. I calmed a bit. "He probably should, but he's definitely paying you more than you'd be making anywhere else, right?"

"I'm here to talk about you," she insisted. "Not me. How you can help make it all easier."

"There's nothing I can do. I don't know anything about physical therapy."

"Oh, I'm not asking you to do anything like that. Just . . . give him the sense that he's welcome," she suggested. "It will please your grandfather, and in the end, you won't be so . . ."

"Angry all the time?"

"Exactly," she said, smiling.

I thought a moment. I had no doubt that my grandfather had sent her up here, but I wasn't sure if I should be angry about it or pleased that he cared. "Are you going to stay on this job long?"

"As long as I'm needed," she replied, and stood.

"You're going to live here practically seven days a week?"

"Yes."

"Don't you have your own life, your own friends, relatives?" I asked, now curious.

"I am a widow with no children. I have a younger sister who's married and has three children, the oldest being twenty-five. She and her family are in Oregon. I see them only occasionally. When you're taking on private-duty nursing positions, you don't keep as close contact with your friends as you'd like. I've worked all over the state these past years."

"And now you'll have a job for years in one place, maybe," I said.

"I don't think that long. I'm sure he'll outgrow his need for constant care."

"Maybe you should adopt him," I said, as she was turning to leave.

She stopped quickly. "What?"

"William. Maybe you can adopt him. If he has a mother who's a nurse, he'll be better off. I think you should suggest it to my grandfather. Maybe he'll pay you to do it. Buy you a new house."

She just stared at me a moment. I didn't have to be taught what the expression of frustration looked like. I had seen it enough in my own mirror. "Think about the things I told you," she said, and walked out, closing the door softly behind her.

I did think about them. I thought about them so hard and long that I almost didn't get any sleep at all, but when I woke up in the morning, I didn't feel any different about the boy or what Grandpa was doing. Maybe I wouldn't be as vocal about it since Mrs. Camden had spoken to me, practically begged me, but anyone looking at me when I was in this house would know how I felt. I was sure of that. I was just as Grandma Arnold had described me, "a girl who printed her thoughts on her forehead as she thought them."

It was the same with my classmates, no matter how hard I tried to resemble the girl I was before Willie's death. I did wear red, and I did enjoy the look of shock on Mr. Leshner's face when we all walked into his classroom. Every time he saw one of us during the day, he started to laugh, and the story spread quickly through the school. It seemed to make everyone a little happier, and I kept telling myself that I had to stop feeling guilty for every smile, every laugh, and every bit of interest I had in my social life.

Aaron Podwell homed in on me again. He had been just as standoffish and timid about talking to me as everyone except Lila had been, but there was obviously a recognizable change in me that gave him the courage. I welcomed it, even though I was never confident of his true motives. I had had boyfriends, gone on dates to school dances, parties, and the movies. I had kissed and petted but never felt much more than the same curiosity about it all that most of my girlfriends expressed. I knew what stopping before it was too late meant and what condoms were, of course. There had been some nasty jokes pulled on a few of us from time to time, usually by immature losers like Stevie Randolph, who was caught writing dirty things on bathroom walls and slipped condoms we learned he had stolen from his father into girls' hall lockers with filthy notes attached.

But I hadn't yet even been bitten by the "crush mosquito." There were boys, especially the older boys, who I thought were cute, even handsome, like Winston Kettner, who was often compared to Troy Donahue but who obviously knew it and moved about as if he was already in college and president of his fraternity or something. He did dress better than any other boy and was probably going to be this year's class valedictorian. I had caught him looking at me a few times, but each time, when I looked back at him, he quickly turned away, as if he had done something wrong. At the moment, he wasn't going with anyone, either. There was a rumor that he wasn't interested in girls, but I laid that at the feet of jealousy.

Aaron was quite different, even though he had been infected with a similar strain of arrogance. He was good-looking, too, but in a more masculine way, more like my grandfather. His features weren't as pretty-boy perfect as Winston's. If anything, his nose was a little too big, and his habitual smile was wry to the point where you felt he was toying with you, but he had his mother's striking green eyes. Under the name Elaine Calvin, she had modeled for major women's magazines. When Aaron looked at you, especially when he looked at me, you couldn't help feeling he was like Superman and could see right through your clothes. He intrigued me, but he often frightened me, too. He was dangerous. I would never tell anyone, especially Lila, what I felt and thought about him.

I couldn't help having similar feelings about most boys. I had the sense that they thought of me as potentially promiscuous because I didn't have parents. They had no idea how tough my grandfather could be with me, but I could feel that there was this underlying belief that unlike other girls, I had no one checking on me, demanding that I behave and obey curfews or even taking interest in what I did socially.

There were two girls in our school who had lost

fathers, one to sickness and one in an automobile accident, both when they were younger, and there was no question that they were what my girlfriends called "loose lips." They weren't referring only to their mouths, either.

In any case, I tried to be friendlier to Aaron without looking too enthusiastic. Like most Prescott residents, Aaron's family was wealthy. They owned an estate that rivaled my grandfather's. His father owned and operated one of the biggest heating-oil companies in Virginia. Aaron's older sister, Tami, was an acknowledged beauty and was in New York trying to follow in her mother's footsteps at the same modeling agency.

Aaron was instantly at my side in the cafeteria, which resembled an upscale fast-food restaurant. Our tables didn't have tablecloths, but the furnishings were kept immaculate and always looked no more than a day old. There was a very active parent-teacher organization whose members my grandfather referred to as more like stockholders. Often parents inspected the building, especially the bathrooms, the locker rooms, and the cafeteria, as if they wore white gloves and were searching for signs of dust. Anyone transferring in from one of the public schools nearby surely felt like they had to wipe their feet before entering. From time to time, we heard their comments, but like everyone else who had been attending the Prescott private school, I took it all for granted. They might as well have been talking about schools in foreign countries.

"Glad to hear you're going to Audrey's party this weekend," Aaron said when he sat beside me.

"I haven't spoken to Audrey yet today. How'd you find out?"

"Lila," he said, nodding at her sitting across from us. She looked as if she had just been caught cheating on a final.

"Lila is my personal public relations officer," I said, looking at her pointedly.

Aaron laughed, and Lila relaxed. "I could pick you up," he offered.

"I think Lila's mother's taking us," I said.

"Oh, I might go with Gerry Okun," she said quickly. "I forgot to tell you. Actually, he just mentioned it this morning." She nodded at Gerry, who was making his way to our table. Gerry was Aaron's Tonto, as we liked to call him. Like the Lone Ranger, Aaron had him at his side constantly. Tall and lanky, with a crooked mouth and small, lazy, dark brown eyes, Gerry was nowhere near as good-looking as Aaron. I think having him as a sidekick helped boost Aaron's ego. He was a nice enough boy, far more timid and insecure. I was sure he wouldn't be doing half the things he was doing if it wasn't for Aaron having him tag along. Of course, I was suspicious of his offer to Lila. As Grandpa Arnold was apt to say, I smelled a rat. Aaron had put him up to it for sure.

"Well, I guess it's all right, then," Aaron said, as Gerry sat beside Lila. "Besides, you'll be the first to ride in my new car. It's my graduation present."

"You have a while to go before graduating."

"Oh, my father got a good deal, and he wanted me to get used to driving it before I'm off to college," he

offered as a rationalization. One thing I noticed about
my friends here was that they were rarely embarrassed
by how much they had.

"How thoughtful," I said.

Aaron laughed. "It's a Plymouth Fury. Ever see
one?"

"I don't pay much attention to cars except when
I'm crossing the street."

"You will to this one," he said, with that smile of
his that was a cross between a smirk and a playful
grin. He aimed those stunning eyes at me like a pair of
pistols.

I shrugged and bit into my toasted cheese sandwich.
Willie would have been just like him when it came to
cars, I thought, and my grandfather would have spoiled
him as quickly as Aaron's father spoiled Aaron. Men
couldn't help but spoil their sons and grandsons. They
saw themselves in them, or maybe they wished they
could relive their youth through them. My father would
have been the same for sure. It suddenly occurred to me
how sad it must be for my grandfather not to feel the
same way toward my uncle Bobby. Surely that was
why he had put so much of his attention on Willie, and
maybe that was why he was now putting it on the boy
in Willie's room wearing Willie's clothes.

I shook the idea out of my head almost as quickly
as I had thought it. I didn't want to find excuses and
explanations like everyone else in my house and in my
life was finding for the things Grandpa Arnold did.
I didn't want to understand it, and I certainly didn't
want to condone it. I didn't want to forgive him for it.

"I might disappoint you," I told Aaron.

He shrugged that Aaron Podwell shrug that made it seem as if he could ignore or disregard an atomic bomb. "We'll see," he said. "It's worth the gamble."

I looked at Lila. She seemed more excited about Aaron and me than I could ever be. "Okay," I said. "If you're willing to take that chance."

"What chance?" Gerry asked. He looked at Lila. She shook her head but kept her smile.

"She might not be as excited as we are about my new car," Aaron told him. Gerry pulled his chin down and in so hard that I thought he would crush his Adam's apple.

I couldn't help smiling, and that felt good, very good.

On the way out to our afternoon classes, Aaron proposed another idea.

"Why don't you call home and tell whoever that you have a ride today and don't need to be picked up. That way, you can experience the car sooner."

I thought about it. My grandfather always wanted to know who was driving me where. He did it more often than not. I rarely had done anything without first getting his approval. Suddenly, this seemed a good way to assert myself, even though it was a small transgression.

"Okay," I said, and stopped at the principal's office. We could ask to use the phone if it involved getting in touch with our parents or, in my case, grandparent. I intended simply to call the house and leave the message with Myra, declaring it a fait accompli.

Mrs. Heinz, the principal's secretary, nodded when I asked her permission to use the phone to call home. "You're not feeling unwell?" she followed quickly.

"Why? Do I look like it?" I snapped back. It wasn't something I would ordinarily do.

I could see the surprise widen her eyes. I was sure she was wondering if I was still too deeply in mourning to participate in my schoolwork. "No, no, of course not," she said quickly, and looked back at her paperwork.

Myra answered the phone as I expected.

"Please cancel my pickup today, Myra," I said. "I have a ride home with a friend."

"Does your grandfather know?"

"He will when you call him," I said. "I don't have time for another call, or I'll be late for class."

"But . . ."

"Thank you, Myra," I said, and hung up. I thanked Mrs. Heinz, who just nodded, and then I joined Aaron waiting in the hallway. "All set," I told him. "Impress me."

"Will do," he promised.

The parents of most other students wouldn't think of it as a big deal, but after all that had happened in my family and what was happening now, my grandfather wasn't like other parents.

Aaron couldn't tell as we continued on to class, but I was trembling a bit.

How would my grandfather react?

8

As I left my last class slowly, Lila smiled at me; she knew I was going off to be intimate with Aaron.

"He's just taking me home, Lila," I said.

"Watch for detours," she warned, then laughed and walked off quickly when we saw Aaron waiting for me in the hall. I was hoping he couldn't tell how nervous I was about his taking me home, something that should have been no major event. It wasn't for any other girl in my class, even though it was something special. You could only go with a senior who had parental permission in writing that guaranteed their child would not speed or drive recklessly. The dean, Mr. McDermott, was usually out there watching like a traffic cop.

I had done my best to make it seem like nothing, but when the bell had rung to end class, my heart had begun to pound. I was even holding my breath on and off like someone going in and out of deep water as we walked through the hallway to the exit and the school parking lot. I kept my head down and wrapped my arms around my books, which I was sure resembled some sort of shield over my breasts. Aaron was running on about the amount of homework Mr. Fine had assigned in math, "as if we have no other subjects." My worst fear was that when we walked out that door, my grandfather would be waiting with little streams of smoke pouring out of his ears. I would never be more embarrassed.

I felt my whole body soften with relief when I realized that he wasn't there. The reason was obvious when we arrived at my grandfather's estate. A large van delivering physical-therapy equipment was backed up to the front entrance, and two men were wheeling something up the newly constructed ramp. Grandpa was there with Jimmy to supervise, and apparently, he didn't even realize we had driven up to the house.

Prescott was small enough so that anything as significant as what Grandpa Arnold was doing would ordinarily be at the top of the chatter pile, heating up telephone lines so much that the birds stayed off them; but from the way Aaron reacted and from the fact that no one at school had asked anything about it, I concluded that Grandpa had not told anyone about the boy in Willie's room and what he was doing for him.

"What's going on?" Aaron asked. Until now, he had been talking about his new car and fishing for me to give it and him more and more compliments.

"I bet you'll keep it cleaner and nicer than your room at home," I had told him after he had described every gauge and every dial and knob as if they were expensive jewelry.

"You bet I will," he had confessed. "I'll probably spend more time in it, too. The first night I got it, I seriously considered sleeping in it. I love the scent of a new car."

Now that we were here, his attention drifted away from his car. His eyes narrowed as he studied the pieces of equipment.

"I know that's a leg machine. Builds up your thighs. Your grandfather putting in a personal gym or something? My father was considering doing that. When he hears about this, he probably will. He's always in competition with your grandfather. I don't know why they play golf together. They're always accusing each other of cheating. So what is this?"

I just sat there, thinking, watching and wondering if I should just let it go at that, a new personal gym. I decided to tell the truth—first, because it probably would get out soon anyway, and second, because I was interested in how Aaron would react to the story. Was I being unreasonable and cruel? Would my complaints sound petty? I knew I couldn't get a true reaction from Lila. She would do or say anything to please me. Keeping my friendship was more important to her even than being true to her own feelings. It wasn't easy to find people who were true to themselves. In fact, it was Grandma Arnold who had told me that one of the things that attracted her to my grandfather was his inability to lie to himself. I did realize that if Aaron heard any unhappiness in my voice, he might be just like Lila and say whatever I wanted him to say. He wanted to go out with me, didn't he?

"Another boy about my brother's age was brought to the hospital practically at the same time," I began, leaning on the facts and reciting it like a history report to subdue my emotions.

"Another car accident? Who was it? I didn't hear anything about anyone else in Prescott."

"He wasn't from Prescott. No one knows where he's from. It was no one we knew, and it wasn't a car accident. He had been poisoned."

"Poisoned? Deliberately?"

"No one knows for sure. Kids can eat the wrong things on their own, I suppose."

"What kind of poison?"

"Arsenic. Rat poison."

"How can anyone eat that on his own?" Aaron asked. "Wouldn't it taste bad?"

"Not necessarily. I looked it up in the medical encyclopedia my grandfather has in his library. He has nearly one thousand books of all kinds."

"He's read all of them?"

"No, I doubt it. He and my grandmother accumulated them over the years. He has a beautiful library in his office. It's three walls from floor to ceiling of books, many leather-bound and collector's copies."

"I wonder if my father knows that. He probably has only a few hundred. So what did you learn? What about its taste and smell?"

"Depends. If it's mixed in with something, it might not be so easily discovered."

"So . . . mixed in with something looks more like

an attempted murder, doesn't it? Who would want to murder a kid—and with arsenic?"

"We actually need small amounts of arsenic in our bodies. There are small amounts of it in apple juice, for example."

"I don't drink that too often."

"There are small amounts in other fruits and vegetable, grains and fish. We excrete it."

"Huh?"

"Pay more attention in science."

"I know what it means. I'm just . . . a little shocked. You think he might have drunk too much apple juice?"

"Very unlikely."

He thought a moment. "What does all this have to do with that, anyway?" he asked, nodding at the truck.

"My grandfather felt sorry for the boy. He arranged for him to have the best medical treatment, which probably saved his life."

"Why your grandfather? Where were the kid's parents?"

"No one knows . . . yet," I said.

"Huh? What do you mean? It's been a while. How did he get to the hospital, anyway?"

"Some man dropped him off at the emergency room and ran away before anyone could question him. It was so chaotic there at the time that no one can even give a good description of him."

"Wow. And your grandfather did all that while . . ." He turned to me. "While your brother was dying?"

I looked away.

"I'm sure he made sure the best was done for him, too?" he added quickly.

"Willie really died in the ambulance," I said, amazed that I could even say it. "They were trying to revive him."

"Wow."

We were both silent.

"I still don't get it," he said, nodding at the men now unloading another piece of equipment. "What's this have to do with arsenic and all that?"

"The boy's life was saved, but there were some serious injuries, side effects of the poison. He was undernourished as it was, apparently. As a result, he had some neurological problems, and that's affected his motor skills. What you see there is physical-therapy equipment."

"Neurological problems? Motor skills? Are you going to be a doctor or something?" He was more surprised than impressed.

"As I said, I read about things."

"But this physical-therapy stuff is all going into your grandfather's house, not the hospital. He wants that?"

"Yes. He brought the boy here."

"What? Why?"

"He wants to . . . take care of him."

Aaron just stared at me and then looked at the house. "Well, don't his parents care?" he asked after a moment.

"I told you. No one knows who they are—or any relatives, as a matter of fact. He had no identification on him, and no one is looking for him, apparently. At least, that's what the police have said."

"Why doesn't the kid just tell them?"

"He's suffering from amnesia," I said, now unable to disguise the disapproval and even the disbelief in my voice.

"Amnesia . . . can't remember his own parents?"

"Or his real name."

"Bull."

"They call it psychological trauma. It causes you to forget things, block them out of your head."

"That's what happened?"

"If you want to believe it."

"So let me get this," he said. "There's a kid moving into your grandfather's house who was poisoned either accidentally or deliberately, and until the police figure out who he belongs to, your grandfather's keeping him and helping him with stuff."

"Including a private-duty nurse," I said. "Who has moved in."

He shook his head.

"And a psychiatrist as well as the other doctors, not to mention the professional therapist who will be here daily."

"Wow. Where's Dick Tracy when you really need him?" he muttered, and I laughed. He gave me his best Aaron Podwell smile and then shrugged. "I guess, good for your grandfather for caring about the kid

I don't think my father would do it. I don't think my mother would even do it, although they do give money to all sorts of charities."

"Some people say charity begins at home."

"Huh?"

"Thanks for the ride in your new car," I said, opening the door. "It is beautiful."

"Beautiful car for a beautiful girl. Looking forward to Friday night."

"Me, too," I said. I closed the door and started toward the front entrance.

"Hey," Aaron called, leaning out of his window. I turned. "If he doesn't remember his own name, what do you call him, Arsenic?" He smiled.

"My grandfather has decided to call him William," I said.

He lost his smile. I turned and walked to the house. When I reached the steps and the ramp and looked back, he was already gone.

Grandpa Arnold stepped out the front door and stood there with his hands on his hips. "Myra said you hung up on her before she could learn who was bringing you home."

"Myra's not my mother," I said, walking past him. "Or my grandmother," I muttered. I didn't look back. Out of the corner of my eye, I saw everyone working with the deliverymen. The chair lift had already been installed. There was a wheelchair just off the bottom step. I glanced at it and then started up the stairway.

"Just a minute, Clara Sue," Grandpa called, walking after me.

I stopped. "What?"

"Since when don't you tell me what you're doing and with whom you're doing it?"

"You were too busy," I said. "It was only Aaron Podwell, anyway. Jack the Ripper had other things to do today."

I hated talking to him like this, but it seemed to come out of a well inside me that I didn't know existed, a well filled with ugly, deformed creatures of rage, their faces bloodred. They danced in glee around my heart, which felt like it was on fire. The heat propelled me forward.

When I walked past Willie's room, I saw Mrs. Camden helping the boy out of his other wheelchair and back into bed. He looked at me over her shoulder. He did seem fragile and helpless, his eyes pleading for some sympathy, but I looked away quickly and went to my room. I had put on a good front before my grandfather, but inside myself, I could feel a small earthquake. For a while, I just lay there staring up at the ceiling and trying to calm myself. I was glad when the phone rang. I knew Lila wanted a report about my ride home with Aaron, but for now, I welcomed the distraction. Besides, I was finding I liked talking about him.

"Did he take you anywhere else first?" she asked as soon as she heard my voice.

"No, but he did take a longer route so I could appreciate his car."

"Did he park for a while?"

"We didn't start groping each other, if that's what you mean."

"But did you want to?" She giggled after asking. She was going to live her own fantasy through me, I thought. Suddenly, I felt very mean about it. I was eager to tease her.

"Oh, yes," I said breathlessly. "I was getting hot and wet just thinking about his hands slipping under my blouse, his fingers undoing my bra. I wanted his lips all over me. You know, his face between my thighs."

I heard her gasp. "You did?"

"Almost," I added, dropping back to my usual tone. "But then I started thinking about My Faith's cookies."

"What?" Her disappointment brought a smile back to my face.

"But everyone was too busy with the preparations for the new William's therapy to suggest that I have any. My grandfather is setting up the room for all the equipment."

"Equipment?"

"The therapy equipment. Now we have a nurse and a therapist and a psychiatrist and doctors parading through the halls."

"Oh," she said.

"Anyway, Aaron now knows all about it, so you don't have to keep your lips zipped. Maybe if more people ask my grandfather about it, he'll realize what he's doing."

"I already told my parents," she confessed.

"Good. And what about Gerry? Did he try to park with you?"

"Oh, no."

"Did you want him to?"

"No!" she exclaimed. "Ugh, Gerry? Please."

"Then why did you let him take you home? Never mind. I know why. I'll call you later," I said.

"You'd better. You did really well on that math. I'll need your help."

After I hung up, I freshened up in the bathroom and then went downstairs. I really had a craving for one of My Faith's cookies. As it turned out, she had made them, but more for the new William than for me.

I paused to watch the men setting up the equipment in my grandfather's den. He had left for the office to finish some things. Mrs. Camden surprised me. I was thinking so hard that I didn't hear her approach.

"Would you like to know about all this?" she asked, nodding at the equipment.

"Not really."

"He was asking some more about you," she said.

"Who?"

"William," she said.

"Really." I tried to sound as if I didn't care, but a part of me was very interested.

"It's a good sign. He's reaching out. It's like someone folded up inside, the way you might make a fist, and gradually, the fingers relax and the hand begins to open again. You could be a big part of that happening."

"Whoop-de-do."

"Aren't you in the least bit interested in him, in where he comes from and what happened to him?"

"If it leads to him going home, yes," I said. "He's living in my brother's room and using my brother's name."

She considered. "Well, it might lead to that," she said. I looked at her hopefully. "Depending on whether it would be a good idea for him to be sent back to that home, of course. It also could lead to an investigation that would result in his going to live with relatives or someplace else."

"Someplace else? Like a foster home? An orphanage?"

"Possibly."

"My grandfather wouldn't permit it, I bet."

She looked at the equipment. "Well, it's nice, rewarding, to help him find his way. Just give it a chance, and you'll see what I mean." She smiled at me and walked on to the kitchen.

"Not everyone dreams of being a nurse," I called after her. I was sure she was pretending she didn't hear me. "Forget this," I muttered, and went back up the stairs to begin my homework. As I passed Willie's room, I thought I heard a small voice call my name.

"Clara Sue."

I stopped and listened, but I didn't hear it again, or maybe I had imagined it. Maybe I wanted to hear it, because it did sound like Willie calling me the way he used to when I tried to ignore him because I wanted to talk to friends or get homework done. Whenever I had done that, I had suffered aching guilt. There was no doubt that he missed our parents even more than I did and that after Grandma Arnold passed away, he sank even deeper into himself, moving about like someone who had been stung so many times by angry bees that he was terrified of stepping outside. He was still a child at heart. He needed more love than I could give him, and to be truthful, I doled it out the way travelers in a desert rationed water.

Hearing nothing more, I continued to my room and closed the door. I attacked my homework with a vengeance. Every ordinary thing I did now seemed fueled with just as much anger as ambition or responsibility. I was still striking back at the world. I wondered if I would ever stop.

As if he could hear my thoughts hundreds of miles away, Uncle Bobby phoned me. "Hey," he said. "How's my Clair de Lune?"

"Surviving," I said.

"That's a start. You're back in school, right?"

"Right. I'm going to a party on Friday, too," I said, as if something like that was an amazing accomplishment. Perhaps it was.

"Good. Get back into the shake and roll of things. We had a good opening with the show, and I can tell you for sure that I'll be in New York next year."

"I'm so happy for you, Uncle Bobby."

"Thanks. So how's the general?"

"Busy. You'll have to check visiting hours before you come next time."

"What?"

"He's moving therapy equipment into the den.

He's hired a private-duty nurse and a therapist to be here daily. And there's the psychiatrist. I'm not sure how often she comes yet. I live in another world."

"What's the nurse like?"

"She's . . . she's okay. She wants me to help her with the poisoned boy, who, you know, is now William."

"Just because he uses his room?"

"No, Uncle Bobby. Grandpa wants him to be called that until he remembers his real name, if ever. He's William Arnold the Second right now."

"He didn't mention that," Uncle Bobby said. "I guess he has to be called something, but . . ."

"But not my brother's name!" I practically screamed.

"Take it easy, honey. Go with the flow for now. I'm sure things will change once the boy improves."

"Maybe," I said. "Are you coming for Thanksgiving?"

"Can't. It's a big weekend for us here. Maybe Christmas," he said. "I sent the playbill to you today. You should get it soon."

"Thank you."

"Keep your chin up. Have a good time at your party. I want to hear some nitty-gritty details when I call next time."

"I'll work on them," I said.

He laughed. "Love you, Clair de Lune."

"I love you, Uncle Bobby. More than ever," I said, and he was silent until he managed a good-bye.

After I hung up, I lay there thinking. It was all

going so fast, this recuperation from grief. The presence of the poisoned boy only sped that up. Willie was in danger of fading away. How could I stop it?

I looked at my desk, and then I rose slowly and sat. Was this silly, even sick?

I took out my perfumed stationery and uncovered my special fountain pen. And then I began.

Dear Willie,

I wonder if you can look down and see us, and if you can, if you are as unhappy about what Grandpa is doing as I am. I think you are. I know how precious all your things were to you. You should know that I've hidden what I knew to be the most precious, and this new boy, the poisoned boy, won't get his hands on them. I promise.

I wish I had been able to say more to you at the cemetery, but I couldn't stand seeing you closed up in that coffin and being lowered into a grave. My Faith tells me that your soul had already left your body and it would never be imprisoned. She claims you were most likely standing there beside me. Sometimes I laugh at the things she tells me, but I didn't laugh at that. I wanted it to be true.

Grandpa and Myra and My Faith, maybe even Uncle Bobby, want me to care about this strange boy Grandpa has decided to rescue. I'm afraid that if you can see us and hear us, you

*now know Grandpa has given him your name,
too. I feel so bad about it. I swear, I'll never call
him Willie. I will try not to call him William,
either. I'll call him "you" or something if I have
to speak to him for any reason.*

*I'm back in school. I'm back with friends.
I'm going to attend a party, not because I've
forgotten all about you but because I can't help
what has happened. The truth is, I want to
think about other things so I don't cry so much,
and I certainly don't want to think about the
boy in your room.*

*Don't be sad about it. I decided tonight
that on Saturday, I'm going to the cemetery to
visit your grave. I will never forget you or stop
thinking about you. I'm sure I'll think about
you every day forever or at least until I can't
think anymore.*

*If you can still think and feel, please think
of me. Please still care about me.*

*Love,
Your sister, Clara Sue*

I reread my letter and then folded it and put it in the
envelope. I dropped it into the drawer with the others.
I was sure I would write many more.

I returned to my homework until it was time to
go to dinner. I was surprised to see that Willie's door
was nearly closed completely, but I didn't pause to see
why. I hurried downstairs, then stopped just before I

entered the dining room, because I could hear laughter coming from Grandpa Arnold's office. I hadn't heard him laugh since Willie's accident. I recognized Mrs. Camden's laugh. They both turned to me when I stepped into the doorway. He wasn't behind his desk. They were both sitting on the pearl leather settee, and it looked like they were having a cocktail. The stunned expression on my face wiped the smiles from theirs. I wondered what had made them laugh.

"How was your day at school?" Grandpa asked. "We didn't get to speak very much when you got home."

"It was okay," I said. "Isn't dinner ready?" I asked, looking more at Mrs. Camden.

"We were about to go to the dining room."

We, I thought. *So she's a regular at the table from now on?*

"I want you to know that I'm going to a party Friday night," I said. "It's at Audrey O'Brian's house."

"That's very nice," Mrs. Camden said.

"You don't even know who she is," I snapped back.

"I just meant it's nice that you're getting out, seeing your friends," she said.

"Am I taking you?" Grandpa asked.

"No. I'm going with Aaron Podwell. He'll pick me up and bring me home."

"By eleven."

"Eleven?"

"That's a bit early, William," Mrs. Camden said softly. "She's old enough to be Cinderella."

He looked at her and nodded. "It's hard to think of these kids growing up so quickly."

"These kids?" I said.

He lost the softness in his face. "Twelve, then," he said. "And don't be late."

"Or Aaron's new car will turn into a pumpkin," I said.

Mrs. Camden widened her smile.

"Worse than that," Grandpa said. "His father will hear about it."

Mrs. Camden held on to her smile.

I turned and walked on to the dining room.

What I hated about her was how hard it was becoming to hate her at all.

9

They were too chatty at dinner, but I finally had my old appetite back, especially when it came to My Faith's cooking. We had often had dinner guests, especially when my grandma Lucy was alive, but since she had died, I rarely saw my grandfather as interested in anyone as he was in Mrs. Camden. By now, they were both addressing each other by their first names, Dorian and William. It was Mrs. Camden more than my grandfather who tried to include me in their discussions, but they were talking about singers and actors I never knew. When I said so, they both seemed surprised.

"If we didn't teach history in our schools, kids today wouldn't even know who George Washington was," Grandpa quipped. I couldn't get over how quickly he was returning to himself.

"Not true," I said. "We'd know every time we had a dollar."

Mrs. Camden laughed so hard that I couldn't keep a smile off my own face. Grandpa laughed, too.

"She's very clever," she told him.

"Her mother was sharp like that, too, and her grandmother wasn't anyone to trade witty remarks with and come away without wounds to your pride."

He paused as if he could see her sitting across the table. Then he shook his head and returned to their conversation. After one of My Faith's famous lemon tarts, Mrs. Camden turned to me and asked, "What do you girls wear to house parties these days? We used to get so dressed up that you'd think we were going to the Waldorf or something."

"Nothing very fancy," I said.

"She probably needs something new," Grandpa said. "Never saw a female who didn't use an occasion to get something new."

"I have enough," I said.

"If you'd like someone to go shopping with you after school this week, I'd be happy to do it. Not that I know what's in style these days," she told my grand-father.

"You can be sure I don't. I haven't bought myself much of anything since . . . since I lost Lucy," he said.

"The offer is good for you as well," Mrs. Camden told him.

I had never seen Grandpa Arnold blush, not like this. He mumbled something and then announced that he had some financial homework to do. Before he left, he complimented My Faith on her dinner. Mrs. Camden added to the praise, and then Myra appeared and the three of them began to talk about the week's menu for the boy in Willie's room. My Faith said she had kept his dinner warm. Apparently, Mrs. Camden had thought it better to let him sleep.

"He's still mending so much," she said. "The poor thing probably doesn't weigh fifty pounds. He must be about nine or ten. I feel like I might break his bones when I lift him."

"And that's not all from the poison, is it?" Myra asked.

I sat there, unable to feign disinterest, especially with Mrs. Camden's response.

"It could have damaged his appetite, of course, but Dr. Friedman believes he was kept on a diet lacking in the basic caloric intake a child that age should have, probably for some time. It's stunted his growth somewhat. We're treating his pituitary gland."

"Sounds like he was kept imprisoned or something," Myra offered.

Mrs. Camden shook her head. "I hope we'll know someday, but that part has to come later." She looked at me. "When he feels more trusting."

I rose. "I have to finish my homework," I said.

"That offer still stands," Mrs. Camden called after me. "Whatever day you choose. I'll work it out."

I didn't reply. I kept walking away, even though my body was fighting to turn around on its own to accept her offer. It had been so long since I had gone shopping with my grandmother and, of course, way longer since I had gone with my mother. On a few occasions, Myra accompanied me, mainly to get some necessities. She was all business, in and out. Lingering over displays, seeing new fashions, and window-shopping were things she never wanted to do. She always had something waiting for her to do at home, even on her day off. What I had bought lately I usually had bought with some girlfriends, especially Lila, whose mother took me along with them. But a special day for myself was something that seemed lost forever.

I didn't pause. I intended as usual to walk quickly past Willie's room, but as I approached, I could hear the boy moaning. I stopped to listen and then looked back to see if Mrs. Camden was coming up. There was no sound of footsteps on the stairway. Slowly, I went to Willie's door and pushed it slightly open. The boy's moans were a little louder. Should I go back and call for Mrs. Camden? I wondered. What if he was dying? If he died here after all my grandfather had done for him, how would that affect my grandfather? Would he think he had been wrong even to have begun all this? Would he blame himself? A terrible part of me wished for it as vengeance for his giving so much of Willie to this stranger. I didn't like that mean and vicious part of me, but I couldn't deny those feelings.

I opened the door farther and stepped into the room. Mrs. Camden had left the curtains open, but the late-afternoon sun had fallen by now, and the sky was just past twilight. I could see some stars growing brighter. My Faith had once told Willie and me that the stars were the souls of the beautiful and good. Willie was always asking me which ones I thought might be our parents.

The stars weren't bright enough yet. The spill of

hallway illumination was all the light in the room. The
boy wasn't moving. He was on his back, his head sunk
into one of Willie's big, soft pillows, his face so pale
that it was ghostlike. Sometimes Willie fell asleep with
his arms wrapped around that pillow, clutching it as if
it was our mother, who slept beside him when he was
sick or frightened. Grandma Arnold never did, but I
had often after our parents were killed.

I heard the boy moan again. Was he dreaming or
calling for help? What if he was dreaming, and in his
dreams, he was talking about his family and what had
happened to him? I could overhear it and then tell everyone what I had learned, I thought. I inched closer.

I was standing right beside the bed when he
moaned again and then shook his head with his eyes
closed and clearly said, "Mickey sick."

Mickey? "Who's Mickey?" I asked. His eyes were
still closed. "Mickey who? Are you Mickey? Is that
your real name?"

He didn't speak.

I looked back at the doorway and listened. I didn't
hear Mrs. Camden coming, so I touched his shoulder
gently and asked again, "Are you Mickey? You're sick,
right?"

His eyes looked sewn shut. His lips opened
slightly, and he shook his head again and again said,
"Mickey sick."

I shook him harder. "Who's Mickey? Talk. Are
you Mickey? Talk!" I said much louder.

A burst of light brightened the room when the
overhead fixture went on, surprising me. I turned

toward the door. Mrs. Camden was standing there. "What's going on?" she asked.

The boy moaned and this time opened his eyes. He looked up at me, visibly terrified at how I was looming over him.

I straightened up quickly. "He was moaning, so I came in to see why."

She nodded and walked toward the bed. I stepped back. "Hi, honey," she said to him. "Getting a little hungry, maybe?"

He looked at me and then at her and nodded.

"He said 'Mickey.' I heard him say it. He said, 'Mickey sick.' That's probably his real name. Ask him. Ask him!"

"Calm down, Clara Sue. It's not good to shout at him. That only frightens him and closes him up faster and tighter."

"Ask him," I said more softly, choking back my excitement. "Go on," I challenged, and folded my arms over my breasts defiantly.

She looked at me and then turned to him. "Is your name Mickey, sweetie?"

He didn't speak, but I could see that he was surprised to hear the name.

"See? He knows that name. It is. I bet it is," I said.

"We'll see," Mrs. Camden said. "Let's let him calm down a little so that he'll eat well, okay?"

"Right," I said. "Let him calm down. *He's* the one who has to calm down."

I turned and marched out of the room, but I felt I had learned more than anyone else, and I was confident that it would mean something, perhaps enough to get him out of Willie's room and bed and name.

When I started to do my homework, I found it difficult to concentrate. Fortunately, Lila remembered I had promised to help her with math. She called, and we got into it enough for me to finish my own work. We talked a little more about Audrey's party, and then I hung up, but before I could turn to my English assignment, the phone rang again. This time, it was Aaron.

"Hey, how's the Prescott General Hospital doing?" he asked.

"Very funny. What did your father say when you told him what my grandfather was doing?"

"Oh, I didn't say anything about it yet."

"What? Why not?"

"I didn't want to start anything and get your grandfather mad at me just when I was working on seducing his granddaughter."

"Seducing? You're a comedian. You can tell anyone you like about what my grandfather is doing. I'm sure it's getting known anyway, so my grandfather can't complain that you spread the story."

"You sound like you want me to."

"Whatever," I said. He was silent a moment. "I didn't thank you for bringing me home."

"It's the other way around."

"What do you mean?"

"Thank you for letting me, which is why I'm really calling. Can I pick you up in the morning? It's an easy swing by."

Things were moving between us quickly. Was I being swept off my feet by the school's Casanova? Was I up to the challenge?

"Am I going to find out that this is just another excuse to let you drive your new car more?"

He laughed. "I won't deny that's a part of the reason, but it's a minor part."

"I'm going to have to ask my grandfather," I said.

"Tell him I got an A-plus in driver's education."

"Don't be surprised if he has us followed to be sure. I'll call you in a little while. Oh, what's your phone number?"

"Make sure you write it on your hand and never wash," he said, and gave it to me. "That's why there are so many girls with dirty hands in our school," he added, laughing.

"I have a good memory," I said. "I won't forget it unless I want to."

"Tough girl, huh?"

Was I? "We'll see," I told him, and hung up.

I thought for a moment and then started for Grandpa's office. Mrs. Camden and Myra were in Willie's room, talking to the boy as he ate his dinner. It was Myra's voice that caught my attention. She had that sweet, loving tone that she had whenever she spoke to Willie, and she was calling him "love" and "sweetie," which was what she always called Willie. The pathetic little imp was winning everyone over, and as they moved closer to him, they moved further away from my brother.

Grandpa looked up when I entered. I didn't walk

all the way to his desk. I stood just inside the doorway, as if I wanted to be able to make a quick getaway.

"Hey," he said. "You need something?"

Where should I begin? I thought. Yes, I needed plenty. I needed my parents back. I needed Willie back. I needed to be told that everything for years was just a bad dream, and I needed to be promised that I wouldn't see so much sadness during the rest of my life. I shouldn't be afraid of tomorrow or afraid of any more than anyone else.

"Aaron's picking me up for school tomorrow," I declared. "I don't need the driver to take me."

I tried to sound as tough and determined as I could, like someone who had firm control of her own life, but every muscle in my body tightened in anticipation of his burst of anger at my declaring what I was going to do without even pretending to ask his permission. It wasn't like him to be silent. His face seemed to harden into cement. He didn't grimace; he didn't raise his eyebrows. The silence awoke butterflies of panic in my chest. I wasn't sure if I should just turn and leave or wait for him to speak.

Finally, he sat back. "I seem to recall a rule requiring a student's parent or guardian having to give permission for her to ride in another student's car. That's why I was surprised today when you came home with Aaron Podwell."

"You only have to give permission if I leave before the school day ends."

"I see. So is this going to become a regular thing?"

"I don't know," I said. "It could be."

I could see a wave of sadness wash over his eyes and pass through his face. That took me by surprise, and for a moment, I felt sorry for my tone and attitude. But I was determined not to be treated like a little girl anymore. He nodded to himself and almost smiled. "Your grandmother warned me," he said. "She said you'd suddenly grow into a young lady, practically overnight, and I'd better be prepared to hold my breath. She said it would be scarier than riding a bull in the rodeo."

"There's nothing scary about it, Grandpa. I'm not getting married or anything."

"What's *anything* mean?" he shot back, and then shook his head. "Okay. I'll tell Bill to take tomorrow off. We'll play it day by day."

I started to turn to leave but stopped. "By the way, I think the poisoned boy's name is Mickey," I said. "Have your detective check it out."

Before he could say anything, I turned and walked out, practically running up to my room to call Aaron, who answered on the first ring, as if he had been hovering over the telephone.

"It's okay," I said.

"Great. I'll take you home, too, of course."

"Of course."

"Maybe one afternoon, we can take a ride to Butler Heights and have one of those famous waffle cones. It's about an hour each way, but it's worth it."

"The cone or going with you?"

"Ha-ha. So how is the boy?" he asked. I was glad he didn't say "William."

"I think he uttered his real first name in a dream. I heard him when I was walking by my brother's room."

"What was it?"

"Mickey."

"Mickey? Sounds like a nickname. It could be Michael or something. People don't list their nicknames on official documents."

"Oh," I said with a little disappointment.

"Or . . . just maybe he was named after Mickey Mantle. Find out if he's a Yankees fan," he said. I knew he was joking now, but a lead was a lead.

"Maybe I will. Thanks."

He laughed. "Okay, then, less then twelve hours."

"Until?"

"I see you," he said.

"Are you always this romantic?"

"Now, don't ask me to give my techniques away."

I didn't just smile. I also felt an exciting tingle run through me. The possibility of going out with him didn't really begin until shortly before Willie's death. I never had the chance to fantasize about what it would be like, but now, having his voice slip softly into my mind, I knew tonight was the night when I would dream about us. I was more eager than ever to get to sleep. "Got to get back to my homework," I said.

"Homework? Is that what this is on my desk? I thought someone left it as a joke."

"The joke will be on you if you don't do it," I told him. "Don't be late. I'm never late for school, and my grandfather would consider it a capital offense."

"Aye-aye, ma'am," he said.

I sat by the phone, thinking about Aaron for a while before turning to my homework, which was all that stood between me and my dreams. At least, that's all I thought was in the way. But after I washed up and brushed my teeth, got into my pajamas, and started to crawl into bed, I heard some commotion out in the hallway and went to see what it was all about. My grandfather had come up the stairs with a doctor carrying his bag, and Mrs. Camden was standing outside Willie's room waiting for them.

"What's happening?" I asked.

Mrs. Camden glanced at me, but no one answered. Grandpa Arnold and the doctor went into the room, Mrs. Camden following. I stood there listening, but I couldn't really hear anything, so I approached and stood just outside the door. I picked up some words here and there: "panic attack," "hyperventilation," "no heart trouble." I heard the doctor talking softly to the boy and Mrs. Camden adding words of reassurance. Apparently, there had been some concern that his rapid breathing was from some pain or a lung problem, but the doctor was assuring my grandfather that was not the case. Their voices got lower. I returned to my room and closed the door softly.

A flood of selfish thoughts began. Why did we need all this, especially now? The boy didn't belong here; he belonged in some sort of hospital or mental clinic. This proved it. What had happened to Willie wasn't enough to turn this house upside down? *Go contribute thousands to some children's charity,*

Grandpa. Or pay for whatever the boy needs outside of our home. Do anything but this.

But then the image returned of him tiny and helpless in Willie's bed, his head sinking into the big pillow, and I turned over to close my eyes hard and squeeze out the negative thoughts. I didn't like being so mean and hateful. I knew that half of my reaction to him was probably out of jealousy. I wanted all of my grandfather's attention now. I needed it, too. But it was difficult to deny that the poisoned boy needed so much more.

I thought I would fall asleep quickly, but there was a knock on my door that I knew could only be Grandpa Arnold. He didn't knock softly when he wanted my attention, that was for sure. I sat up just as he opened the door. He stood silhouetted in the hall light.

"This business with the name Mickey," he said. "Don't you mention it to him again."

"I thought you wanted to find out who he really is."

"I don't want you going in there and speaking to him until you speak to Dr. Patrick."

"Dr. Patrick? The psychiatrist?"

"She'll be here tomorrow in the afternoon when you return from school. Come directly home," he ordered. "Call if you want Bill to bring you."

"Well, what just happened?" I demanded.

"There are things that can stimulate very bad memories for him and cause what Mrs. Camden calls hyperventilation, a fit of rapid breathing. It can be terrifying. It's usually because of panic, but it looks like a few bad things could be happening. He'll be fine now," he added. "Remember what I said." He closed the door. I sat there in the darkness.

Now he wanted me to see the psychiatrist? What happened was my fault?

What was I supposed to do next, tiptoe past Willie's room?

Don't mention Mickey? I'll be damned if I'll ever speak to that boy again, I thought, and slammed myself back on my pillows. I looked up at the vaguely starlit ceiling. Maybe I would just ask Aaron to drive up to Butler Heights tomorrow and leave that psychiatrist talking to herself.

My body felt like a rubber band stretched too far. I was so tense I might just snap. My bed felt like a rowboat caught in a hurricane as I tossed and turned before finally falling asleep. Usually, I woke before my alarm sounded, but that morning, it thundered, and I snapped my eyes open. I had planned on looking especially good this morning for Aaron and for my friends when he and I entered the school building. Other girls, especially the older ones in our school, seemed to bloom when they were in happy romantic relationships. I could feel and see the envy in the ones who didn't have boyfriends. The happier girls had voices full of excitement. They were far more animated, and their eyes sparkled as if they lived in a world where every day was Christmas or their birthdays.

In minutes, I would go from someone to be pitied and treated gently, as if I were made of thin china, to someone who was the object of jealousy. And no matter what any of my girlfriends claimed, they all wanted other girls to be jealous of them. They competed constantly for that trophy, wearing the most exciting clothes they could find, having their hair cut and styled to resemble the hairdo of some young actress, showing off their latest jewelry and bragging about the phone calls they received from a boy. To be modest was to be forgotten.

Now I regretted not having spent more time last night choosing what to wear. Some of my friends were wearing knee-length skirts, taking some risk. The school's unwritten rule for skirts was that if you knelt and your skirt didn't touch the ground, you could be sent home. I wished I had one that didn't touch the ground, but unfortunately, all of mine did. The newest outfit I had was a light green Bermuda-collared shirt with an A-line plaid wool skirt. I had a cable-stitched dark green sweater to wear over my shirt, instead of the jacket I always wore. I put on a pair of cable-stitched kneesocks the color of my sweater and slipped on a pair of red oxford tied shoes and inspected myself in the full-length mirror on my closet door. My cheeks did look rosier than they had in the past dreadful days. I turned this way and that, imagining being looked at from different angles.

When Grandpa had told me that my grandmother had warned him that I would turn into a young lady practically overnight, I was reminded of how suddenly my body had begun to develop curves and sweep me into adolescence. The boyish figure I had begun to hate seemed to sink beneath my budding breasts and tighter waist. I would stand in front of a mirror and admire the way my rear end was filling out. My legs were more shapely with each passing month, it seemed. I smiled to myself, recalling how shocked Willie had been when he had first realized my maturity.

"You look more like Mommy," he once said.

Running through my memory and sifting through our family albums, I constantly looked for the resemblances. Uncle Bobby was right when he had said it: I was looking more and more like my mother. Did I dare think it? I would be as beautiful as she was.

This morning, I'd wear more lipstick, I thought, but I wouldn't put it on until I got into Aaron's car.

I hurried down the hall, not even glancing at Willie's bedroom door, and found that my grandfather had already left for work. Mrs. Camden was in the kitchen with My Faith and Myra, preparing breakfast for the boy. I charged in and poured myself some orange juice. I was already only minutes away from being picked up, so I grabbed one of My Faith's homemade buttermilk biscuits and gobbled it down with a glass of milk. They were all complaining about how fast I was eating, Myra the most vocal, but I acted deaf and dumb.

Everyone apparently knew that Aaron Podwell was coming to pick me up. When he buzzed at the front gate, I pressed number five to have it opened, and that drew a moment of silence.

My Faith shook her head. "No boy's more important than your health," she said.

"Some boys might improve your health," I told her.

Both Myra and My Faith widened their eyes together, but Mrs. Camden just smiled. "Let us know which it is," she called after me, and the three of them laughed.

We'll see who laughs last, I thought, and on a wave of defiance woven tightly with currents of rage, I sailed out of the front entrance and reached Aaron's car just as he opened the door for me and said, "Ma'am, your chariot has arrived."

"Take me to Rome," I said.

He laughed and closed the door. As he came around to get in, I began to put on my lipstick. He sat behind the steering wheel, watching me with a big look of surprise and amusement.

"Nearly overslept," I explained.

"You look good to me," he said.

I leaned over and kissed him on the cheek. "Sorry. I had to blot my lipstick," I told him.

His eyes nearly exploded with delight, and I knew as he pulled away that he'd be in trouble with my grandfather if he had been there to hear the squeal of Aaron's tires. "Oops," he said.

"No worries. My grandfather is already at work," I told him. He nodded, but when I looked to my right, I saw Jimmy Wilson looking back at us with disapproval that would certainly find its way to my grandfather's ears.

10

Surprisingly, Aaron did not wipe my lipstick off his cheek before we entered the building. When I pointed it out to him, he stopped and, with a wide and dramatic sweep of his arms, declared he'd wear it like a medal of honor and fight to the death before wiping it away. We certainly didn't need any other way of attracting attention. We had that the moment we walked in holding hands and everyone realized that he had picked me up for school. I kept my eyes forward, but I could feel everyone looking at us, their conversations stopping and then starting quickly as he walked me to my homeroom. Our school had a rule against boys and girls doing much more than holding hands. Kissing anywhere inside the building was especially frowned upon, so we just parted when the bell rang to go to our first classes of the day.

"Got a new limo driver, I see," Sandra Roth said as soon as I sat at my desk in homeroom. It was no secret that the strawberry blonde with the biggest boobs in our class had been chasing after Aaron from the start of the school year. She had done everything but throw herself at his feet. "What did you do to get him?"

I spun on her as if she had pinched the back of my neck. "What makes you think I had to do anything?"

She smirked. Lila was listening at the desk right beside me.

"Did you do something to try to get him?" I asked, trying to sound as innocent as I could. "Something you're ashamed of, maybe?" I looked at Lila and then at her. "Why so silent? Don't you know that confession is good for the soul?" I asked. It came to me quickly because My Faith was so fond of saying it.

Her blood rushed to her face so fast that she looked like a cherry Popsicle. Lila laughed. I glanced at her and turned around to listen to the daily announcements, but I had no doubt that the table was set for today's chatter. Sandra would seek a way to get back at me. I was in the game again, keeping my head above the surface of the pool of gossip. There was no longer anything off-limits about me now. The jealous could direct their rumors and lies toward me without restraint. Envy had shoved pity aside.

However, the remainder of my school day went better than I had anticipated. Aaron and I spent as much time together as we could, with him being in senior classes and me being a junior. Lunch and walks between classes were enough. I continued to toy with the idea of standing up Dr. Patrick, but I was worried that Grandpa would be angry and punish me by not letting me go to Audrey's party. By the end of the day,

Aaron revealed that he had sensed that I was in deep, if not troubled, thought about something from time to time. I could see that he was trying to navigate carefully through the minefield of my moods.

We had just started away from school when he turned and asked, "Okay, so what's bothering you, Clara Sue? I mean, on top of all the other reasons for you to be upset. Three times today, you didn't hear a word I said, and usually girls take notes when I speak."

How much am I willing to trust him? I wondered. I wasn't happy with how everyone at home was reacting to my feelings, and Lila just wasn't enough.

"Taking this boy into our home and putting him in Willie's room isn't just a minor thing for me. I can't help thinking about it."

"Yeah, I could see that when I dropped you off yesterday. Anything new happen this morning before I picked you up?"

"I haven't been very cooperative about it, and everyone is giving me grief, and now . . ." I hesitated, but I was like someone who jumped off a diving board and had second thoughts too late.

"Now what?"

"My grandfather wants me to talk to the boy's psychiatrist this afternoon."

"He's taking you to a psychiatrist?"

"No, she's waiting for me at the house."

"But why you?"

His surprise didn't surprise me. I was worried that he might think I was a head case myself and that would scare him off. And then I thought, *Is that really why Grandpa wants me to talk to the psychiatrist, too?* Did he think I was mentally unstable? Did Mrs. Camden advise him to have me examined by Dr. Patrick? Until this moment, I was thinking it was solely to convince me to be kinder to the boy, but Aaron's tone gave me second thoughts.

"It's no secret in my house that I don't want the boy to be there. I guess I sound very cruel and mean," I said. It sounded like a weak explanation for my seeing a psychiatrist.

He nodded, but he didn't really look like he agreed.

"Do you think I'm mean and cruel to want him someplace else? Do you think I need a psychiatrist now?"

He shrugged. Then he smiled. "I don't know you well enough yet. Do you enjoy pulling the wings off of houseflies?"

"It's not funny, Aaron. If you're going to ask me serious questions, be serious when I respond. Otherwise, don't ask."

"Okay, okay. Take it easy."

He was quieter, so I decided not to suggest Butler Heights today. When he did start talking again on our way to my grandfather's estate, he talked about the other kids in school, some of his friends, who liked whom, and then he went on to tell me about his sister's new opportunity at a magazine in New York. I thought he was talking more than usual, babbling, actually, because he had suddenly become very nervous around me and hated the silence between us.

Maybe he was regretting taking on the challenge and was trying to think of a way out. Who could blame him?

"You don't have to pick me up every morning," I said when we pulled up in front of the house.

"Don't you want me to?"

"Only if you really want to," I said.

"I wouldn't do it if I didn't want to."

"Okay."

"Okay. I'll call you tonight."

I started to get out but stopped. I sat there thinking a moment. He waited, watching me. "There's more," I said.

"More?"

"The boy was moaning last night. I went into the room and heard him say 'Mickey' like I told you, only I tried a little too hard, maybe, to get him to say whether that was his name."

"A little too hard? What does that mean? What did you do to him?"

"I shouted and poked him, and Mrs. Camden, the nurse, was a little upset about it."

"Poked him? With what? A knife or something?"

"No, just my hand. He was like in a daze, but when he woke and saw me, he was . . ."

"What?"

"Really scared. Later, he had an episode, and my grandfather blamed me. I think that's why he wants me to see Dr. Patrick today."

"What sort of episode?"

"Hyperventilation. They had to get the doctor. They said he had a panic attack or something."

"Oh. That's when you have trouble breathing, right?"

"Yes."

"And they think it was because of you?"

"Yes."

"Wow."

"Now you do think I'm cruel, right? I mean, who would do that to a sick little boy, right?"

He was silent just a little too long to please me.

"You don't have to pick me up, and you can take Sandra Roth to Audrey's party. She'll be easier, for sure, because she doesn't have all these problems that will spoil your fun," I said, and I got out of the car before he could reply.

"Hey," he called after me.

I kept walking, tears burning my eyes, and entered the house quickly. I never looked back. Mrs. Camden was sitting in the living room with a tall, thin, dark-brown-haired woman who looked like she had a pair of microscope lenses for eyes. Maybe that was my imagination, because I knew she was Dr. Patrick and her job was to get inside your head. She wore an ankle-length dark blue skirt and a slightly lighter blue blouse that I thought looked more like a man's shirt. She had her long legs crossed and was sipping a cup of tea. Her thin lips softened into what looked like a crooked slice in her lean face. Then her eyes softened, too, as a full smile rippled. Mrs. Camden stood as soon as she saw me.

"Hi, Clara Sue. This is Dr. Patrick," she said. "Why don't you come in? I was just going up."

"Maybe I should put my books away and change," I said.

"Oh, we won't be that long," Dr. Patrick said, holding her smile but commanding with her eyes. She put her cup of tea down on the side table and unfolded her legs as she sat back on the sofa. "We should start by getting to know each other."

"Start what?" I asked, not moving.

Mrs. Camden kept smiling but continued to walk out of the living room.

"Just give it a chance," she whispered as she passed me.

I turned back to Dr. Patrick.

"Just a conversation, Clara Sue. Please. Won't you sit?" she asked. She had the sort of authoritative voice that made requests sound more like commands. Mrs. Rosner, my business education teacher, sounded like that. Even the toughest boys in our class jumped when she snapped an order.

Nevertheless, I was determined not to be intimidated. Not even attempting to hide my annoyance and reluctance, I approached the chair across from her like someone on death row approaching the electric chair. I flopped into it and slammed my books onto the table beside it so hard that the lamp shook. She didn't lose her smile. Ironically, her tolerance for bad behavior made me even angrier.

"You're in the eleventh grade?"

"I'm sure you know that. You probably know everything about me."

Her eyes blinked, but she otherwise didn't reveal a note of displeasure. I was beginning to hate that smile. It seemed like a mask. I could feel the way she was taking measurement of me, making me self-conscious of my posture, the way I opened and closed my hand, and even how I was breathing. I really was under a microscope.

"I never take anything anyone says about someone else for granted," she said. "I have the feeling you're the same way. You like to make up your own mind and not let others do it for you."

"That's right. That includes everyone."

She nodded and finally lost her smile, ready to get down to business. "I understand you do very well in school. What's your favorite subject?"

I looked away and then turned back to her. "What's my favorite subject, what's my favorite color, what kind of music do I like? Let's not dance around what's happening here, please. I know my grandfather wanted you to see me because he thinks I'm seriously disturbed or mentally ill because of all this."

"He doesn't think you're mentally ill, Clara Sue."

"He wanted me to see you. You're a psychiatrist, right?"

"I am. A child psychiatrist," she said, leaning forward. "People generally think young people don't need treatment. Most people believe all they need is more discipline. At least, I get that most of the time."

"Is that what my grandfather thinks?"

"He wouldn't have had us meet to talk if he believed that, would he? And he didn't ask me to talk to
you because he thought you were mentally ill. We're
just talking. I'm not giving you all sorts of diagnostic
tests. There's no reason for you to be afraid of me."

"Don't flatter yourself. I'm not afraid of you."

"Good. I'm simply talking with you to see if
there's something we can do to make things easier for
you. You've been through a great deal of shock, and
you're full of rage. It doesn't take a psychiatrist to see
that. There's nothing wrong with having professional
help. It's a lot to go through. Most adults would be
just as troubled, if not worse."

"The guidance counselor in our school already
spoke with me. She's supposedly a psychologist, too.
I think."

She widened her smile. "She could be, sure. A psychiatrist has a medical degree, and a psychologist has
a doctorate in psychology. Our methods sometimes
seem similar, but I don't do counseling as much as di-
agnose mental illness and often prescribe medication."

"So they really do think I'm mentally ill," I insisted.

"Of course not. I'm not here for you. You're not
my patient. I'm here because of the child your grandfather is helping."

"So I was right," I pounced. "The boy's mentally
ill? He belongs in a clinic or something, then, doesn't
he?"

"At the moment, he has severe paranoia," she said,

"but a clinical setting could do him more harm than good. Do you know what that means, paranoia?"

"You just told me I was a good student."

She smirked, and I relaxed a little.

"He's afraid of stuff all the time? Doesn't trust anyone," I said.

"Lots of stuff," she said. "It's having an effect on his physical well-being. Just getting him to eat well is an issue."

"Well, he was poisoned. Why shouldn't he be afraid to eat? I would be, too."

"Exactly. But I don't think he fully understands that he was poisoned."

"But I told him."

"Or wants to believe it when he hears it," she added.

"What's that mean?"

"Maybe someone he loved and trusted did this to him, or maybe he's ashamed that he did it to himself."

I grimaced. "Please. I don't believe all this. The doctors surely asked him about it when he was in the hospital."

"He doesn't remember being brought there. It took a while before he realized where he was, and when he did, he didn't reveal anything helpful, Clara Sue. He knows he was sick, of course, but that's about all I can get from him now."

"So he's speaking to you?"

"A little, very little. It will take time."

"Time," I muttered. I hated the sound of that word now. For me, it had become profanity. I leaned forward. "How do you know he's not lying about being unable to remember his name or what happened to him or his family or anything?" I demanded.

She thought a moment. Was she pretending I had asked a good question, or had she thought that, too? I decided to pursue it. Maybe I could make her see what was really happening, and she would tell my grandfather, and that would end all this.

"He could have come from a very poor home, and he sees all we have here, and . . . and he sees how easy it is to take advantage of my grandfather because of Willie's death, take advantage of everyone in the house, everyone except me."

"All that is a little bit sophisticated for a boy who looks about nine or ten, don't you think?"

"No."

"I do, but I will admit that what your grandfather has given him is a way out of his turmoil, the conflict raging in him from what were obviously traumatic events. He has to like and want that, but he's not conniving."

"If he hasn't said much, how do you know all that?"

"I have treated children who were caught in wars and have seen horrible violence. It's not much different. That's why I suggested your grandfather hire Mrs. Camden. She's treated war victims."

"He's not a war victim. There's no war here."

"There are different kinds of wars, Clara Sue," she said. "Family wars."

"Right. Like right here, right now."

"Oh, it's not that bad," she said. "Everyone is concerned for you as much as they are for the little boy."

"Says you."

"Is it that you don't want to believe it?" she asked softly. "Because if that's true, it's understandable," she added quickly. "You are not at fault here for anything. And I want you to believe me when I say that I don't believe you have anything wrong with you that would require me to examine and treat you. If anything, what you're feeling is understandable, normal."

"Good. Tell my grandfather."

"But you are also feeling threatened, and that's a little paranoid, too."

"A *little* paranoid? What's that, like being a little pregnant?"

She widened her smile and nearly laughed. "Maybe. Look, Clara Sue, you're a very important part of this effort to bring him back, if you will. You will be far happier if you accept that. It's easy to see you're not happy now."

"Yes, everyone says that, but I lost my little brother, and this . . . weird kid is living in his room, wearing his clothes, taking everything that was his, even his name!"

"Why don't we think of it more in terms of borrowing it, sort of like hitching a ride from the darkness into the light? You'd give someone in desperate need a ride, wouldn't you?"

"I don't believe my grandfather simply wants to give him a ride. I think he's . . ."

"He's what?"

"Replacing my brother," I said. "And that's not a little paranoid. *He's* the one who needs your help, not me."

"I've been helping him," she said. It stunned me for a moment. My grandfather was going to a psychiatrist? "He's seeing me twice a week now."

"Good for him. He might need to see you five times a week," I replied.

"I'm sure you don't mean to sound this way, Clara Sue. Don't you think he's suffering with the loss of your brother, too?"

I looked away. "Not enough," I muttered. "Not when he has this weird boy in Willie's room."

"What if it was the other way around? What if it was Willie who had been poisoned and who was helped by someone like your grandfather? Would you be happy for him or angry?"

"It's not the other way around! I'm not going to play mind games with you about it, either," I said, standing. Tears were starting to burn under my eyelids, but I was determined not to give her the satisfaction of seeing me cry. I scooped up my books. "Do whatever you want. I'll stay away from him. You can tell my grandfather that I promise I won't hurt him. I won't spoil anything for him. I won't even look at him."

"But no one wants you to stay away from him. It's exactly the opposite. Everyone wants you to work with us to help him. I think deep down, you want that, too."

"I don't. I don't care. I just want to be left alone."

"Can we talk about this again?"

"No," I said, and I walked out of the room and up the stairs. As I passed Willie's room, I saw Mrs. Camden turn away from the boy, who was sitting up in bed, to look toward me. Before she could say a word, I was in my room. And so she'd understand how I felt about it all, I slammed my door closed.

I flopped onto my bed, pressed my clenched fists against each other, and looked up at the ceiling. Why was I the only one who saw the injustice? My Faith, Myra, Mrs. Camden, and now Aaron all thought I was being unfair. In their minds, I was the one who needed to change, not my grandfather. The only ally I had was what Grandpa Arnold called a "weak sister," Lila Stewart, who probably said one thing to my face and another to our girlfriends, anyway. And now this psychiatrist . . . she infuriated me, and yet I couldn't deny that she had planted some doubt in my mind. Maybe I was being a little paranoid.

I turned over and pressed my face into the pillow, wishing I could smother myself. That would teach them all. Nothing seemed more important than spiting them, getting even, making them regret every word they had uttered against me, every critical syllable. I fantasized about what it would be like. The house would be a morgue again; only this time, there would be reason for someone in it to feel guilty—actually, everyone in it. They'd all be sitting there moaning and groaning, wishing they had been different and kinder to me. Most of them would look at my grandfather angrily now. *Why did you have to bring this boy here at this time? And when you saw how it disturbed Clara Sue, why didn't you remove him?* Uncle Bobby would actually stand up and ask these things out loud. Grandpa Arnold would stammer and stutter and then get up and run into his office. He wouldn't be able to look at the picture of my grandmother, and the pictures of my parents would be like thorns in his heart.

All these images made me feel better. I took a deep breath and sat up, wiping my face to be sure there wasn't a single tear of self-pity trickling down my cheek. Then I went to my stereo and turned it on, deliberately making it louder than ever. I started to change my clothes and then got a new idea. On the floor of my closet, I had my mother's personal makeup kit. It was old, and most of it was dried out, but with a little water, I might revive the mascara and the eye shadow. Certainly, I could use the lipsticks. Maybe the makeup foundation and the blush were fine. I brought the case into the bathroom and sat before the vanity mirror table in my bra and panties and began. *I'll show them*, I thought. *I'll go down to dinner all made up.*

In a frenzy, I began. My memories of watching my mother do it were vague, but I did recall how easily and confidently she put on her makeup, and when she was finished, she looked like a movie star to me. Grandma Arnold was not fond of using much makeup, so I learned practically nothing from her. My girlfriends and I did experiment with it, of course, but the school rules kept us from using it frequently. I wasn't in quite the mood to be careful about it.

Actually, anyone watching would think I was attacking my face. I added too much water to the mascara and the eye shadow. They began to run. The foundation didn't seem to be the right shade, and the blush, if anything, looked too pale. Adding more seemed to compound the clownish appearance I was building. I knew I had put on too much lipstick, and in wiping it off, I smeared some on my cheek.

The sound of heavy knocking on my door finally caught my attention. I rose and went to it. "What?" I demanded before it was half open.

Mrs. Camden stood there, a wide look of astonishment on her face. She looked like she couldn't speak for a moment. "Your music," she managed first. "You can't mean for it to be this loud."

I turned and realized what she meant. Somehow, I had not heard it while I worked on my makeup.

"They can hear it downstairs. Your grandfather just shouted up for me to see what is happening."

Without replying, I went to the stereo and lowered it considerably. "Happy?"

"What are you doing, Clara Sue?" she asked, stepping in.

"I'm putting on my makeup for dinner," I said.

"Oh, no. Can I help?" she asked.

"I don't need anyone's help," I said.

She stood there staring at me. "You're not feeling well," she said. "You're getting yourself too upset."

"Getting *myself* upset? That's a laugh. Look, I'm busy." I returned to the bathroom. I sat at the vanity mirror again and looked at my face. It was streaked now. Everything seemed to be running into everything else. I looked like a clown who had gone insane.

There was nothing to do but take a washcloth and begin scrubbing it all off. I turned when I sensed she was still there, standing in my bathroom doorway.

"My mother forbid me to wear any makeup, even lipstick," she said. "I used to sneak it on at school and then wash it off before I went home. Do most of the girls at your school wear makeup?"

"No. There are rules against most anything but a little lipstick," I said. "Most schools are built on a cement foundation. Mine is built on cement rules."

She laughed. I looked at her, surprised. "You don't really need much makeup," she said. "Wait until you're my age."

"My mother used makeup."

"Yes, but I'm sure not for everyday life, right? I bet she didn't use that much when she went shopping."

"Still, she used it when she went to parties and shows."

"You're going to a party this weekend, right?"

"I don't think so."

"Why not?"

I didn't answer.

"You've got to stop punishing yourself, Clara Sue. It won't change anything. If you change your mind and decide to go, I'll go shopping with you for something to wear, and I'll share whatever I know about doing makeup, too."

I turned to look at her again. I could feel my eyelids narrowing, the flush coming up my neck. "You

know that it won't do you any good, don't you?" I
said.

"Pardon?"

"Trying to be my pal. It won't change how I feel
about him being here. Don't waste your time." I went
back to scrubbing my face.

When I turned to the doorway again, she was
gone. Half of me felt delight, but the other half felt
regret. I sat there in confusion, not knowing whether I
should start crying again or start laughing. Thankfully,
the phone rang before I needed to decide. I expected it
to be Lila, but it was Aaron.

"Just tell me what I did wrong," he began. "I like
to learn from my mistakes with girls."

"You decided to date me."

"Huh?"

"That's what you did wrong. I'm sure you were
undecided about it."

"No, I wasn't. I've been trying to get your attention since the first day of school. I just backed off
when your brother was killed."

"I don't make anyone happy," I warned.

"I'm already happy, and don't say you'll make me
unhappy. I was vaccinated against it."

"You're such an idiot," I said, but softly. I looked
at myself in my full-length mirror on the closet door.
"Do you think I need to wear makeup? I mean, more
than just lipstick?"

"I don't know anything about makeup, but I
wouldn't want to change anything on your face."

"I could be sexier."

"My heart can stand only so much excitement," he replied, and I had my first laugh of the day.

"Okay. I'm sorry I was so cold before. Come get me in the morning."

"Did you hurt the psychiatrist?"

"She won't be the same. I pity her next patient."

He laughed.

"Let's not talk about it. Let's not talk about any of it, Aaron."

"Fine with me," he said. "I'm satisfied just talking about you. See you in the morning."

"Okay. Now you can wash your car for the tenth time in two days," I told him.

After I hung up, I did feel better. I didn't put on anything special for dinner. It was still early, so I started some homework, and then, when it was time to go down, I sucked in my breath, gazed at myself in the mirror, and decided right there to leave that sweet little girl who was once in my body behind. Like a pair of shoes gone out of style.

Suddenly, that made it far easier to walk past Willie's room and treat it as if it had been boarded up. *There's no one in there*, I told myself. *There's no lift on the stairway and no wheelchair at the bottom. There is no physical-therapy equipment in Grandpa's den.*

And Mrs. Camden? She was simply some guest Grandpa had invited to stay for a while.

I could feel the coy new smile on my lips. I would probably become so difficult to tolerate that they would all ignore me. It would be easier for me to forget what was happening here.

But I wouldn't forget Willie. Oh, no. Everything I did from now on would be to help me remember him.

I bounced down the remaining steps and headed for the dining room. When everyone saw me and stopped talking, I smiled again.

"I'm absolutely starving," I said, and sat quickly. I reached for a piece of bread and practically shoved it down my throat.

No one spoke.

The looks on their faces were priceless.

It was as if a total stranger had just walked into the house and taken my seat.

11

At dinner, Grandpa Arnold didn't ask me anything about my conversation with Dr. Patrick, nor did he mention anything she had told him about our tense little discussion. Perhaps she had told him that the best way to handle me was to ignore me. I knew that was what everyone was doing now, handling me. They had been doing that since the day Willie died. I had resented it until now. *Handle me*, I thought. *Cater to my every whim and need.* I could be as selfish as anyone else, if I had to be.

As if to underscore what I was thinking, my grandfather and Mrs. Camden talked about everything else but me and the boy in Willie's room. I didn't know if he was putting on a show for me to demonstrate that he could be just as aloof about it all as I was, but Grandpa Arnold was even more interested in Mrs. Camden, her early life, her education, some of her nursing experiences, and how she had come to live in Prescott. It was almost as if I wasn't there, but I was interested in her answers.

Shortly after her husband had died, Mrs. Camden said, she had taken a private-duty nurse position at the home of one of the founding families of the community, the Brocktons. The matriarch of the family had been a vigorous woman in her early eighties, but she had rapidly fallen into what Mrs. Camden called dementia. It had gotten so she didn't even recognize her own children and certainly not her grandchildren.

Of course, I wondered how you could forget your own family. I almost unintentionally turned the conversation to the boy when I asked, "Isn't that just amnesia?"

"Amnesia," she said, "is the loss of facts, personal experiences. Dementia is the loss of mental functions like cognition, the ability to reason, to understand what's being said or done. There's loss of memory and even language skills, but it's a far more severe situation. Amnesia victims can and do eventually remember things," she explained.

I looked at Grandpa while she spoke. He was staring at her with such admiration. It really surprised me, because I knew it wasn't easy to impress him. I think he realized that I was looking more at him than at her while she spoke. He cleared his throat and turned back to his food.

"Well, I'm with the Eskimos when it comes to that condition," he said. "Time to put you on a shelf of ice and set you sailing off into the sunset."

"Oh, you don't really believe that, William," Mrs. Camden told him. I saw how she reached over to put her left hand over his for a moment. He didn't pull his away. She lifted hers, and they got started on a new topic.

Well, they're happy peas in a pod. Good for them, I thought. I finished my dinner and excused myself to go up and complete my homework. I was so proud of the way I could walk past Willie's room and not have the slightest temptation to look into it. Perhaps the boy would see how indifferent I had become to his existence and that would discourage him enough to consider returning to his own family. I pushed all that aside, finished my work, and began to think more about Audrey's party. I wanted to wear something special, something different, something that clearly said *She's no little girl anymore.*

I knew I could have Aaron take me shopping, but I was sure he would be bored, and besides, I wanted to surprise him with what I wore. I was half-tempted to take Mrs. Camden up on her offer to go shopping with me. It would be interesting to see how much of an effort she would make to do it or if it was just something she had said to sound nice, not only to me but to my grandfather. Then I thought, *Why is that even slightly important to me? Once the boy goes, she goes out of our lives with him, doesn't she?*

Just before getting ready to go to bed, I thought about it again and decided to test her and see what she would do if I said I'd like her to shop with me tomorrow after school. If she did come, would she direct me only to clothes she thought my grandfather would approve? I imagined the boy had gone to sleep and she had gone to her room, the room that had been my parents' room. I listened just outside my door and heard nothing coming from Willie's room. Moving quickly past it, I went to Mrs. Camden's door. I was just about to knock on it when I heard my grandfather's distinct laugh followed by hers. I was frozen for a moment, my fist inches from the door.

What was he doing in there? Why was the door closed? I was happy I hadn't knocked. I couldn't make out what they were saying, but whatever it was brought more laughter. I stepped back as if the door had caught fire. There was something about my grandfather's laugh that was different. I hadn't heard it since my grandma's passing. Sometimes, despite their ages, they could act and sound like young lovers. He sounded too much like that.

Maybe it was wrong for me to be angry about it, but I was. How could they be enjoying themselves so much and so soon? What happened to the worry about me? Even the worry about the boy? A new suspicion reared its ugly head. Had my grandfather known Mrs. Camden before all this? I wondered as I turned and walked quickly back to my room. Maybe all that talk about her being experienced with patients who had suffered serious physical and psychological traumas was hogwash, as Grandpa Arnold would call it. Maybe his real reason for bringing the boy to our house was to get Mrs. Camden here.

I closed my door and sat on my bed, thinking. Lila's comments about my grandfather being such a catch returned. It had bothered me to think of him being romantically involved with anyone back then, and it really bothered me now. I thought about all those references he continually made to my grandmother. Didn't he mean them? Didn't he miss her as terribly as he claimed? How could he want another woman, and in this house especially? Grandma had decorated it, decided the arrangement of everything that was in it. Mrs. Camden was sleeping in the bed my grandmother had chosen for that room!

Love, I thought bitterly, it was as easy to file away as a library card.

I was fuming until I was in bed and closing my eyes. Even then, I couldn't stop thinking about their laughter. What were they doing now? Having a consultation about the boy? *Hardly that, Clara Sue*, I told myself. *Grow up. They're not playing spin the bottle.*

That's what I would do. Starting tomorrow, I thought. I would grow up. I couldn't grow old enough to leave this house for college fast enough. I chased after sleep for at least an hour before I could wrap my arms around it and make it take me into my new fantasies.

On Thursday, I asked Aaron to take me shopping after school. I told him to go busy himself while I went about choosing a new outfit to wear.

"I don't want you hovering around me. It will make me nervous," I said.

He laughed. "That's what my mother always tells my father," he said, and went off.

The clothing store I went into had just gotten some new fashions out of England. I was surprised at how short the skirts were. When I tried one on, it was half-way between my knees and my thighs. *You don't bend over in this unless your back's to the wall*, I thought. No way I could wear it to school. It was certainly different. I liked the crimson color and decided to match it with a top that was also just a little too tight to wear to school. Feeling reckless with the money Grandpa had given me, I bought a pair of red boots to match and some new red panties. It was all bagged up for me by the time Aaron returned.

"Will I be surprised?" Aaron asked as we left.

"Oh, I think so," I said. "Along with everyone else."

As Friday came around, excitement began to build. All my girlfriends kept asking me what I was wearing, but I told them I hadn't yet decided. Only Lila was a little suspicious, because she had found out that Aaron had taken me shopping. I hadn't told my grandfather or Myra anything, either. On Friday, Mrs. Camden came to my room in the late afternoon. I had bought myself some new foundation, blush, eye shadow, and mascara. The salesgirl in the store had given me some tips on how to put it on, especially the eye shadow. She had helped me pick out a new lipstick, too. I had just showered and done my hair when Mrs. Camden knocked and stepped in.

"Hi," she said. "I was wondering if you needed any help with your makeup for tonight."

"How would you know, really? You hardly wear any," I said.

"Not while I'm at work, no."

I turned away from her and continued to brush out my hair. "You're not always at work here," I muttered loudly enough for her to hear.

She was silent. I waited a moment and then looked at her. She was staring at me with the strangest expression on her face.

"What?" I said.

"Nothing. I hope you have a good time," she said, then turned and walked out.

My emotions were tied in knots. On one hand, I was proud of and satisfied with myself for cutting her off at the knees, as Grandpa might say, but the pained look on her face stirred the softer part of me, a part I had come to believe was more of a weakness. I wanted to ignore it. I was tired of crying, of protesting, of feeling alone and abused. I was tired of playing the victim. *Let them be victims for a change,* I thought. *Tonight I rule.*

I started on my makeup.

After I dressed, I stood there looking at myself in the full-length mirror. It really was like looking at a complete stranger. Of course, I was aware of how my body was developing. I saw the eyes of my girlfriends study me in the locker room, just the way I studied some of them, always comparing and being afraid that I wouldn't be as pretty or as sexy as most of them. I actually admired the girls who were not as self-conscious. I wanted to be just as indifferent about the curves developing, the way I was being molded into a young woman. I wasn't as crazy as some, who I knew were measuring everything weekly, if not daily. The girls who were still quite flat-chested looked mournful and envious sometimes.

I had bought two new bras, one I wondered if I would have the nerve to wear. In size, I was somewhere between an A cup and a B cup. The padded bra

I had bought gave me the look of a woman with a definite B size. In the slightly tight blouse, I looked quite voluptuous. Was it too much? Did I dare?

Defiance was still raging in me. I swallowed back any hesitation and, now quite pleased with my hair and my makeup, walked out confidently. Aaron would be here any moment. Mrs. Camden, Myra, and my grandfather were sitting in the living room and talking. I paused in the doorway. They all looked at me, but no one spoke. My grandfather actually blushed. Mrs. Camden looked at him and then at me.

"And who could this be?" Myra finally said.

I knew my grandfather well enough to realize that he was about to voice his displeasure, but Mrs. Camden beat him to the microphone.

"You look very pretty, Clara Sue," she said. "Very grown-up."

"Why shouldn't I?" I shot back.

"Clara Sue!" Grandpa said. "You thank people when they give you a compliment."

They all stared at me.

"Thank you," I said. "I'm going out to wait for Aaron. He'll be here any moment."

"Remember to be home before midnight," Grandpa warned.

I looked at my watch and then at the grandfather clock. "That's five minutes fast," I said, and walked out of the house.

My legs were trembling, but I felt so good about myself that I nearly broke out in laughter. I did laugh when Aaron drove up. He got out, took one look at me, and put his right hand over his heart as he pretended to battle back a wave of dizziness.

"Idiot," I said, moving to the car.

He rushed around to open the door for me. "Are you trying to kill me with beauty?" he asked.

I looked at him, our faces inches apart. "Proceed at your own risk," I said.

He smiled, looked back at the house, and then kissed me softly. "I think we might have a good time tonight."

"Depends on your definition of a good time," I said, and got into his car.

He nearly tripped over himself rushing to get back behind the wheel.

As we pulled away, I looked up at the window of Willie's room. I knew it was my imagination, or at least, I thought it was, but I saw that little boy looking down at us mournfully, the way Willie used to whenever I went anywhere without him. I quickly leaned over and turned up the volume of the radio. Aaron accelerated as soon as we were clear of the gates, and I felt as if I had been launched into space.

Audrey's house was about half the size of my grandfather's, but it was still quite a large ranch-style home, with that famous big basement furnished with fun things like a pool table, a jukebox, and a Ping-Pong table at the far right end. There was a bar, too, but her father had done a funny thing with all the visible bottles of liquor. He had put a piece of tape at the top of any bottle that had been opened so he could tell immediately if Audrey had permitted any of her friends to have a drink of rye, vodka, gin, scotch, or bourbon. The bottles of beer were in a locked cabinet. Only soft drinks were visible. Charlie Martin immediately suggested that Audrey simply add water to any bottle of liquor we sampled.

"That's what I do at home, and my parents have never noticed," he said.

"If my father does, I'm grounded for the rest of the year," Audrey replied.

She was the shortest girl in our class, doll-like, with diminutive facial features and crystal-blue eyes. She had been going with Ted Davis for months. He was a junior, nearly six feet two, and a star on our basketball team, and the sight of them together always brought smiles. Audrey said her father called them Mutt and Jeff, after some old cartoon.

There were twenty of us at the party, and when Aaron and I appeared, it was like the parting of the Red Sea. My girlfriends, led by Lila, immediately surrounded me to find out where I had bought my skirt and blouse and boots. I could feel how some of them were actually happy to see me so upbeat since Willie's tragic death. They all ranted about how horrible our strict school dress code was. Everyone but me vowed to have her parents go to the next PTA meeting to protest for us. I couldn't even begin to imagine my grandfather doing such a thing.

As it turned out, Audrey didn't have to sneak any of her father's liquor. Tommy Koch had brought two flasks of vodka. He explained that vodka didn't smell as much on your breath as the other liquors. Everyone was anxious to try it, but some couldn't hide their nervousness, especially Audrey.

"Nobody had better throw up in my house," she warned.

Of course, the boys assured her that wouldn't happen. While Ted was dancing with Audrey and the lights were low, Tommy and two other boys snuck some of her father's vodka, replacing it with water, and the drinking continued.

I felt a little dizzy and even a little nauseated after eating some pizza and anchovies. By now, Aaron and I were dancing very close. I was practically sleeping on him. I could feel his lips on my cheeks and my neck, and at one point, disregarding anyone else in the basement, we kissed like they kiss in the movies.

Audrey stepped up beside us. "If you don't make a mess," she said, "you can use my bedroom."

The suggestion excited and frightened me simultaneously. I had never ever been in a bedroom alone with a boy, not even my own. In fact, I had never had a boy visit me at my grandfather's house. Aaron's excitement took over his face completely. His eyes lit up as the possibilities seized him. I could easily imagine that he was already getting a boy's eagerness, the famous "erection fantasies" we girls teased one another about when we could talk in secret. Everyone always tried to outdo everyone else with some sort of experience, the most common being "It happened to him while we were dancing." Most claimed they pretended not to notice—"I was too embarrassed"—while others bragged about how they had pressed themselves closer and tighter, enjoying how uncomfortable it made the boy. It was happening in public, after all.

"What do you say?" Aaron whispered in my ear now.

I had deliberately sought out clothes that would make me sexy. I had put on makeup and been snippy with my grandfather and Mrs. Camden, even Myra. I had been thinking I might even violate the curfew Grandpa had imposed. Why not do this? "Okay," I whispered back.

I could feel his quickened breath. It excited my own. We turned gracefully and, without looking at anyone, started for the stairway out of the basement.

"Where are you going?" Lila asked before we got to the first step.

I looked at her. "I'll let you know after I get there," I said.

Her mouth locked open. Aaron laughed.

I had been in Audrey's house enough times to know where her bedroom was. We were there in seconds. Aaron closed the door behind us. There was enough moonlight streaming through the opened curtains to outline her bed clearly. We didn't turn on any lights. Aaron turned me toward him, and we kissed again.

"I have what we need," he said.

No girls in my class or in the class ahead of mine were ashamed that they were still virgins. Some were more suspected than others of having lost their virginity. Whether it was true or not, they seemed to have a more sophisticated air about them, especially less patience for "childish flirtations." We had our girls' health classes and were taught enough to know what to expect and how dangerous it could be to have un-protected sex. I had read as much as I could find about it on my own. Without a mother, an older sister, or even a grandmother, I was really on my own as I ma-tured. I was on my own tonight. How far would the rage against my grandfather and my unhappiness at home take me tonight?

We kissed again. Aaron guided me to Audrey's bed and gently lifted me onto it. He got beside me, and we kissed, his hands moving to unzip my blouse. There was resistance in me, but I covered it the way you covered a pot of boiling milk and let him undo my bra and bring his lips to my nipples. How many times had I fantasized about this and wondered what it would feel like? Now it was happening. A rush of warmth curled around the insides of my thighs. His fingers were struggling with the zipper on my skirt. I put my hand over his hand.

"This is Audrey's bed," I whispered, as if everyone was listening at the door.

"So? She invited us to use it."

"I'm a virgin, Aaron."

Did he understand? How sophisticated, really, was he? Boys were more apt to fabricate their sexual expe-riences. They were always proving themselves to one another, strutting like peacocks when they were con-vincing. "So? Let's put an end to that disadvantage," he joked.

"I could stain her bed," I said, and he stopped try-ing to undo my zipper.

"You could stain mine anytime," he said, and kissed me again, but I heard the disappointment in his voice and felt it in his kiss.

I sat up, pulled my blouse over my head, and dropped it and my bra beside me. He took off his shirt quickly. Then I slipped out of my skirt, and he took off his pants. How far could I go without going too far? I wondered. I was exploring myself as much as we were exploring each other. We were lost in the wonder of our passion. I was already past boundaries I had set for myself with every boy I had ever been with at a party.

We were simply holding on to each other now. He paused to take another deep breath, and then he brought his lips down between my breasts, to my stomach, to inside my thighs. I could hear myself moaning as if I was listening to someone else. I heard him unwrapping his protection. I tightened, but he said, "It's all right. I'll wait for the next opportunity, but a guy needs relief."

We moved against each other. I was building toward that climax I had brought on myself in my most secret moments. We both reached it together, and then we held on to each other like two people afraid they would sink or fly off if they didn't. After a few more moments, he turned onto his back, and I turned onto mine, but he continued to hold my hand.

"You're not just using me, are you?" he asked.

"What?"

He leaned up on his right elbow and looked down at me. "I've been with girls who wanted to get even with someone or something."

"I wouldn't be here with you if I didn't want to be here with you, Aaron. Sound familiar?"

He laughed. "So you'll respect me in the morning?"

"You're such an idiot," I said. But I was really whirling with how close he had come to my deepest emotions.

"Sure you don't want to reconsider home base?" he asked.

"Home base?"

"We've been all the way to third. You know what's going to happen now, don't you?"

"Enlighten me, my know-it-all."

"Audrey's going to inspect her bed and then tell everyone you weren't a virgin."

"I'll take my chances," I said.

He laughed and lay back again, this time putting his arm around my shoulders. I turned and rested my head against his chest. "I've decided to do whatever I can to help you," he said.

"With what?"

"Your situation at home. Whatever you need me to do, I'll do it."

"There's nothing to do. Except wait."

"For what?"

"For him to remember who he is and where he came from."

"And if he doesn't?"

"Then there will be something to do."

"What?"

"Help him remember," I said.

12

Aaron brought me home well before midnight. We were among the first to leave Audrey's party. As we started out, I saw Steve Marks poke Aaron playfully in the ribs and overheard him say, "Leaving early? I guess you got what you wanted tonight."

"Worry about yourself," Aaron told him.

It was actually Aaron more than I who was concerned with the time.

"I'm not risking your getting grounded," he told me, half joking. "I'd end up moaning like a dog in heat under your bedroom window."

I was glad Aaron had drunk very little vodka. I'd had more but stopped before I would get sick. Lila didn't look too well when I saw her after Aaron and I had come out of Audrey's bedroom. She was holding her stomach and lying in a corner with her eyes closed. That was all I'd need to do, and I wouldn't just be grounded, I'd be incarcerated. I wasn't exactly winning sympathy at home these days.

"You'd better make sure no one goes home plastered," Aaron told Tommy Koch. "They'll trace it to you, and Audrey will get into big trouble, too."

Tommy laughed but looked a little worried.

"What are your plans for tomorrow?" Aaron asked when we drove away from Audrey's house.

I told him I was riding my bike to the cemetery in the morning, and he offered to take me. "Thanks, Aaron, but it's my private time with Willie," I said.

"No problem. I'll wait for you in the car," he said. "What's the difference how you get there as long as you get there?"

"Okay. I'd like to go about nine."

"I'll be here." He leaned over to kiss me goodnight. "I had a great time," he said. "I've got the hottest girl in the school. And besides, you're now the big topic of conversation for sure."

"In my house, too, I bet," I said.

He got out and came around to open the car door for me. I wondered if he had treated every girl he dated the way he was treating me. He reached for my hand to help me get out. "Your grandfather isn't watching us from some window, is he?" he asked, his back to the house.

"No," I said, smiling. "He's hiding in the bushes."

"What?" He laughed. "Okay. See you in the morning."

I started toward the front entrance. I could feel him still standing there watching me walk away. Did all girls wonder what the boys who stared at them or watched them walking in the hallways were thinking?

Was it always some sexual fantasy? Aaron was my first
real boyfriend. I almost felt like I was learning a new
language. I turned at the door. He waved, his signature
wave that began as a salute and then careened above
his head. He got back into his car. I waited until he had
driven slowly down the driveway and out, and then I
entered the house, eager to go to bed and relive every
moment in Audrey's bedroom.

All the lights in the house were dim. I had seen the
house this way late at night, but it looked different tonight. *My home really has changed for me*, I thought.
I didn't feel it was my home as much as I had. Shadows seemed deeper. The rooms were vacant, despite
the elaborate furniture. Was I being overly dramatic
in thinking that love had left this house? The silence
seemed to say yes. I expected it would follow me to
bed. However, as soon as I closed the door behind me,
I heard my grandfather call my name from the living
room.

He was sitting in his favorite big, cushioned easy
chair. I could tell he had dozed off and just woken. He
wore his light blue robe over his pajamas and slippers,
all Christmas presents from Grandma Arnold, from
the last Christmas before she died. We had all gotten
up at the crack of dawn to gather around the tree. Willie still believed in Santa Claus.

I glanced around. There was no one else in the
room. I was expecting to see Mrs. Camden, maybe
even Myra. Normally, she would be up waiting for
me, but she was still recuperating from her broken arm
and bruises.

"So how was your party?" he asked.

"It was all right," I said.

"All right? Funny way to put it. When I was your age and I went to a party, it was either great fun or boring."

"It was great fun," I said. I knew I said it like he was pulling it from me.

"Good. I want you to be as happy as you can be, Clara Sue. I know you're not happy with how things are at the moment, but I'm hoping you'll settle down."

"Settle down? I've lost everyone in my family, Grandpa."

"You haven't lost me."

Oh, how I wanted to answer that, but I didn't. I looked down instead and pressed my lips together so hard that it hurt.

"Now, I was hoping your uncle Bobby would be here for Thanksgiving, but apparently, that's a very busy time for his show, so he can't come."

I looked up sharply. "We're having Thanksgiving?"

"We've always had Thanksgiving, Clara Sue. There were many years when your parents came here for it and, although you were too young to remember, when your grandmother and I went to your home."

"How could we have Thanksgiving? What are we thankful for?" I asked him. It was on the tip of my tongue to add, *the poisoned boy?*

"Do you think your grandmother or your mother and father would want us to ignore it? You and I are still alive and healthy. We have much more than most people in America. Should we just pretend that isn't true?"

"Who would be at our dinner?" I asked.

"Well, My Faith will make quite a dinner for us, I'm sure. I'll ask Myra to sit at the table, and Mrs. Camden will be here, and maybe . . ."

"That boy? He'll sit at our table?"

"If he's able to. It can't hurt him. Dr. Patrick thinks it might stimulate more healing."

"So you think a turkey might help him remember who he is?" I asked.

He just stared at me for a moment. I could see the conflict going on in his mind. He wanted to shout and send me to my room, but he didn't want to create any more tension and anger in this house, either. "Thanksgiving is more than a turkey, Clara Sue," he said softly.

"Right. I'm tired, Grandpa."

"Okay."

I started to turn but stopped. "Aaron is coming for me at nine tomorrow."

"You going on some picnic?"

"No, Grandpa. I'm going to Willie's grave. I'm going to go there every weekend I can," I said. I waited for him to reply. He didn't, so I turned and walked away, the silence fleeing at the sound of my footsteps as I pounded my way up the stairs. I had no intention of pausing at Willie's room, but Mrs. Camden, in her nightgown, stepped out and closed the door partway behind her.

"Oh," she said, because I surprised her. "How was your party?"

"Fine and dandy."

"He had a troubling nightmare," she said, nodding toward Willie's room.

"What was it about?"

"I don't know, exactly. More or less a typical nightmare a young child might have. You know, some monster hovering over him."

"So he didn't say anything important?"

She hesitated.

"He did, didn't he? What did he say?"

She smiled and shook her head. "Nothing that makes any sense, at least to us. I'll share it with Dr. Patrick."

"You should share it with the police," I said, and walked on to my room, thinking, *Why should I trust her?* She would keep everything a secret as long as she could so she could stay on this job . . . and maybe be with my grandfather. *One way or another*, I thought, *I'll let her know I'm on to her.*

I was more wound up than I had expected to be before I went to sleep. I wanted to think only about Aaron and me. *That poisoned boy ruins everything for me*, I thought, *even my dreams*.

I made sure to rise early enough in the morning to be ready for Aaron at nine. Grandpa Arnold was at breakfast, but we didn't say much to each other. While reading the newspaper, he was mumbling about some congressman pushing to have tighter restrictions on the trucking industry, especially regulations about drivers and how long they could go without time off. He left before Aaron arrived, and there was no mention of where I was going. When Aaron pulled up and got out, I thought he still looked half-asleep. He wore his school baseball cap, a school sweatshirt, and jeans.

"Do you sleep-drive the way some people sleep-walk?" I asked him when he opened the car door for me.

"I'm awake. I dreamed about you so much last night that it carried into the morning. My mother said I ate breakfast in slow motion and ruined her appetite. My parents make a big deal of weekend breakfasts. Sometimes they go out to brunch." He looked back at the house and then leaned in to kiss me, pausing to look closer. "You look wide awake."

"I'm probably just running on rage," I said.

"Oh? Now what?"

I waited until he got in and we started down the drive. "We're having Thanksgiving."

"So?"

"I think my grandfather wants it mainly for the boy. They think it might help him recuperate faster."

"Ah," Aaron said. He thought a moment. "Who else will be there?"

"His private-duty nurse and Myra. My uncle can't come. He's in a successful show." I looked at him. "Why? Do you want me to have you invited to my house?"

"I'd love it, but I don't think I can get out of ours. My sister will be home, and my parents invite friends. It's a big deal."

"It always was for me, too, but unlike my grandfather, I'm not very thankful this year."

He nodded. "Maybe you should think of it like this. If it does help the boy, he'll be out of your life that much faster."

I grunted.

"You don't think so?"

"No. I think my grandfather sees him as never leaving, no matter what he says to anyone else."

"The boy might not feel that way after a while. His life before can't have been so bad that he doesn't want anything to do with anyone in his family. Hell, he probably misses his mother or father, don't you think?"

"I don't know what to think," I said. "And if I voice an opinion, everyone practically jumps down my throat. I'm trying to ignore his existence, but it's not easy with stair lifts and wheelchairs and therapy equipment, not to mention a nurse parading about as if she is already part of the family."

We grew quiet as we approached the famous Prescott cemetery. He drove in slowly. I told him where to turn, and then I told him to stop. He turned off the engine and sat back. I got out of the car and walked the path to Willie's grave. There was just a marker on it now. The monument was being prepared. It was going to be very special.

I couldn't even conceive of Willie being down there. He hated being contained, especially kept in his room when he was sick. He even disliked being in a car too long. I recalled how he would charge out of the house as soon as he could and race around the front, holding a toy sword or a cap gun, pretending to chase some villains. Every part of his body needed to move, to be exercised, to grow. He despised clothes that were too tight, and when Grandma Arnold used to put him to sleep and tuck him in, folding his top sheet under the mattress as if she thought he might fall out during the night, he would complain. I always went into his room after she had left and loosened it up for him.

I couldn't loosen anything for him now. I went to my knees and lowered my head.

"See," I said. "I promised you I would be here, and I am. I know I treated you like a pain sometimes, and I was probably cruel, but I miss you very much. I miss you more than anyone, Willie. Believe me, more than anyone."

I paused and looked around. It was a partly cloudy day. The breeze was stronger, and I could feel the underlying winter air invading. It wouldn't be long before we had our first snow, something Willie always looked forward to. It was as if the flakes had bells and played a wonderful tune as they fell, inviting him to go out and roll about in them. It was never cold to him. Would it be now?

I glanced back at Aaron. He was deliberately not looking my way. Were his eyes tearful? Was he afraid of how I would be when I returned? *He must really like me to want to do this*, I thought. I couldn't imagine any other boy from school doing this. I couldn't blame them. Who would want to be with a girl who was still mourning heavily and was so angry, much less go with her to a cemetery? This was very nice of him. *Maybe he just has a bad reputation developed by the girls he's dropped*, I thought. Sour grapes make for a bitter drink.

"I have a boyfriend now, Willie. I think he'll be my boyfriend for a while, maybe even the whole school year. You didn't really know him, but you would have liked him, I'm sure.

"We're going to have Thanksgiving this year, Willie. I will hate it because you're not there. I'll write my letter to you afterward, and then, when I can, I'll return to tell you more.

"Never think I might forget you. Never," I said. I touched the marker with his name, and then I stood up, took a breath, and walked slowly back to Aaron's car. I saw a crow fly over it and then past me. I turned as it flew lower and landed on Willie's marker.

He has a pet, I thought. *That will make him happy.*

Aaron didn't say anything after I got in. He started the car, and we drove out slowly. He didn't speak until we were back on the street and heading to my grandfather's estate.

"You want to do something this afternoon?" he asked.

"Like what?"

"Sort of a picnic. I thought we might drive out to Three Wrens Lake and go rowing. We can get some sandwiches and sodas at the shop on the lake."

"Okay," I said. "The less time I have to spend in my house, the better."

"You want to go back to change or something?"

"I'm good. Just go," I said. He turned to me, looking surprised. "My grandfather will figure it out," I said. "Or not."

Three Wrens Lake was a good hour's ride south.

I knew Aaron was desperate to get me talking about anything except what was happening in my home and what had happened to Willie. He tried one subject after another, talking about school, his classes, our teachers, and his plans for college next year. He was hoping to be accepted at the College of William & Mary in Williamsburg. His father was an alumnus and made significant contributions, so he had a pretty good chance of that happening. Baseball was his sport, and William & Mary had a good team.

"My father wants me to major in economics," he told me. He talked almost continuously for the first half hour of our trip. I wasn't talking, because I was having trouble getting the sight of Willie's grave out of my head. "He's always telling me I don't sing and I don't dance, so I'd better have a good head on my shoulders for business."

He paused, waiting for me to say something. I didn't know what to say. I didn't think I'd had one thought about my future for weeks. "That's nice" sounded stupid, so I just kept silent.

"You ever go rowing on Three Wrens Lake?" he asked, trying a new topic.

"No." I thought about it. "I don't remember ever going rowing, actually."

"Really? Great. I'll teach you how, and then I'll lie back and let you row us for hours."

It was like a small crack in the ice. I smiled and sat back, a little more relaxed.

As the day continued, the clouds were swept out of the sky, and it grew warmer than I had expected.

It was obvious that Aaron had been to the lake many times. The clerk at the shop even recognized him. He ordered our sandwiches, some potato chips, and sodas, and then we went down to the dock to rent a rowboat. Three Wrens Lake was a little more than two miles long and a mile wide. There were light motorboats on it and dozens of people in rowboats and small sailboats. The man renting the boat insisted that we put on the life jackets provided. Aaron got us off with graceful and rhythmic rowing. His obvious effort to impress me was working.

"Dad bought me a rowing machine for our little basement gym," he said. "Makes me a stronger hitter. I had four home runs last year. Did you know that?"

"No. I didn't go to any games."

"You will this year, or else," he said, and I laughed. I could feel my body loosening up. I closed my eyes and bathed my face in the sun. Then I undid my hair and shook it before I reached over the edge of the boat to feel the cool water.

"I see little fish," I said.

"Let me know if you see any sharks."

"What?"

He laughed. "You want to try this?"

"Sure."

Carefully, I moved to the seat. He put the oars in my hands, showing me how to hold them. He sat right behind me, his arms against mine, and began to show me how to lift and pull the oars, how to turn the boat, and how to avoid splashing. "You're doing well," he said, but he didn't move away. He pressed his lips to my neck and then gently moved them along with small kisses.

"I can't concentrate on my rowing."

He laughed and sat back.

I was really enjoying it now and feeling like I was accomplishing something. A motorboat came a little too close, the waves in its wake bouncing us about. I screeched with delight.

"You should rest," he said. "You'll get blisters on those dainty palms of yours."

I paused and looked at my hands. They were red.

"Let's just drift for a while," he suggested.

He came forward and lifted the oars out of the water, resting them on the sides of the boat. Then he lowered himself to the floor of the boat and urged me to do the same, with my upper body against him. It was peaceful and warm, mesmerizing. The sounds of other people laughing and shouting floated gently over the lake, and the engines of motorboats droned softly around us. A very pretty little sailboat passed by, the man and the woman waving. I closed my eyes again. Aaron moved his fingers over my face to my lips. Then he slipped down beside me, and we embraced and kissed.

"Feeling better?" he asked. I was, but I didn't want to say it. He could tell. "Don't feel guilty for feeling better, Clara Sue. Surely no one wants that."

I nodded. He was right. It just wasn't easy.

"I know what could really make you feel better," he said. He was moving his hands under my skirt.

"People can see us," I protested.

"Not really. Besides, making love on the water adds something. You know, the bobbing and all."

Casanova raises his head again, I thought, and squirmed away. "Let's get back to what we came here for," I said.

"I was." He smiled. "All right, all right."

He rowed again. We talked about other lakes he had been to and then about some other things we might do when our Christmas holiday began. His family wasn't going to travel this year, because his sister was coming home again, although there was a chance they would go to New York City to see a show. I told him about my uncle Bobby's show, and he said he would go to New York to see it with me. It seemed like we could make an endless list of promises and plans. He was even thinking ahead to when he went to college. William & Mary wasn't far away. He would come home on weekends to see me so we'd never break up.

Is any of this real? I wondered.

Our rowing and the clear, crisp air made us hungry. We gobbled up everything he had bought. Nearly three hours later, we turned the boat around and began to return to the dock. I told him it was the best day I'd had since Willie's death.

"We'll just have to pile on some more," he said. "What say we go for pizza and a movie? We'll be home by six. I'll drop you off to change and go home to change and come back. Think you can?"

"Yes," I said.

But that was before I entered the house nine hours

after I had left without telling anyone about anything I was doing.

Grandpa must have been watching the front gate. When we drove up, he stepped out of the house onto the portico and stood there with his steely arms folded, his hands tucked in under his arms, which was his usual posture when he was very, very annoyed. Except for his hoisted shoulders, his body was so straight and tense that he looked like a statue someone had just left there with the words "Angry Grandpa" carved into the base. As we drew closer, I could see how deep the lines in his face were. They seemed to be drawn on with a black crayon.

"Uh-oh," Aaron said. "He doesn't look happy."

I wanted to be as defiant as ever, but there was something so new and fierce about Grandpa's look of anger that I could feel my spine twinge and my confidence wither. In seconds, I was a little girl again, the very thought of challenging one of the adults in my life terrifying. My mind began to weave and spin excuses.

When Aaron didn't get out of the car to open my door, I felt his fear, which only put the icing on mine. I got out slowly.

"Should I say hello?" Aaron asked.

"Not right now. Just drive extra slowly out of here and call me later tonight," I told him, and closed the door. He looked relieved.

I turned to face Grandpa Arnold, taking a few steps toward him. When he spoke, I stopped.

"You don't even call to let anyone know where you are for more than nine hours," he began.

"We went for a picnic on Three Wrens Lake."

"Telling me a little late, aren't you? I've already spoken with Aaron's father. For your information, he was just as upset about it."

It was unrealistic to expect that was it. I walked forward and stopped just in front of him.

"I've put up with a lot because you're hurting, but that doesn't mean you can be irresponsible and disrespectful, Clara Sue. I'm your guardian. I love you, but I won't put up with this sort of behavior. You go to your room, and you think about it. For now, you're to go to and from school with Bill. Don't make any plans for any weekend activities until I say so. You can invite your girlfriend or girlfriends over, but that's it until you demonstrate you're responsible enough for anything more." He opened the front door and stood back.

"That's not fair," I said.

"That's what it is," he replied. He didn't even sound like my grandfather. The sternness in his voice and the firm way he held his posture quickly subdued any other comment I could think to make.

I walked in quickly and paused when I saw Myra standing there beside My Faith.

"You had us very worried," Myra said.

"Oh, child," My Faith said, shaking her head.

"I'm not a child!" I cried, and ran up the stairs.

I paused at Willie's doorway. Mrs. Camden was pushing the boy out in his wheelchair. The sight of him sitting up, his golden hair brushed neatly, startled me. I quickly recognized Willie's shirt and pants. I glanced down at his shoes and socks and then looked up at her.

"He's the same shoe size?" I asked. To me, it was the most astounding thing.

"Yes," she said.

I looked at the boy. His face seemed fuller, his cheeks rosier than ever. The blue in his eyes was the most exquisite blue I had ever seen. It was as if his body was emerging from the depth of his great pain and sorrow stronger than it had been. He started to smile at me. Nothing I had done or said apparently frightened or discouraged him. He smiled like a little brother might at the appearance of his sister, waiting for some kind or friendly remark.

"No!" I cried, and ran to my room.

When I shut the door behind me, it felt as if I had lowered the lid on my own coffin. I flopped onto my bed, the tears rushing out of my eyes as if they'd been shut up for weeks and weeks and could finally break free.

"Willie," I whispered. "Willie."

I rose and went to my desk, quickly pulling out my stationery and peeling a sheet off the top. It was going to be a short letter.

Dear Willie,

I hate Grandpa. I want to run away, only I have no place to go, and I hate the idea of never going to your grave.

*I won't talk to anyone in this house. No one
is on my side.*

Clara Sue

I folded it and put it in the envelope and in the drawer.
Then I took a deep breath and went into my bathroom
to take a shower and disguise my tears with the water
that ran down my face.

No one would see me cry.

Especially my grandfather.

13

When I didn't go down to dinner, Myra came up to see me. I was lying on my bed, staring furiously at the ceiling.

"Everyone's at the table," she said. "We're waiting for you, Clara Sue."

"I'm not hungry," I replied without looking at her.

"Now, you know this is not the way to behave, love."

I didn't answer or move.

"Jesus, Mary, and Joseph. You and your granddad are two peas in a pod. I don't know who can be more stubborn. You know he's not happy punishing you."

I turned to her. I could feel the heat in my eyes spreading through my face. "I don't know what makes my grandfather happy or unhappy anymore. And I don't care." Before she could reply, I turned over on my bed and looked at the wall.

"No one is terribly happy in this house right now, Clara Sue."

"He is," I muttered, loudly enough for her to hear.

"Who?"

"That boy my grandfather wants us all to call William."

"I don't know how happy he is. For him, a smile is like a drop of rain in a drought right now," she said. "I think he has some time to go before we can say he's happy. He's at the table tonight," she added.

I spun around again. "In whose seat?"

"Well, he's in the wheelchair, Clara Sue."

"At whose place, then?"

"He's beside Mrs. Camden," she said.

"That's where Willie would sit."

"She needs to be beside him for now. Did you want him beside you?"

I turned around again, giving her my back instead of a reply. I knew she was standing there, staring at me and trying to come up with something that would please me, but I was even angrier now.

"I'll send something up if you don't come down," she said, and left.

When the phone rang, I debated answering it, but then I thought it was probably Aaron. Unfortunately for me, it was Lila. I was definitely not in the mood for what she wanted to talk about.

"I've been calling you all day. I kept getting your answering machine, so I didn't leave any more messages. Didn't you see I called? Where were you all day?"

"I was with Aaron," I said. "I haven't bothered looking at my answering machine."

"All day?"

"Most of my waking hours, yes."

"What did you do?"

"I went to the cemetery in the morning, and then we drove up to Three Wrens Lake to row and have a picnic. Now you know it all."

"Not all, I'm sure." She giggled. "You had lots of fun last night."

"When I left, you looked like you had too much," I said.

"I had a headache until an hour ago, but I didn't throw up," she added quickly, "and my mother didn't realize a thing. She waited up for me. My father never does."

"Good for you."

"But anyway, there's a reason I've been trying to call you all day."

"What?"

"Audrey and Sandra Roth inspected her bed right after you two left. Then Sandra spread the story around the party that you were definitely not a virgin before you went up to her room with Aaron last night."

"Maybe we didn't go all the way."

"Really? Everyone says Aaron Podwell wouldn't give a girl ten minutes of his time if she didn't go all the way. Some people at the party have been telling everyone what Sandra said today. Sara Combes was the first to call and tell me that she had heard about it, and you know what a big mouth she has. I thought you should know what they're saying to everyone."

"Sick if that's the way they get their jollies. Both of them but especially Sandra," I said.

"They all keep asking me as if I know all your secrets, like who was the first time, where did it happen, stuff like that. I'm getting calls all day, but they don't believe me when I tell them I don't know." She sounded like she was really fishing for information. Did she think I was lying about Aaron and me, or did she wish it was true so she could enjoy the details?

"It's a terrible responsibility to put on your shoulders. I'm sorry for you," I said.

"No, I didn't mean . . ."

"Look, I have to go, Lila. I'll see you Monday."

"Monday? What are you doing tonight? Going out again with Aaron?"

"No. I have to do some ironing," I said. I wasn't interested in telling her all about my grandfather and how angry he was. She would find out soon enough.

"What? Ironing?"

"I'll see you Monday," I repeated.

"I could come by tomorrow."

"I have too much to do. 'Bye," I said, before she could ask another thing, and practically slammed the receiver onto the cradle.

Her phone call only heightened the flame of rage burning inside me. I was being accused and tried in gossip court, and I hadn't even enjoyed the fruits of my supposed fall from innocence. The things that were being said about Aaron didn't surprise me. I had heard them, but I was hoping that they were embellishments of fantasies other girls had about him, especially Sandra Roth. But I couldn't deny that I liked the fact that besides being handsome, charming, and bright, he was also considered dangerous to girls. Going on a date with him had the added excitement that came from going too fast or drinking too much alcohol. How quickly my reputation had been challenged. I should have been angrier.

I was tired of pouting about what was happening to me at home, but I wasn't in the mood to do homework or read and especially not to go downstairs to watch television. Besides, I couldn't get the things Lila had said out of my mind. As if he could hear my thoughts, Aaron finally called.

"How bad was it for you?" he asked as soon as I said hello.

"I'm grounded until further notice, so doing anything tonight is out. You can't pick me up for school and take me home, either. I have to go with the limousine driver."

"My father won't let me use the car for a week, anyway. I have to hitch a ride with Paulie Richards. He lives just down the street from me. My father and his father play bridge together. He's always trying to get me to be friends with him. He still plays with an Erector Set. That's the only erection he's ever known."

I smiled and fell back onto the bed with the phone pressed to my ear. It felt like a lifeline. In this house, I was drowning in wave after wave of pity, sorrow, and anger. I wanted Aaron to do something magical and pull me right out of it.

"Why was your father so mad at you?" I asked.

"Were you supposed to tell him where you were going, too?"

"A little of that, but I think it was more your grandfather raking him over the coals for permitting his son to go off with a girl only sixteen without permission. Can you grow older faster?"

"How I wish."

"Grounded. How hard is it to sneak into your house?"

I laughed. "It's easier for me to sneak out."

"Would you?"

"We'll see," I said. "I was thinking of going on a hunger strike."

"Somehow I don't think that would impress your grandfather. He's a tough cookie. He'd have you force-fed or something."

"I know. I guess if I have to, I'll trade."

"Trade? Trade what?"

"Being friendly."

"Friendly?" I could practically hear him thinking. "To the poisoned boy?"

"If there's no other way."

He was quiet a moment. "You'd do that for me?"

"For us," I said. "I'm involved in this, too."

"I'm sorry I got you in trouble," he said. "My father and your grandfather are right, you know. I should have made sure you checked in and got permission first. In two weeks, I could go to prison if I took you over the state line or somewhere else we almost went last night, since you're officially a minor."

"Your eighteenth birthday is in two weeks?"

"Yes. So maybe my father will ease up in less than a week. I'll play on my mother's sympathy. Have to get you out from house arrest before then so you can help me celebrate. I've been planning it since I was five."

"I will, no matter what," I vowed.

"No matter what?"

"Yes."

"Hmm. Can I count on an extra-special birthday present?"

"We'll see."

He laughed.

Actually, I thought, in the back of my mind, I was always planning that I wouldn't lose my virginity until I was eighteen. Somehow, no matter how immature we were, we would be considered adults at eighteen.

"Sorry I got you in trouble. I mean, you have enough going on."

"You didn't kidnap me. It was just as much my fault. Stop thinking that way." I thought for a moment and then asked, "What are you going to do tomorrow?"

"Dream of you all day, what else?"

"You know that children's playground not too far from my grandfather's estate?"

"Yes. So?"

"I'll ride my bike there at two. Can you get there?"

"Swings or seesaw?"

"Sliding pond," I said, smiling, "and then merry-go-round."

He laughed. "I'll be there even if I have to walk. You've given me reason to undo the hangman's knot."

"Don't even joke about it." There was a big story about a teenage boy who had hung himself in his room after his girlfriend of three years broke up with him.

"Okay. Till then."

"Till then," I said.

I did feel a little better after I hung up. I looked at the plate of food again and began to nibble on it. After I finished what I wanted, I picked it up and started to bring it down to the kitchen. I looked into Willie's room on the way and saw that no one was in there. As I passed Grandpa's office, I heard voices and paused to look in. He was showing some of his plaques and pictures to the boy and Mrs. Camden. The boy was in his wheelchair. The boy was sitting up in his chair and listening attentively, but he didn't say anything. Grandpa's voice was colored with the pride he had from knowing and meeting the powerful politicians who had posed for pictures with him. I wondered what he would say when he reached the picture of Willie and me, but when he noticed me standing there watching, I quickly walked away.

As if I had caught them doing something wrong, Mrs. Camden followed me into the kitchen to explain. Myra and My Faith were sitting at the kitchen table, enjoying some of Myra's imported British tea. Myra smiled when she saw that I had eaten most of the food. We all turned when Mrs. Camden stepped in, too.

She looked at everyone when she spoke, but I knew it was mostly for my benefit. "Dr. Patrick thinks it will be very helpful for William to get a sense of the

Arnold family, the warmth in this home. It will help build his confidence."

"William," I said disdainfully, and looked at Myra especially. "Are you calling him William, too?"

"We're all just trying to do what we can to help him recuperate, love." She smiled. "My granddad used to say, 'Call me what you want, but don't call me late for dinner.'"

My Faith laughed, and Mrs. Camden smiled and said, "Wise advice."

"Did you ever ask him if his real name was Mickey?" I demanded.

"Mickey?" My Faith said.

"She never told you two? I heard him say it when he was having a dream."

"I discussed it with Dr. Patrick," Mrs. Camden said. "He doesn't react well to the name. Whoever it is revives very bad memories for him. It's definitely not his name, Clara Sue."

"William's definitely not his name, either," I said, and put the dish on the counter so hard that I almost broke it.

"Well, please don't refer to him as the poisoned boy, Clara Sue. If and when he hears that, it'll just reinforce the terrible things done to him."

"We never called Willie William very much," Myra said. "It's almost like a different name."

"Not to me," I said. "His teachers called him William, and I heard Grandpa call him that many times."

They were all quiet.

I stood there for a moment, thinking, and then

turned to Mrs. Camden and asked, "What did he do when my grandfather showed him pictures of Willie and me?"

"He became very sad. We could see it, so your grandfather quickly moved on to other pictures and his trophies."

"Didn't he say anything?"

"No."

"Don't you think it's weird that he still won't talk much after all this time, even when you're being so nice to him?"

"There have been cases of prisoners of war who didn't speak for months and months after they were freed. It takes a lot of tender loving care."

"Yes, I know. Like easing him into a warm bath," I said disdainfully.

Both Myra and My Faith scowled. I didn't care. Maybe they would stop talking about him in front of me.

"We're thinking of taking him for a ride tomorrow," Mrs. Camden said. "Dr. Patrick thinks it would be a very good thing. New scenery might revive his memory. Would you be interested in going?"

"Didn't you hear? I'm under house arrest," I said, and walked out past her. When I reached Grandpa Arnold's office this time and looked in, I saw that he was taking some of the models of his trucks off the shelves and showing them to the boy. He never let Willie play with those. He bought him different ones. I saw him put one into the boy's lap. The boy looked up at him with admiration, and my grandfather smiled. When he looked toward me this time, he kept his smile.

It won't be long, I thought, *before he loves him more than he loved Willie and especially more than he loves me.* Forget about trading even false acceptance for Grandpa rescinding his punishment, I thought. I wasn't that good a liar.

The boy saw where Grandpa was looking and turned to me. Suddenly, he smiled, too. I believed it was a smile of self-satisfaction. He was showing me that he was winning his place in my grandfather's heart despite me. But I was sure that Mrs. Camden, Dr. Patrick, and everyone else in this house would tell me that he was just reaching out to me, hoping that I would like him, maybe even love him like a brother.

Never, I thought. Someone had poisoned him, and now he was poisoning almost everyone in this house. But he wasn't poisoning me. *You're all too stupid to see it*, I wanted to shout, but I swallowed back the words and returned to my room.

I tried doing some of my reading for English class, but I was having too much trouble concentrating and found myself rereading the same pages. I hadn't closed my door completely, so I heard Mrs. Camden and my grandfather bringing the boy up to Willie's room. The two of them were laughing. I listened for the boy's laughter, too, but I didn't hear it. They took him into his room, and Mrs. Camden started to prepare him for sleep. While she did that, my grandfather came to my room.

"Dorian said she told you we're taking William for a ride tomorrow. It looks like it's going to be a very nice day. We thought after lunch, we'd go toward Richmond. Dr. Patrick thinks it would be beneficial to get him out for a while. She suspects he wasn't permitted to go anywhere or do much before. So if you would like to come along . . ."

"I have too much to do for school," I said. "I might just take a bike ride."

"A bike ride?"

"Yes. I would like to get some air and exercise, or do you want me to end up like him in a wheelchair? If that happened, you'd get me a private nurse, too, wouldn't you?"

He jerked his head back as if I had spit at him. "Don't make it too difficult for me to be your guardian, Clara Sue," he said, his voice full of warning.

"I don't think of you as my guardian, Grandpa. I think of you as my grandfather. At least, I used to," I added, turning away.

He didn't respond.

When I looked back, he was gone. I lay there for a while, wondering how all this had happened. There was so much darkness now between today and all the wonderful yesterdays that Willie, my parents, and I had once enjoyed, wonderful memories like the sound of laughter or my parents singing some favorite children's song they shared from their own youth while we drove somewhere. Willie would fall asleep against me back then. He was so little. I would put my arm around him like Mommy did, and when she looked back and saw us, she would smile brightly enough to light up a room.

All those memories were so distant. They were slipping away like smoke caught in the cold wind that had rushed in under the bruised and angry clouds of my great sadness. Reaching out for them was like reaching into wisps of haze, grasping nothing. I fell asleep like someone falling down a tunnel whose walls were lined with tears.

The following morning, I deliberately went to breakfast later than usual. By then, my grandfather had finished eating and was outside doing things with Jimmy on the property. Mrs. Camden was busy with the boy and his physical therapist. My Faith had left for her church work in Charlottesville, and Myra was in her room. They had left out the orange juice and my favorite cereal with a banana. I ate alone and then returned to complete my homework and pick out something to wear for my bike ride and my rendezvous with Aaron.

No one came looking for me at lunchtime. I was sure they were all preoccupied with the big adventure with the boy, but when I went down, Myra was there to make me a toasted cheese sandwich. She tried to talk about my behavior and my attitude, but I wouldn't say anything, so she gave up. At one thirty, I left the house, got on my bike, and headed for the playground. I didn't even tell her where I was going. I was angry at everyone. It felt good to get away from the house. I paused only when I was near the place where the truck had hit Willie and Myra. Then I rode faster.

Aaron had gotten Paulie to drive him there and pick him up in two hours. The park was busy with families, dozens of young children on the rides. Two teenagers drew some passing attention. Some of the parents knew who we were, but most weren't interested.

"Now I know what Romeo and Juliet felt like," Aaron said when we met. We started walking away, me walking alongside my bike.

"That didn't end well," I said. We had just read it in my English class.

He laughed. "You know the creek down here?" he asked when we made the turn south of the park.

"No."

He led the way through an empty lot. When we reached a patch of woods, he told me to leave my bike, and then we followed a path for about half a mile to a hill that looked down on the creek. We sat at the top and watched the water flowing over the rocks and dead tree stumps.

Aaron played with a blade of yellowed grass and then took a tiny branch and held it with both hands. "See this?" he said.

"So?"

"My father's got this expression. 'A branch that doesn't bend breaks.'" He demonstrated by bending it but not breaking it.

"What are you saying?"

"You have a little war going on at your house now."

"No kidding, Dick Tracy."

He smiled and shook his head. "I've been thinking about it all morning. My guess is that if you won and your grandfather shipped the kid out, you wouldn't be all that happy, because you wouldn't like how everyone at the house thought of you, including your grandfather. I'm not saying he's done the right thing by giving him your brother's stuff and putting him in your brother's room so soon," he quickly added.

I was quiet. He wasn't saying anything I hadn't thought. I just didn't want to think about it now or ever.

"I have a selfish motive for bringing this up," he added when I didn't speak.

"And what's that?"

"If you were a happy camper at home and your grandfather wasn't on your case, I wouldn't have to be dreaming about you so much. I could see you more. Get it?"

I nodded. I liked what he was saying. Right now, I didn't think anyone was as happy being around me as he was. I hoped it was for the right reasons. Was I an easy target, or did he mean it? Lila and the gossips had stirred up my natural paranoia. He saw how deeply I was thinking.

"I mean, you were suggesting it, too, when you said you might do a trade to get the chains off, right?"

"I thought I could do that, but I got angry again right afterward. Today they wanted me to go for a ride with them. They were taking him out for the first time, at the doctor's suggestion."

"Oh. Might have helped."

"I wouldn't have been able to see you right now."

"But for sure next weekend, I bet."

"You're not going to tell me not to cut off my nose

to spite my face or anything, are you? Everyone is running about spewing proverbs in my house. I feel like it's feeding time at the chicken coop, and I'm the only chicken there."

He laughed and fell backward to look up at the sky. I gazed down at him. *What are you so worried about, Clara Sue?* I asked myself. *You're going to lose your virginity someday, aren't you? Isn't Aaron the boy you'd really like to lose it to? You don't have to have a ring on your finger first, do you? Boys don't think like that. Why should girls?*

It was like I was in the girls' locker room listening to the great debate, only this one was happening in my head. Aaron must have been listening in, I thought.

"What would you have done if we weren't in Audrey's bedroom?"

"Done?"

"You know, if we were almost where we were when we were in Audrey's bedroom."

"I don't know. You're just going to have to wait to find out."

He braced himself on his elbow. "What about now?"

"Now?" I looked around. We were far from any road, far from any house, and there was no one walking below beside the creek.

"What's better than here? It's like the Garden of Eden or something," he said. "We're like the only people on earth."

"Like Romeo and Juliet? I told you, that didn't end well, either," I said, and he laughed.

He took off his jacket and laid it behind me, bunching it up into something of a pillow. I looked back at it and then at him. His eyes were electric with excitement. Was it too late to slow him down? Or myself, for that matter?

"Lila called me last night and told me that Audrey and Sandra actually inspected her bed after we left. Now they're spreading stories about me not having been a virgin."

"So let's prove them right," he said, and leaned in to kiss me. I didn't kiss him back. "What's wrong?"

"It feels funny out here like this. I feel like I did on the boat."

"Taking a chance of being seen makes it even more exciting, don't you think? A rabbit might see us and get ideas," he said.

My mind reeled with words of refusal, of caution and reluctance, words I thought every girl my age certainly should have not only memorized but embedded in their brains. *I'm too young. We haven't been going together long enough. What if he breaks up with me a week later? How would I feel then? What if he tells his friends, and I end up with a reputation as bad as someone like Sandra Roth? What if my grandfather and Myra somehow find out?*

Why hadn't I thought of all these things when we were in Audrey's bedroom? Was the embarrassment of losing my virginity the only reason I escaped from his advances and my own driving passion? Was that just a handy excuse helping me to avoid all these questions, an excuse I couldn't use now?

He leaned in to kiss me again. "I've never felt about any girl like I feel about you, Clara Sue," he said. Wasn't that something he was supposed to say?

Once, when Lila and I were talking about such things, she told me she had heard that there was actually an instruction book boys could get, and it had a list of things they should say to get a girl to stop resisting.

But I didn't want to believe that. I wanted to believe Aaron. I wanted to be closer to him than I had been with any other boy. For that matter, closer to him than with any other person since I had lost my parents and now Willie. He would be my lover and my family all at once, I thought. He wanted me even with all my baggage. I might never meet another boy like him. The other girls couldn't be right about him.

Just knowing that my grandfather, Myra, and especially My Faith would be upset over my promiscuity also encouraged me. *I'm on my own now,* I told myself. *I have no one but myself. I have to be in charge of myself. I have to be my own person.*

I kissed him before he could try to kiss me again. It seemed to open the gate for both of us.

But then I heard laughter, and I sat up quickly. It was the laughter of young girls. It was coming from off to our left, and then they suddenly appeared, a group of about ten Brownies and their guide. They paused when they saw us.

Aaron groaned. "Great. That's Mrs. Elliot. She was my third-grade teacher," he said. "She once put me in the cloakroom for an hour because I threw a spit ball."

Mrs. Elliot saw us, too, and quickly herded the

troop in another direction. I recognized Mindy Cooper's little sister when she turned back to flash a smile at us before they disappeared over the hill.

A few minutes later would have been quite a little disaster for us, I thought. I stood.

"Hey."

"This isn't the place or the time, Aaron."

"You wanted to see me. I thought . . ."

"I want to be with you, but look how close that was. For both of us," I added. "Your father would probably take your new car away permanently."

He nodded and stood. "You're right. I knew there was a reason I didn't join the Cub Scouts."

He took my hand, and we walked back slowly.

"Think about what I said," he told me when we reached my bike. "Work yourself back into your grandfather's favor. You don't want to become the Lady of Shalott or something."

"Who's that?" I asked.

"A poem you'll learn when you're a senior, probably," he said as we walked back to the playground. "It's about this lady who was cursed and lives in a castle, where she weaves images of what she sees in a mirror. She never looks directly out the window at the world. Until she sees Lancelot, that is. Then she leaves her tower, puts her name on a boat, and floats down to Camelot. She dies before arriving."

"How sad."

"Right. So don't miss out on reality," he said.

"Or when you do after waiting so long, you'll die?"

"Something like that."

"Are you my Lancelot?"

"I'll be anyone you want." He smiled and kissed me.

Would he be?

And did I live under a mysterious curse, too?

14

We sat on one of the pinewood benches at the playground and talked until Paulie returned for him. Aaron revealed more about his family and his relationships with his father, his mother, and his older sister. I had the feeling he was telling me things he had never told anyone else—especially any other girl—about his sister. Stories illustrating how his feelings for her grew stronger as he grew older and he began to appreciate her feelings for him.

In my heart of hearts, I felt something special was happening between us. Gradually, the image of him that other girls were trying to impose on me was crumbling. I thought he was very sensitive and caring, and in some ways, he was as vulnerable emotionally as I was. Was I being too naive, gullible? Or was I simply desperate to be close to someone at any cost?

Now some of the adults who knew Aaron and his family and a few who knew my grandfather and me came by to say hello to us. Two mentioned Willie and how sad they were for me and my grandfather. Others avoided the topic, and I was grateful. One mother, Mrs. Willow, who had twin girls, talked to us the longest. I could see from the way she was looking at us, catching that we were still holding hands, that she was probably thinking about her own youthful romances or maybe just one, maybe the most serious one that had gone in the direction we were heading. Maybe she thought we were already there. She had that know-it-all expression that made me blush when she talked about how cute we looked together. I even thought she was flirting with Aaron. I was happy when her children grew bored and she walked off.

Paulie barely looked at me when he arrived. He glanced at me, smiled when I said hello, and then looked away quickly, as if I was already someone forbidden and he didn't want to be caught smiling at me. *Maybe he's just terribly shy*, I thought. Aaron's kissing me good-bye definitely embarrassed him.

"Think about what we discussed," Aaron said before he got into Paulie's car. To be sure that I knew what he meant, he added, "The Lady of Shalott."

I watched them drive off and then got on my bike and started for home. When I reached the place where the truck had plowed into Willie and Myra, I stopped and stared at it for a while. A few rows of the hedges were still looking damaged. This area had become special now, almost a holy place. On this section of sidewalk, I had seen my brother alive for the last time. At that moment, he had been barely clinging to life, if I understood what had happened correctly. I couldn't be sure if he had heard my voice when I called out to our grandfather. I hoped he had.

Suddenly, I wondered. What if he had lived but had been in a wheelchair like the poisoned boy? What if something had happened to his brain and he couldn't remember us, just the way the poisoned boy couldn't remember his family? Grandpa would have done all the same things for him as he had done for the poisoned boy, for sure. I would have been there for him every day, of course. And I would have cried for him every night. I wouldn't be happy as long as he was ill, and maybe I wouldn't have even gone on a date with Aaron or gone to a party or had any social life at all, for that matter. Maybe I would have been Mrs. Camden's real assistant. I'd like to think that if that had been the case, I would have helped bring him back. The first time he would have said my name would have been like my birthday, Thanksgiving, and Christmas all rolled into one.

Would it be like that for someone who loved the poisoned boy when he finally opened his eyes and said his or her name, clearing the way for his return to them? I had to admit to myself, however, how odd it was that no one was advertising that he was gone and pleading for information that would lead to his return. As Myra would say sometimes, it's a "riddle wrapped in a mystery inside an enigma."

I walked my bike the remainder of the way to the gate and then up the driveway, thinking about all of it. I had to admit that by this time, Willie would have been very interested in the poisoned boy. He was always curious about other boys his age and eager to make friends with them. On his own, he would have shared all that he had with him. He would have wanted me to help. He would have expected it and even believed that I would have made a difference. I could almost hear him say it as I approached the house. *You could help him, Clara Sue. You could make him well again. Don't let him be sick.*

Doctors and psychiatrists, nurses and nannies, all were adults. No matter what my grandfather gave him and no matter how much tender loving care he received from Myra and My Faith, the boy would always be distrusting. I was sure of that even though I had no proof of why. I probably really could make a difference. I was just being a selfish, stubborn little fool because I wasn't helping. No one could help him get back to his family faster than I could if I put my mind to it. Deep down, that had to be something he wanted, didn't it? *Should I really help, I mean, for good reasons?* I wondered. Aaron was probably right. Grandpa would be nicer to me. If I thought this way about my reason for cooperating, I might not hate myself for being such a conniver trying to get what I wanted. That would just be a bonus.

But could I be sincere about it? Could I really care?

No matter what I end up doing, I won't call him William, I vowed. *From the start, I'll let him know that for sure.*

I put my bike away and entered the house. As soon as I did, I knew something was up. I could feel the excitement in the air and saw the way the maids were scurrying along. Myra was cranking out orders and criticism. She was standing in the hallway with her back to me, whipping out commands like a lion tamer. When she turned and saw me, she came hurrying my way.

"What's going on?" I asked.

"Oh, those maids we hired recently get my goat. They dillydally like we're paying them hourly. They're way behind on the upstairs, but we had to move them down here."

"Why?"

"Your granddad didn't get too far with their ride," she continued, obviously excited. "You know the old Farmingham estate on the way to Richmond?"

"Yes. That's the famous haunted house, where Clarence Farmingham supposedly killed his own parents when he was fourteen nearly eighty years ago." My eyes widened as I remembered. "He poisoned them, didn't he?"

"Yes, yes, that's the story, love. No one wanted to live in it afterward, none of the relatives who inherited, and no one wanted to buy it, either. It's lain fallow for years and years, but the Farmingham family has kept it and the grounds around it in fairly good condition. Your grandfather said there was talk once of turning it into some sort of museum, a house of horror where they'd run tours, but the chamber of commerce shot that idea down quickly. It's quite a Gothic mansion with its arches and chimneys. All it needs is a moat. Reminds me of a house near where

I grew up in Surrey. It was quite a popular place the night before All Hallows."

"Yes, yes, Halloween. So what's this have to do with the ride Grandpa and Mrs. Camden took the boy on?"

"Oh, everything was going well, Mrs. Camden says. Until your granddad made the turn in the road where the Farmingham house looms almost directly in front of you, looks like you're going straight at it. It has such a way of suddenly appearing. I remember the first time I saw it . . ."

"I know. So?" I asked, now very impatient with Myra's slow explanation.

"I'm getting to it, dear. As soon as that happened and William saw the house, he began to scream. He became quite hysterical."

"Why?"

"They don't know, dear, but Mrs. Camden thinks he thought they were taking him to the house."

"The Farmingham house? He might be from the Farmingham house? Is that it?" I asked, now really excited, too.

"I don't know. As I said, supposedly no one lives there, but I can imagine squatters finding out about it and maybe camping out there."

"What did Mrs. Camden and my grandfather do?"

"Your granddad turned the car around quickly, and Mrs. Camden held the boy and comforted him best she could. She said he felt like he had turned into ice, and his eyes were going back in his head. It sounded just horrible. They hurried back and called

Dr. Patrick. She's upstairs with him and Mrs. Camden now. As I said, we hadn't really gotten the upstairs done and—"

"Where's my grandfather?"

"He went to see about the Farmingham house, to be sure no one's been camping out in it. The police are with him."

I shook my head, astonished, and looked up the stairway. This could be over in hours if the boy's family was in that house. It made sense to me. Maybe the Farmingham family had put rat poison everywhere. Maybe the boy had been kidnapped and kept in that house. When it looked like he would die, they dropped him at the hospital and fled. Maybe they had brought him in from another state, somewhere far enough away that it wouldn't make local news. It all made sense to me.

"Your granddad carried him up the stairs. He looked like he was unconscious, his arms dangling like a puppet off its strings," Myra said, shaking her head and biting down on her lower lip.

"Did he say anything important when he was screaming?"

"Mrs. Camden said he was incoherent, babbling gibberish. Nothing made any sense. And then he went into a deep sleep. Poor thing."

I nodded. She began barking at one of the maids, so I started up the stairs. The door to Willie's room was closed. I stood a moment listening, but I didn't hear anything, so I went to my room. I wasn't sure why, but Myra's relating of the events made me tremble, especially the description of Grandpa Arnold carrying the boy's limp body up the stairs. It had never occurred to me until just this moment that the boy could actually die here. Little kids could have heart attacks, couldn't they? How terrible would that be? What if he died and we still didn't know who his family was? Or his real name?

Would Grandpa have him buried in the Prescott cemetery with a tombstone that said "William Arnold," too? Would he bury him close to Willie? Would everyone hate me for having been so mean to him? Even if he didn't die, maybe Grandpa finally would realize that he was too fragile to be in this house. Maybe Dr. Patrick would order him back to the hospital or a clinic or something. Should I be happy that all this had happened? Why couldn't I stop shaking?

I heard conversation and rose quickly to look out in the hallway. Mrs. Camden was talking to Dr. Patrick as they walked toward the stairway. I started after them and paused just before Willie's room. When they had both descended, I stepped up to the doorway and looked in. The boy was asleep in Willie's bed. I watched him for a while. He looked dead already. He was so still, and in the subdued light, his face was ashen. How serious was this? Why wasn't he in the hospital now?

After a moment, I walked down the stairs. Mrs. Camden and Dr. Patrick were at the front door. They paused and looked toward me.

"Are you sending him back to the hospital?" I demanded as I hurried toward them. "He can't stay here if he's dying."

"No. He's not dying, Clara Sue. All his vitals are good," Dr. Patrick replied. "He's resting comfortably now. I've given him something that will help him sleep for a while. I'm sure he'll be fine when he awakes."

"But he went kind of nuts, didn't he? He should be in a psycho ward or something, right?"

Neither of them smiled.

"No," Dr. Patrick said softly, "he didn't go *kind of nuts*. That's not the way to put it at all. He had what we call a traumatic flashback, a memory of a traumatic event, experienced as if the event were being relived with all the same intense feeling he had the first time it happened. The patient is forced to process the memory."

"Well, what was the memory? What did it have to do with the Farmingham mansion?"

"We don't know yet," Mrs. Camden said.

"Won't it happen again?" I asked.

"Maybe not this exact one, but yes, it's very possible that some other event, some other memory, might trigger a similar emotional response," Dr. Patrick replied, as if it wasn't really a big deal.

"Isn't that terrible?" I asked, looking from Mrs. Camden to her.

"No. Actually, this is something of a breakthrough," Dr. Patrick said, again in that very controlled, quiet way that made me want to reach out and slap her. She was making me feel foolish for asking anything. "I'll explore this with him as time goes by and make sure that he understands that whatever it is, it's not his fault. Often, that's why the patient sees it as so traumatic."

"What if it *is* his fault?"

"We'll find that out and deal with it." She paused, a tiny smile at the corners of her lips. "Are you interested in all this now?"

I stepped back. I was, but I wasn't eager to say so. I think she saw it in my face.

She widened her smile. "You could be of great help, and you'll learn a lot, too." When I didn't respond, she turned to Mrs. Camden. "I'll stop by late tomorrow morning. Get him up and about as soon as you can. The most important thing," she added, now turning back to me, "is that we don't make him feel bad about his behavior."

Mrs. Camden opened the door for her. Dr. Patrick smiled again at me and walked out. I turned away quickly, my arms folded, my head down, as if my thoughts were too heavy now.

"I don't think your coming along with us would have changed anything," Mrs. Camden said. "You shouldn't feel bad about it."

"I wasn't blaming myself, Mrs. Camden," I snapped back at her.

"Call me Dorian," she said. She walked past me and up the stairs. I watched her until she disappeared, and then I went into the living room and flopped onto the large settee. I was fuming, but mostly at myself. I wanted so to dislike her. I wanted to despise Dr. Patrick. I even wanted to dislike Myra and My Faith. Most of all, I wanted to hate my grandfather now, but suddenly, none of that was really happening, and I was blaming myself for having wanted to dislike everyone in the first place.

Who was more alone in this house at the moment, the poisoned boy or me?

Minutes later, I heard the front door open and close and looked up as my grandfather appeared. He looked upset, flustered. I had the feeling that he was blaming himself for what had happened. He stood in the hallway, pulling off his leather driving gloves and mumbling. Then he saw me sitting in the living room. He walked in.

"What did you find out about the Farmingham house?" I quickly demanded, before he could utter a complaint about my behavior.

"You heard about it?"

"Yes. So? What did you find out? Did you find his real family, or was he kept there by kidnappers?"

He considered whether he should talk to me and then sat in his favorite chair and unbuttoned his black leather jacket. His hair was a little wild, looking like he had been running his fingers through it madly. He pushed some strands back.

"There was no sign of anyone squatting in the old place now or ever. In fact, it's in remarkably good shape. Someone's looking after it regularly. Prime property, actually."

"So he wasn't there? He didn't come from there?" I asked, disappointment practically dripping from my lips.

Grandpa shook his head. "No, but that house would probably frighten any child the first time he saw it. I remember it frightened you because we came upon it at twilight, and it looked like . . . you said a home for ghosts."

"Apparently, it didn't frighten me like it frightened him. I didn't start screaming. Dr. Patrick called it a traumatic flashback."

"Oh? Dr. Patrick is still here?"

"No, she left a little while ago."

"How is he doing now?"

"She gave him something for sleep."

"Good. I guess I'll go see Dorian and see what's what. It's terrible to see anyone that small that frightened." He started to rise.

"I'm sorry about him," I said quickly. "I don't want to see him suffer or anything."

He nodded and remained frozen in place, expecting me to say more, maybe apologize for my behavior, but I wasn't ready to do that and maybe never would be.

"I miss my brother," I said instead. "A lot. I'm sure he was very frightened after that truck ran into him and Myra."

His face softened. "I know, Clara Sue. Believe me, not a day passes when I don't think about him or what I could have done to prevent it."

I pressed my lips tightly together. I didn't try to swallow or breathe, and I didn't want to start crying again.

He sat back down. "I don't want to spend whatever I have left of my life in constant mourning, Clara Sue. I've had more than my fair share, but I'm not whining about myself. That gets you nowhere, and even friends, people who like you, get turned off by all the damn self-pity. It sounds cruel to think like that, but that's the way it is. I've got you, I've got your uncle Bobby, I've got my business, and now I've got that boy upstairs to look after. Whoever did this to him should be burned at the stake. I think about that, and it gets me angry, and I want to do something about it. I believe I was meant to."

He looked as enraged as ever. Then he paused and took a deep breath.

"You've heard me say some of this before. But that's all there is to it. I don't love you or Willie any less. I hope you can live with that," he said, and stood up.

I watched him leave, his shoulders a bit more slumped than usual. Then I took a deep breath, wiped some tears away before they could reach the middle of my cheeks, and got up and went to see what My Faith was making for dinner.

I could tell she was very nervous in my presence, probably because of all the nasty things I had said, especially now when everyone was on edge about the boy.

"I'm sorry if I said anything mean to you, My Faith."

She paused and looked at me. "You're not a mean and sassy girl, Clara Sue. I know that. Everyone has their times. And nothin' you could say or do would change my opinion of you, child. Don't you know that?"

I smiled and nodded at the stove. "That's your famous corn pone you're making, right?"

"It's not really anything special."

"Yes, it is. You have a secret ingredient. Grandma Lucy told me so."

She laughed. "Well, if it's a secret, I can't tell you, now, can I?"

I nodded. She held her arms out, and we hugged.

"I know you're hurting," she said. "And you know we are, too."

I nodded and looked at the stove again. I could smell what was being prepared for dinner. "Orange baked ham?"

"Your granddad asked for it yesterday," she said. "It's his favorite."

"Mine, too. I'll be hungry tonight," I told her, and I hurried back upstairs. I was eager to call Aaron and fill him in on all that had happened.

"The Farmingham mansion," he said as soon as I'd finished babbling at Superman speed. "That has to be a big clue."

"I know, but they didn't get anything sensible out of him. I guess it was really terrible. My grandfather looked like he did when Willie died. Everyone did."

"Except you. You're like the odd man out now."

"We'll see," I said. "Maybe I'll just bend that branch and not break it."

He laughed. "You know you're in trouble if you start taking my advice."

"I trust you," I said. How close to "I love you" was that? Wasn't it a better thing to tell someone you were very fond of, anyway? There couldn't be love without trust, could there? That would be just sexual attraction.

Myra talked about putting guineas of affection into a bank account with the name of someone you cared for on it. "Real friendships don't just happen, love," she told me once when I was complaining about some of the girls in my class being snobby and unfriendly. "You can invest in people like you invest in stocks and bonds."

"So you'll believe me when I tell you I'll respect you in the morning?" Aaron joked now. Or *was* he joking?

"Depends on how much you respect me at night," I countered.

He laughed and was silent a moment, so long a moment that I thought we had been disconnected.

"Hello?"

"You know, I started to watch you when you were in ninth grade. There was something I saw that told me you were going to be special, and then you just bloomed like a rose overnight."

"Are you reading from some book called *How to Win the Heart of a Girl*?"

"Honest. You can ask Skip or Brad or even Paulie."

"If you were caught robbing a bank, they would testify that you were in their houses at the time."

He laughed again. "Okay. I'll just have to find a way to prove it."

"Do that. I gotta go. I want to help set the table tonight. See you tomorrow."

"Ah, the coming out of the Lady of Shalott," he said. "I'd better get prepared."

I felt so excited and happy. It was like I was intoxicated on hope again. I practically bounced out of my room and then paused at Willie's door to look in. The boy was awake. He was sitting up and slowly turning the pages of one of Willie's picture books of fables. The one he was reading was "How the Beggar Boy Turned into Count Piro." I knew it well, having read it aloud to Willie from time to time. It was one of his favorites. It told the story of a clever fox that helped a poor boy marry a princess and become rich.

"Do you like that story?" I asked now. The boy was so engrossed in it that he hadn't heard me enter the room. He looked up quickly. "Do you think you're like the Beggar Boy?"

He looked down at the book and then at me again. He didn't answer, but there was no doubt in my mind that living here—with my grandfather laying on gifts and all the servants waiting on him—made him feel like a prince. I shouldn't blame him for it, I thought.

"It's better when you hear someone read it to you," I said, and plucked it out of his hands. Then I sat on the bed and began. "Once upon a time, there lived a man who had only one son, a lazy, stupid boy, who would never do anything he was told . . ."

As I read, I kept an eye on him to see if anything I was reading was having a personal effect on him. He blinked a lot, but he didn't smile or look sad. He looked more like Willie had when I read it to him, his eyes widening with amazement at some of the magic in the story.

I was so into it myself that I didn't hear Dorian step up behind me at the foot of the bed. After a few moments, I sensed her presence and paused to look at her. She smiled, turned, and walked out. The boy stared at me, anxious for me to continue. I read to the end of the story and closed the book.

"That was one of my brother's favorite fables," I said. He nodded as if he had known. "Would you like me to read you another one sometime?"

This time, he smiled and nodded.

"Someone used to read to you, too, right?"

He blinked rapidly and then looked like he might cry or scream, so I got up quickly.

"I'm not going to call you William," I said. "That's not your name, and you know it's not. It's my brother's name." I looked at the fable I had just read to him. "I'm going to call you Count Piro."

I thought he was smiling, although it wasn't easy to tell. He also looked like he was about to cry.

"I'm going down to help with dinner," I said, rising. "Are you getting hungry?"

He nodded.

I had an idea. "When you get better, do you want to go back to where you were?" I asked him.

His eyes widened, and he shook his head.

I smiled to myself. If anyone else had asked him that, he hadn't replied. I was making a difference already.

At least I knew that he remembered where he'd been. And that he didn't want any part of it anymore.

Now, if I could just get him to tell me where.

15

Myra was overseeing one of the recently hired maids setting the table for dinner when I entered the dining room. She paused in her instructing as soon as I came in and looked at me with a broad smile on her face, her jackpot smile, as she called it, but she said nothing. She didn't have to. I knew that look well. It always came quickly when she was proud of me.

"I'll help bring things out," I said, and went into the kitchen to get some of the condiments. I often tried to do something helpful in the house, even though it seemed like we had an army of servants. As soon as I was old enough, I always did something to help my mother at breakfast and especially at dinner. Doing things now that I used to do with her helped keep my memories of her vivid and alive.

My Faith looked up from the large salad bowl and flashed her special smile at me, too. I was ashamed of myself for having been angry at both of them. They were the best cheerleaders any girl my age could hope to have. The condiments were already organized on a tray. I picked it up.

"This is like a Christmas dinner," I said, seeing her elaborate preparations.

"My grandmother used to say, 'Child, nothin' cheers up the troubled soul like a good meal.' And we have our share of troubled souls here," she added.

I carried the tray to the dining room and set up the condiments on the table in exactly the places Myra wanted them to be. Under her scrutinizing gaze, it was like setting up a chessboard. I knew that even though she was instructing the new maid on how to set dishes and silverware on a table, she was watching me. Like a snapped rubber band, her full attention returned to the new maid. She had put the salad fork where the entrée fork was supposed to be. To Myra, that was a capital crime.

"No, no, no, can't you see the difference in the size?"

"Sorry," the young woman said. She couldn't have been more than nineteen or twenty. Myra was also particular about how the napkins should be folded and placed in the Arnold monogram napkin rings. I watched the poor, flustered girl work at it until my grandfather entered.

He was smiling at me just the way Myra and My Faith had done. Obviously, Dorian had told everyone what I had been doing with the poisoned boy.

"I could eat a horse tonight," he said, slapping his hands together and rubbing his palms.

"I believe it's more like a pig," Myra said, and he

threw his head back and roared with laughter, an outburst I hadn't heard since Willie's death.

The new maid looked like she had come to work for the Mad Hatter in *Alice's Adventures in Wonderland*. Her head down, she quickly followed Myra into the kitchen. I went around and sat at my place. Grandpa took his seat and looked at me with those steely eyes he could bring out whenever he wanted to be stern.

"So where did you take your bike ride today?" he asked.

From the way he was waiting for my answer, I had the feeling that he already knew. Perhaps he had run into one of the women who had been with their children at the playground.

"I went to the children's playground on Jefferson Street," I said.

He said nothing, obviously waiting for me to continue. If he knew I had been there, then he knew whom I had been there with. I was going to tell him anyway.

"Where I met Aaron Podwell. His father took away his driving privileges for a week after you called him, but his friend drove him there. You didn't say I couldn't see him," I quickly added.

"And if I did, would you listen?"

"No." I held my breath, expecting him to go into another rage, but instead, those steely eyes softened into not so much a pleasing look as a look of quiet resignation.

"No doubt whose daughter you are. Between your

grandmother and her, I was about as effective and in control as the driver of a twelve-wheeler dump truck without brakes going down Devil's Run."

Before either of us could speak, Dorian entered. Grandpa turned to her, smiling in a way I hadn't seen him smile since Grandma Lucy passed away. There was a special look of appreciation in it, something much more than a man would give an employee.

"I'm going to prepare his dinner tray," she said. "Better he eats upstairs tonight. I'll eat with him."

Grandpa nodded, but I thought he looked disappointed. Dorian flashed a smile at me and went into the kitchen. Moments later, with Myra looking over her shoulder, the maid began to serve our dinner.

"Well," Grandpa said, starting on his salad, "since I have little to say in the matter, when Mr. Podwell gets his privileges reinstated, maybe I'll have you bring him around for dinner one night."

"Really?"

"Your grandmother used to tell me you can't fight city hall. City hall is a piece of cake compared with a woman who makes up her mind about something or someone."

I smiled. He was being more like the grandfather I knew, loved, and trusted.

"But don't misunderstand me, Clara Sue," he said, waving his salad fork at me. "I'm still your grandfather, in charge and responsible for your welfare. We follow rules here. No more of this gallivanting about without letting me know where you're going, who you're going with, and how long you intend to be away."

"Okay, Grandpa," I said. "It won't happen again. I promise."

He grunted and ate for a moment. "His father cheats at golf, you know," he said, as if that was worse than murder. "I hope he's made of better stuff," he added, and then went into a speech about how he could understand a man's true character by playing golf with him.

As I listened to him elaborate on the true natures of different business associates and lessons he had learned in his life, I felt we were back to the days before Willie's death, even before Grandma Arnold had passed away. He could go on and on, and we'd always pretend we were glued to his every word, until Grandma finally would say, "Come up for air, William Arnold, before you wear out our ears."

He came up for air tonight when his favorite baked ham was brought out on a platter. Everything was delicious. My Faith's grandmother was right about the power of a good dinner when it came to restoring troubled souls.

Just before our dishes were being cleared away, Dorian brought down hers and the boy's, pleased that he had eaten well.

"He's putting weight back on quickly," she told us. Usually, she directed herself solely to my grandfather when she talked about my Count Piro, but tonight she was including me. She reminded us that Dr. Patrick would be coming in the morning, and I reminded them both that I'd be at school.

"We might think about getting him a tutor," Dorian suggested. "I brought it up with him tonight."

I thought it was interesting how quickly Dorian Camden had become part of everything in our home. She acted and spoke as if she was more like a family member than hired help, but Grandpa was obviously pleased about it.

"Yes, that would be smart now," he said. "Did he say anything about school? What grade he was in, anything?"

I perked up to hear her answer.

"Nothing that makes sense, except maybe . . ."

"Go on," Grandpa told her.

"It sounds like he was homeschooled." She looked at me. "Someone was often reading to him. That was about all I could gather."

"Interesting," Grandpa said. He turned to me. "You read him some of that children's story?"

"I saw he was reading one of Willie's favorite fables, 'How the Beggar Boy Turned into Count Piro.'"

"Whatever. Could you tell if he could read well?"

"He could read. I don't know how well. Probably not as well as Willie could for his age," I said. "My brother loved to read and be read to," I told Dorian. She smiled.

We were all quiet for a moment. The miniature grandfather clock in the living room tapped out the hour. Was it my imagination, or was the house raising its head which had been bowed in sorrow and mourning? Would deep shadows retreat? Could this ever really be a home again?

"I'll look into a tutor tomorrow," Grandpa told Dorian. "I'll speak with the grade-school principal.

His wife is a bookkeeper for Arnold Trucking."
Grandpa always referred to his business as Arnold
Trucking instead of "my business." It was as if he
worked for some invisible owner besides himself.

"Great. The faster we get him doing regular things
kids his age do, the faster he'll recuperate."

"Will he ever walk again?" I asked, wondering just
how much he could recuperate.

She looked to Grandpa Arnold to respond.

"They don't sound very hopeful about it," he said.

"He's getting stronger. We'll see," Dorian said.
Maybe it was her job, but she seemed to like being
more optimistic than most people. "I'll just take this
into the kitchen and go back up. Have to give him a
bath tonight."

Then My Faith surprised us with a peach pie.
She made her pies from scratch, as Grandma Arnold
would say.

"This is like a Thanksgiving dinner tonight," I said.

"Oh, she'll outdo this for Thanksgiving," Grandpa
assured me.

It was still difficult to get excited about that
holiday, but it seemed wrong now to do anything that
would darken the mood or block out the light that had
come trickling into our world with the promise of a
better tomorrow.

Later, feeling bad about how mean I had been to
Lila, I called her and explained why I had been upset
and how both Aaron and I had been punished. I
didn't mention what I had done with Count Piro,
and she seemed to know not to bring him up in our

conversation. We gossiped instead about the others at Audrey's party, and I finished by promising to do more with her during the week, especially since Aaron wouldn't have his car. I decided not to mention the possibility of my inviting him to dinner. She would wonder why I wasn't inviting her, too.

Aaron was waiting for me in the lobby at school the following morning. Probably before we had reached my homeroom, the story about our "unauthorized" Saturday all-day date had spread with hurricane speed to all our classmates. I hadn't sworn Lila to secrecy, and Aaron had told some of his friends, because he knew they'd be asking about his car and why he wasn't driving it. Before the day ended, we had become the "hot couple." I saw it in the expressions and heard it in the voices of my girlfriends. Apparently, no one needed my confirmation or would believe any denial concerning how intimate Aaron and I had become. For most of my girlfriends, I seemed to have grown in stature. I enjoyed the way they were treating me and decided to let them embellish my romance.

The rest of the week wasn't going fast enough for either Aaron or me. We had to spend our time after school talking only on the phone, and a few times, I had to do it while Lila was visiting and doing homework or studying for a test. She pretended not to be listening closely, but I knew she was hanging on every word. Aaron was getting his car privileges back on Friday, and although Grandpa didn't mention inviting him to dinner again, I began to drop hints with him that Friday would be nice, since the following week

[x]ly

was Thanksgiving and we'd break for the holiday at midday on Tuesday. Grandpa didn't say yes or no.

I thought that might be because he seemed to be having a busier week than usual, and his mind was occupied with other things. On top of what was happening at the trucking company, he was apparently meeting regularly with Dr. Patrick and had, with Dorian, arranged for a tutor, a Mrs. Crystal, who was a retired grade-school teacher. She was gone before I got home after school every day, but I saw how Count Piro was diligently working on what she had given him to do. She had brought him workbooks for vocabulary and English grammar, math and science, and reading. Dorian would be helping him, too. By Wednesday, I saw how alert he had become because of all this new interaction. He was sitting at the table again for dinner.

At Dr. Patrick's request, no one pressured him with questions about his past or his identity. The first time I referred to him as Count Piro caught everyone's attention. Looking right at him across the table, I explained how much he had enjoyed the fable and how, just like Willie liked to be called Batman sometimes, he didn't mind being called Count Piro.

"Am I right, Count Piro?" I asked him.

He nodded. Grandpa looked at Dorian, and they both seemed pleased. I certainly was. I had found a way never to call him William.

I hadn't realized it, but Grandpa was waiting to discuss with Dr. Patrick whether it was wise yet to invite a stranger to dinner, especially a teenage boy. On

Secret Brother   285

Thursday afternoon, as soon as I entered the house, Myra informed me that Dr. Patrick was waiting for me in the living room, the way she had been the first time we met.

"Hi," she said immediately. I thought she looked more relaxed and friendlier.

"Hi." I stood for a moment and then sat in Grandpa's chair. "Anything wrong?"

"Oh, no. Just the opposite. I'm so happy to hear you've embraced the situation more. To me, that shows real maturity, Clara Sue. There's so much in life that annoys us or disturbs us, and it's how we handle those things that makes the difference in the end and helps balance our emotions."

"You mean, like you're handling me," I said, and she laughed.

Then she put up her hands. "No more psychiatrist's lingo. I promise."

"Some of it I don't mind," I said with a shrug. I had been doing some reading on the side to see if I could determine how much Count Piro was really suffering and how much was pretend. I even began to wonder if pursuing a career in psychotherapy was possible for me.

"Okay. I think you've broken through a little with him, and I think that will lead to some promising results. Your grandfather has told me that you want to invite a boy to dinner tomorrow night, and chances are, William . . . oh, what do you call him? Count . . ."

"Piro. After the fable I read him."

"Right." She smiled "Very clever." She nodded at

me. "I promise another thing, not to underestimate you. Anyway, getting back to exposing our Count to more people, especially a teenage boy. I think that could be very good. What I would like to see, however, is no one cross-examining him. For now, no direct questions about him or his past. Too much pressure on him can set him back. Can you explain that to . . ."

"Aaron, Aaron Podwell. He's a senior, and he's sensitive enough to understand, especially in the presence of my grandfather," I added. "Anyway, it's more of a truce dinner between him and my grandfather and me."

"I heard."

"Yes, I'm a real rebel. But with a cause," I said, tucking in the corners of my mouth.

She nodded, obviously thinking about what to say next. "I'm not here to give you any personal advice, but . . ."

"But?"

"But I'm also a woman who has a history full of disappointments and successes, anger and elation."

"You're not going to tell me now that you've been to a psychiatrist, too?"

"Oh, yes. That's part of our training, our education."

"Really? Okay, what personal advice do you have for me, Dr. Patrick?" I challenged.

"Call me Katherine."

"Katherine."

She leaned forward. "When we're unhappy with what we think is unfair treatment of us or simply angry at people we think don't love us as much as they should, we sometimes do self-destructive things as a way of striking back. We do things we would not normally do and things we know in our hearts we shouldn't. On the surface, it looks like we're doing it to get even."

"Why do you say 'on the surface'? Maybe it is."

"Your grandfather tells me you have always been a very responsible person. You take care of your things. You don't procrastinate when it comes to your homework. You took on the responsibility of looking after your little brother when your parents died in that horrible accident and consequently sacrificed a lot of your own time and fun. That's a lot for a girl your age. He is very proud of you. In fact, he tells me he couldn't have gotten by until now without you. Maybe he's guilty of not saying it enough, but I believe him."

I saw where she was going, and it did make me feel bad, but I didn't like it. "I just did one bad thing by not telling him where I was all day. I didn't kill anyone," I said. "Why make a federal case of it?"

"Oh, I agree. In proportion to some of the things young people your age do, it's relatively minor, but it's a start in the wrong direction. It makes it easier for something more."

"'Steal a pencil, and someday soon you'll steal a car.' We hear that all the time."

"Well, maybe there's some exaggeration, but it's out there like the forbidden fruit waiting to be plucked, especially by a rebel with a cause."

She sat back, and we just stared at each other for a few moments. My heart was beating faster, and I thought my temperature was rising, but I tried to look unaffected by her comment.

"I make a living trying to figure out why people do things, young people. Almost always, I discover they don't always do things because they really want to do them. With young people especially, they do them because their peers do them or they want to be liked or, yes, they want to get back at their parents. All I'm saying, advising, is that whenever you're thinking of doing something you wouldn't ordinarily do, ask yourself why you're doing it. Do you really want to do it? Stay in control. Don't let anything or anyone else make decisions for you," she concluded. She stood up and smiled. "It ain't easy, especially with those hormones raging."

"Is that all from some textbook, or did you live it?"

She held out her hand. "Go on, touch it," she said. I pulled my head back and smirked. "Go ahead."

"Why?"

"Humor me."

I touched her hand. "So?"

"Notice? Flesh and blood. I've been there," she said. "Invite your boyfriend to dinner," she told me, and started out.

I watched her go and heard her leave the house. The truth was, I couldn't stand how well she had gotten under my skin. She was right about what Aaron and I had done. I had kept my grandfather worrying about me all day just to get back at him. There was no question that I had been more sexually active with Aaron than I had been with any other boy, too. I had almost gone all the way. Was it like she had said? Had I done things because I wanted to, or was I looking for another way to strike back at everyone who was my family now?

I hated having to think of all this. It made my life so much more complicated. You don't worry about a pain so much if no one tells you it could be cancer or appendicitis, something to keep you up at night. *Who needs her to come here and peel away my scabs?* I thought.

But another part of me thought that maybe I should be grateful. If I wanted to be honest about it, I *would* be grateful. She didn't have to waste her time on me . . . or was my grandfather paying her to do so? Had I unknowingly become another one of her patients? I didn't deserve that, or was it necessary?

I hurried upstairs, feeling like I had suddenly been turned into my own parents worrying about me. I felt more like someone's parent. I cursed fate and the devil for making me grow up faster than I wanted. My childish smiles and laughter were gone long ago, along with my childish, innocent body. She was right. My hormones were raging, demanding to be heard and recognized. Every part of me was changing just when my whole world seemed to crumble around me. How would I reform it? I wanted to like who I was, but I feared looking in the mirror now.

I rushed to my room without looking into Willie's

and, as usual, began stripping off my school clothes as if they were contaminated with bedbugs or something. I was down to my bra and panties when I turned toward my open doorway and paused in shock.

Count Piro had wheeled himself to my room. He remained there staring at me. The way he looked at me made me want to grab something to cover myself. It was as if his face, the expression around his eyes, was suddenly more mature, as if some vivid memory of sexual things had risen to the surface. The embarrassment I felt receded as my interest in him sharpened.

"Come in," I urged. "I'm just changing out of my school clothes."

He thought a moment and then wheeled forward. I didn't look at him. *Act casual*, I thought. *Don't frighten him*. I went to my closet.

"I hate my school clothes. Did you have to wear school clothes, a uniform or something? We don't wear a uniform, but we might as well."

I plucked a pair of jeans off its hanger and looked at him. He was nearly to my bed. He looked around my room and then at me.

"Boys usually don't come into girls' rooms when they're dressing, not even brothers and sisters, you know. You don't have to leave," I added quickly.

He shook his head.

"What? Do you have a sister? Did you go into her room when she was dressing?" I held my breath and practically froze in position, my jeans on but not zipped.

He nodded.

"You have a sister? What's her name? Where is she?" I demanded. "Don't you want to go see her, go back to her?"

A trembling seemed to rise from his neck and ripple through his face.

Oh, God, I thought, *he's going to howl or scream, and everything I've done will be destroyed in an instant.*

Grandpa would be very angry at me again. Dr. Patrick had just made a big point of our not pressuring him with questions. They'd all think I was doing this deliberately.

"Wait!" I cried. "I have something I wanted to give you very much."

I went to my closet and grabbed Willie's Superman figure.

"You know who this is?" I asked him. He shook his head. "You don't know who Superman is? Faster than a speeding bullet? What kind of a childhood did you have?" I asked, of myself more than him. I brought him the figure. "Superman can fly. Bullets bounce off him. He's the strongest man in the world."

I put the figure in his lap. He took it and looked at it closely.

"I'll tell you all about him," I promised. "He was my brother's favorite hero. See the cape? My brother had a Superman cape, too. I know where it is. I'll be sure you get it so you can wear it when you want, okay?"

He looked at the figure again and then nodded.

"I'll find one of Willie's Superman comics, and I'll read it to you."

He wasn't smiling, but the trembling was gone. I took a deep breath of relief.

His eyes were on my breasts now. He looked interested but not so much sexually. *His memory is stirring*, I thought. What was his sister like? Was she older? Did he have more than one? What about his mother? How was nudity treated in his home? So many questions were bouncing about in my head. I was just as driven by my own curiosity about him and his past as I was by the desire to get him to remember and go home.

"I'll finish dressing," I said. "Then we'll go back to Willie's . . . to your room, and I'll find Willie's Superman comics and read one to you. You know what a comic book is, right?"

He shook his head.

He's from another planet, I thought. *That's it. We have an alien creature in our house.* I laughed at the idea, found a blouse, and put it on while he watched me, seemingly fascinated with everything I did for myself and everything about me. I wasn't feeling embarrassed by it anymore, either. I was feeling . . . important.

Smiling at him now, I got behind his wheelchair and began pushing him out of my room.

I'm going to solve all this, I thought. *I'm going to do what private-duty nurses and psychiatrists haven't done. I'm going to find out exactly who he is. And how he came to be here.*

But until I did, it was probably better if I didn't tell anyone anything.

I didn't want them to come up with a reason I should stop.

16

At dinner, my Count Piro was more fascinated by Aaron than he was by me or anyone else. He stared at him and hung on to every word he said. Aaron knew he was under a spotlight and a microscope and had come prepared. He just didn't expect that spotlight to be held by the poisoned boy. He was thinking more about my grandfather. That was clear the moment I greeted him at the door.

Grandpa Arnold only wore a tie at dinner when we had his business associates and their wives for dinner or someone from the government. He dressed up for holidays, but usually, if he still wore a sports jacket, he didn't wear a tie. Aaron had come in a dark blue jacket and slacks and a light blue tie, and he wore an expensive-looking watch I had never seen him wear.

"Well," he whispered, standing back for my approval, "think I'll pass muster with the old man?"

"You look very handsome, Aaron. He's not an old man," I said, even more sharply than I intended.

He just smiled. "He's older than my father, and my father is an old man to me most of the time."

"Whatever," I said, and led him to the dining room, where everyone had already gathered. When Dorian complimented Aaron on his watch, he explained that it was a gift his paternal grandfather and grandmother had given him on his sixteenth birthday.

"I wear it only on special occasions," he added.

Grandpa didn't say anything, but I could see from the twinkle in his eyes that he was pleased to hear that dinner at our house was a special occasion for Aaron. But I was paying more attention to Count Piro's reaction than to Grandpa's. The boy watched how Aaron ate, eating when Aaron did, and whenever Aaron paused to say something or listen to something, Count Piro paused, too.

Although Dorian knew that I had given him Willie's Superman figure and had read some of the Superman comics to him, showing him the pictures as I did, she knew nothing about my questions concerning his family. Just as something about me had reminded him of someone, I thought something about Aaron now was reminding him of someone, someone he looked up to. Was it an older brother or his father?

Aaron realized how closely Count Piro was watching him. He was cool about it, winking at me when he could but pretending he wasn't as aware. Because I had told Aaron what Dr. Patrick had advised, I hoped he wasn't going to do or say anything that might disturb the boy, even in a small way. He knew that would upset my grandfather, too. I relaxed after the first few minutes. There was no reason to worry. Aaron was working everyone well. He was very smooth and convincing. He even complimented My Faith on the food, claiming she was better than the cook his parents had. Grandpa really liked that. Aaron was so good at handling everyone that I couldn't help wondering if he was handling me in a similar way, saying things he knew would please me but in a way that suggested he had planned. I kept wondering if I was simply too trusting and naive.

Before the dinner ended, however, Aaron surprised me even more by showing real interest in the physical-therapy machinery.

"That's a field that fascinates me," he told Dorian. "Sports medicine, the whole thing. I'm thinking of pursuing it as a career."

"That's very smart, Aaron. It's a growing field. If it's all right with Mr. Arnold, I'd be happy to show you the therapy equipment," she said, and looked at Grandpa.

"It's all right," he said. Then he peered at Aaron more like he peered at someone he didn't believe. I held my breath. Aaron was putting it on too heavily. "Your dad's not trying to get you to become part of his business, get you to go to business school?"

"Oh, he's trying," Aaron said with a smile. Dorian laughed. Count Piro's face even brightened.

"I don't blame him for it," Grandpa said wistfully. I knew he was thinking about Uncle Bobby and how he had refused to have anything to do with Grandpa's trucking company. "A man builds a business to support his family. He feels he has something he can pass on. It's one of the reasons he works so hard at it. You keep that in mind, son," he said. "What you can pass on to your children is what's most important in this world."

Aaron's smile evaporated. He nodded and glanced at me.

Yes, I told him with my eyes, *my grandpa is a tough man, and just being diplomatic isn't going to get you there*. Too many times, he'd told me that he had a built-in bullcrap meter. "It comes with the territory when you're in business," he said. I wanted to whisper to Aaron to stop trying so hard or to be less obvious about it. That could be worse.

After dinner, Grandpa went into the living room to read his *Wall Street Journal* while Dorian, pushing Count Piro, led Aaron and me to the room now dedicated to Count Piro's physical therapy. I was impressed with just how much Aaron did know about the equipment and the areas of the body each device was meant to improve. Was he sincere about all this? Perhaps I was judging him too severely.

While he and Dorian talked about it, both Count Piro, who suddenly looked bored, and I felt as if we weren't even there. Then Aaron turned to the boy and told him how confident he was that if he followed Mrs. Camden's directions, he would get better and better.

"Maybe I'll come here one day and work out with you," Aaron said. "Would that be all right with you?"

Count Piro smiled and nodded. Aaron was making

a bigger hit with him than either Dorian or I had. She looked at me and smiled.

"He works out when we're in school," I said.

"Oh, we can arrange a weekend or two," Dorian quickly suggested.

"Perfect," Aaron told her. "I have nothing better to do on my weekends."

He made a fist and put it next to the boy's hand. Count Piro looked at it and then made a fist, too, and Aaron gently pressed his to the boy's. I saw how impressed Dorian was. She smiled her approval at me. This was going so well, but I couldn't help being even more nervous just because it was.

Afterward, when we all joined Grandpa in the living room, Aaron surprised me again by volunteering to read a Superman comic with Count Piro after I had mentioned my earlier introduction. Grandpa looked up from what he was reading, pleased and surprised. He looked at me. It was obvious that Count Piro was very excited about it, so I ran up to Willie's room and brought down a new Superman comic.

Aaron told Count Piro that Superman had always been one of his favorite comic characters. "When I was your age, I even had a Superman cape, and it gave me powers," he added.

Count Piro's eyes widened.

"Don't we have one of those for him?" Grandpa asked me.

"I gave it to him," I said, and Grandpa smiled.

Before the reading began, my grandfather told us about men he had met in his life who were extraordinarily strong. Of course, he bragged about Jimmy and the things he had seen him lift on our property. Aaron winked at me and turned back to Count Piro, telling him that the comic I had happened to bring was one of his favorites.

He's really piling it on, I thought. *Grandpa's going to realize it and be very displeased.* I anticipated him calling me into his office after Aaron had left to tell me he was just as he expected, a phony like his father.

For now, Dorian and my grandfather sat back and watched Aaron read, show the pictures, and describe the events with such enthusiasm it was as if he really believed there was a Superman. I could see from Dorian's expression that she thought this evening was one of the best the boy had had since he was brought here to recuperate. Would my grandfather agree?

Finally, she decided it was time for him to go to bed.

Count Piro hadn't said anything until now, and no one had tried to draw anything out of him, but as Dorian began wheeling him out to the stair lift, he turned, still clinging to the comic book, and said, "Thank you," to Aaron. He hadn't said thank you to me like that. I looked from Aaron to Grandpa Arnold, who was smiling with the same sort of joy he had shown Willie whenever Willie had done something to please him. He looked at Aaron with respect and admiration, too.

Of everyone, I think I looked the most dumb-founded. Aaron had no younger brother and had never struck me as someone who enjoyed being around children, but Dr. Patrick had suspected that he could make better contact with Count Piro. And maybe not only because he was a boy. *She must know more about the poisoned boy than she's told me, perhaps. He's revealed more, and she's sharing that with only my grandfather and Dorian.* This wasn't the first time I suspected I was being kept in the dark. That wasn't fair. I was just as much, if not more, a part of all this than Dorian. When I looked at Aaron, I even had the sense that he realized more than I did.

The suspicion and annoyance twisted into a small ball of rage that grew hotter and larger inside me. Right now, I felt like the only one who was not part of this.

"Is it all right for me to show Aaron my room, Grandpa?" I asked.

He thought for a moment and shrugged. "Sure. Before he leaves, you might bring him to my office. I think he would enjoy some of the photographs and plaques. He can tell his dad about them," he added with his impish smile.

"Oh, absolutely, sir. Thank you," Aaron said.

I walked ahead of him to the stairway. He paused to look at the stair lift when we reached the top.

"Never saw one of these," he said. "My father was talking about getting one for my grandmother or else selling her house and getting her a single-level house."

I didn't say anything until we were in my room. We both looked at the door. Would I close it? "You can close it," I said.

He hesitated. "Maybe your grandfather wouldn't like that."

"Oh, give me a break, Aaron Podwell!" I cried, and shut the door myself. "You don't have to worry about what you'll be, Aaron. You'll be governor or something."

He smiled weakly. "Why do you say that?"

"You're a natural politician, as smooth as sleet on a country road," I added, which was one of Myra's expressions.

He lost his smile, now either feigning that he was hurt or really feeling hurt. I couldn't tell. "I was only trying to do my best for you, for us," he protested. "I thought you would be pleased. You think I like wearing this suit? Even my mother was shocked when she saw me leaving the house. It's my family straitjacket. Jeez, Clara Sue. I spent twenty minutes getting this tie knot perfect. I figured your grandfather would notice." He flopped into a chair as if I had pounded him with a sledgehammer. However, the fog of suspicion didn't lift from my eyes.

"You never told me you were interested in sports medicine and that sort of thing. Where did that come from?"

"Yeah, well, I've been thinking about it a lot lately." He rose and walked around my room, looking at my pictures and posters, and then sat on my bed and loosened his tie. "I like the nurse. She's not bad-looking, either. Maybe I can get her to come over to my house to give me a bath," he added, smiling licentiously. That was more like the Aaron Podwell I knew.

"Be careful what you wish for," I said.

He reached out for me. "I'm wishing only for you," he said. "C'mon. Loosen up. I'm going to get those chains off you."

I sat next to him, and he kissed me quickly.

"The first step to make my dream come true," he said. "Nice bed." He ran his right hand over my top sheet with his eyes closed and that smile still blooming on his face. "Now I can better picture you dreaming about me."

"You're not just conceited, you're convinced," I said.

He laughed. He continued to run his fingers along the bed and to my skirt, lifting it a little above my knee. "You look more delicious than any of the food tonight."

"I look better than food? Thanks."

"Hey, I'm trying to be romantic. I could live on a deserted island for weeks on just bread and water and you."

"Boy, do you know how to get yourself out of trouble," I said.

"If you're trouble, I don't want to ever get out."

He surprised me by leaning down and kissing the inside of my thigh. No other boy had ever done that. I hadn't even imagined it, but the sensation it sent up my thighs was so fast and hot that it took my breath away. He looked up at me, smiled, and kissed me again, only higher up, moving my skirt as he did. I had been bracing myself with my hands flat against the bed. My arms weakened when he kissed me a third time, again higher, and when I fell back on the bed, he moved to kiss me between my thighs. I couldn't smother the moan. He sat up and leaned over to kiss me on the lips. The fingers of his left hand slipped under my panties. If there was any protest in me, he drove it back with another, longer, more demanding kiss. I felt my whole body soften.

"We can't," I managed, the words reluctant to be spoken.

"I know," he whispered, kissing my ear softly and then my cheek before finding my lips.

His fingers were touching me. I didn't pull away. I lifted myself toward them. He took a deep breath when we heard footsteps in the hallway. I turned sharply and quickly away from him.

"I know what I'll dream about tonight," he said with a moan, and lay on his back.

I quickly straightened out my skirt and sat up. The footsteps stopped. It was either Myra or Grandpa going to Willie's room.

"Sorry," I said.

He groaned, rose, and went into my bathroom. While he was in there, I went to one of my windows and looked out at the driveway and the gate, at the lights and the stars. Every time I was with Aaron, I felt myself moving closer and closer to that moment. I wasn't totally blinded by the light in his eyes and the passion raging inside me. How do you decide when and with whom to do it? Very likely, there was someone else out there for me when I grew older. Aaron was going off to college next year. Even if we vowed to be faithful to each other and Aaron was as sincere as I was, there was so much out there that would challenge such a promise. I knew that.

What if he found someone else while he was in college? And what if I found someone else when I went to college? Would it matter to whoever fell in love with me that I wasn't a virgin? Would his view of me change enough to diminish his feelings for me? Would I regret having given myself to someone who would not mean that much to me years from now? Did my mother have these thoughts when she was my age? When did she lose her virginity? Was it with my father?

It wasn't enough to talk about it with other girls, even Lila. Deep inside, I was skeptical of anything any of them said. We were competing with one another too much for male attention, whether we would admit it or not. Everyone would lie or embellish just to look more sophisticated. My mother was the only other woman I could trust, and she was gone.

Everyone thought that losing your parents was the worst for you when you were young, but that wasn't true. I had never needed my mother as much as I needed her right now. I took a deep breath and nodded to myself. *What decisions you make, Clara Sue Sanders, you really make yourself from now until forever. You have lost the luxury of being able to blame someone else.* That was really what becoming an adult meant. Why were we all so eager for that to happen?

I turned when I heard Aaron coming out of the

bathroom. He looked like he had washed his face in cold water, even his hair.

He shook his head at the surprise on my face. "I felt like a stick of dynamite with a lit wick," he said, and laughed.

"Sorry."

"Okay," he said, slapping his hands together and rubbing his palms. "I have a plan."

"Plan? For what?" Did he mean our making love? When and where?

"For the investigation, silly. I want to help you discover who he is, where he's from, and what happened to him so you can get rid of him," he replied, as if it was obvious. "That's why I was doing all that downstairs."

"Is that what you were doing?"

"Of course. I thought you could see that. I was winning his trust. That's what we'll do together. We'll do a lot better than the psychiatrist and the nurse," he said. He lay back against one of my oversized pillows. "I'll be over more often, too, and when we can do it, we'll take him for some rides or something, so we get as much private time with him as we can, see? We just won't be obvious about our reasons. We'll just come off as sincerely concerned about him. He'll believe it, too, and he'll open up."

"Aren't you the schemer," I said.

"Who isn't? Even him, maybe. You thought that was possible, didn't you?"

"I don't know about that anymore."

He smiled. "See? He's winning you over, too."

"He's not winning me over. Dr. Patrick says he can't be that clever at that age, and I think she knows a little more about it than you do."

"Don't believe it. I was that conniving at his age, especially when it came to handling my mother or getting my father to loosen up the rules. I still am. How do you think I got my new car so soon?"

"Don't you think that's wrong? They're your parents, your family."

"What's wrong? Getting what you want?" He raised his arms.

"It's like lying to them, Aaron."

"It's the American way," he said, and laughed. Then he looked at his expensive watch and leaped up.

"What now?"

"We'd better go down so your grandfather can show me his pictures and plaques. He said he wants me to tell my father all about them. I know why, even though I'm playing innocent."

I looked up at him as he smiled wryly at me. I wanted to do everything he was suggesting, but I felt guilty about it now. Surely my Count Piro was betrayed by people who should have loved and protected him. If we did something like that to him, too, we might hurt him beyond repair.

And yet even having these feelings of conscience made me feel even guiltier, for after all, I was not thinking of Willie. Wasn't it my original purpose to get Count Piro out of our lives because it kept us from mourning Willie as we should?

Aaron was probably right. We could make more

progress with Count Piro than my grandfather, Dorian, or even Dr. Patrick. It was so much easier to fool children, because the world looked so simple to them. There were good things and bad, ugly and beautiful, bitter and sweet, and never once until they were old enough to understand could they imagine anything being both. Black and white turned to gray. Hesitation and distrust were born with the loss of innocence.

My eyes brightened with a thought.

Maybe all that had already happened to my Count Piro. Maybe he wasn't terrified by memories as much as he was terrified of what was in the future. Once he felt safe, he would tell everything.

"Don't look so serious, Clara Sue. It makes people suspicious," Aaron said, reaching for my hand to lead me out of my bedroom.

I rose and followed Aaron down to Grandpa, who, despite his success and his power, was unaware of the deception Aaron was creating right before his eyes.

"Well," Grandpa said, perhaps surprised at the sight of us so soon. "Get the tour, did you?"

"A little. I think the layout of your house is much smarter than ours," Aaron said. "Our guest bedrooms are very close to my sister's, mine, and my parents' bedrooms. Not that we have that many guests," he quickly added. "Dad has this big sign up in the entryway. 'Guests and fish smell in three days. Benjamin Franklin.'"

Grandpa laughed. "Very wise. My office is just down here," he said, rising and pointing to the right.

Aaron took my hand again, something that Grandpa didn't miss, and we followed him out.

Was Aaron right? Was my grandfather showing him all this just because of his constant competition with Aaron's father? There was talk occasionally of my grandfather running for mayor of Prescott, and almost every time I had heard that, Aaron's father was mentioned as another possible candidate.

Aaron was so good at his reactions that I couldn't tell if he really was impressed with my grandfather's pictures of famous Virginia politicians, U.S. senators, and Navy officers. Grandpa had chamber of commerce awards, letters and plaques, and a national Better Business Bureau award. And then there were his pictures with famous baseball players and one with his favorite movie actor, Humphrey Bogart. And of course, there were the trophies for the landscape award. Grandpa had to mention that Aaron's father hadn't won one yet.

"He thinks he will this year," Aaron said. "He's been planning on some dramatic changes on the property."

"Is that so?" Grandpa said. "We'll see."

Aaron looked at his watch. "I'd better get going. My sister's coming home for Thanksgiving a little early, and we're kind of close. I'd never admit it, but I miss her."

"That so?" Grandpa said. His admiration for Aaron seemed to have no limit.

"Yes, sir. Thanks for showing me all this, Mr. Arnold, and thanks for inviting me to dinner."

"You're welcome," Grandpa said.

I walked Aaron out.

"Your grandfather isn't as tough as you think," he said when we were at his car. "Anyone who wants to help a little boy like that has soft spots, Clara Sue."

"Don't underestimate him, Aaron. Those who do regret it."

Aaron looked a little taken aback. Despite everything Grandpa had done that upset me, I had to come to his defense, and quickly, too. Actually, I didn't like deceiving him.

"I'll be careful," Aaron said. "I'll call you in the morning to see if the chains have been taken off you since my political performance. Maybe we'll go to a movie or something."

He kissed me quickly and got into his car. He looked so confident and, for a moment, unattractive. I watched him drive off and then lowered my head and started to walk back into the house.

I looked up quickly when Grandpa said, "Very polite young man."

"Yes," I said.

"Hard to believe he's Lester Podwell's son, but sometimes the apple does fall far from the tree, especially if the tree's at the top of a hill." I knew he was really thinking more about Uncle Bobby.

"Everyone should be his or her own person, Grandpa."

"Hmm," he said. "I like how he was with William. Seeing other young people could help him recuperate faster. When he's more able, you and Aaron might do some things with him, even if it's just around here."

I stared at him. He was walking right into Aaron's plan. Why didn't I feel happier about it?

"Anyway, your punishment's over, but don't let something like that happen again," he warned, and returned to his office.

I started up the stairs. The door to Willie's bedroom was slightly ajar, but the room was dark. I didn't pause to look in at Count Piro. When I got to my bedroom, I flopped onto my bed and looked up at the ceiling.

As I lay there thinking, I felt as if the burden of all my rage had slipped away. Ever since Willie's death, I clung to anger. It was a shield, helping me block any other emotion from taking hold of me. I still wanted to keep sadness at arm's length, leave it outside my door if I could, but what I hadn't expected to feel so strongly right now was guilt.

Aaron's sudden interest and determination were putting me off when I should have been encouraged by them. I had my ally, someone in whom I could confide all my troubled feelings, someone who would sympathize and understand my feelings and resentments, didn't I? He was better than Lila, who, deep down, wasn't really that concerned. Yet the way I had come to my grandfather's defense just before seemed to open another door, one I had been ignoring.

Despite everything that was happening, I really didn't like conspiring against my family, against those who loved me in this house. It even bothered me now to take advantage of Dorian Camden. Yet Aaron was planning that we would go behind Grandpa's back and work on Count Piro until we had the information that would send him away.

But if Count Piro was blocking out his memory of his family and where he came from, even if he was pretending to do that, how horrible must that be? How would I feel if the people who had done this to him drove up here one day and took him away, mainly because of what we had forced him to remember? And there was nothing Grandpa could do about it, either. Would I feel better, successful, happier?

I recalled something My Faith was fond of saying: "God's in his heaven, all's right with the world." Once I overheard Myra ask her what she thought that really meant. Without hesitation, My Faith said, "God's watching over us, but he's not down here making us do the right thing. We've got to do that ourselves and just know he's watching us."

Myra hadn't replied, but I had thought more about it and was thinking about it now.

God didn't stop that pickup driver from killing Willie, and even if the pickup driver ended up in hell, it wouldn't bring Willie back.

And even if Aaron and I found out the truth about Count Piro, that wouldn't bring Willie back.

His room would be empty again.

All would not be right with the world.

17

Aaron was surprised at my lack of enthusiasm when he called me the following morning.

"Are you all right?" he asked.

I was in such deep thought when my phone rang that I didn't hear it until the third ring. I was sure he asked how I was because my "hello" sounded like that of someone who was under hypnosis.

"Yes. Just a little tired. I didn't sleep that well."

"Because you were dreaming of me?"

"No. I didn't sleep enough to dream."

"Sorry. We'll have to do something about that. I was thinking I would come over."

"Not today. I have too much homework to leave for Sunday night, and I've got to make significant progress on my history term paper. Fortunately, my grandfather has some books I can use in his library."

"Sounds like a perfect way to ruin a Saturday. Are you sure? It's nice out. Maybe they'll let us wheel the kid around the property or something, and we can pry the truth out of him."

"Not today," I said, my words as final as death itself.

"Okay. You still want to go out tonight, though, don't you? We have plans to make for the immediate future."

"I don't think so. My grandfather is thinking of getting our Christmas tree today. It was always a big thing for all of us to decorate it," I said. "We'll be doing it all day and tonight. We always had a little pre-Christmas dinner when we finished the tree."

"We've never done that. My mother gets it delivered all done by some decorator."

"How cold," I said. I didn't mean to say it so critically.

"Yeah, I guess," he said. "I've always been more interested in presents, anyway, and barely noticed the tree, but maybe I should come over to help you with yours. It'll give me an appreciation for what I've missed."

I didn't say yes.

"But I imagine it's something you want to do with your grandfather," he added after my silent response.

"This time, more than ever, I think," I said.

"Sure. I understand," he said, his voice dropping off with the weight of disappointment and clearly indicating that he didn't understand or didn't want to understand. "Well, maybe I'll catch you tomorrow, and we can do some planning then. I mean, you can't be doing homework all day Sunday, too, right?"

"Maybe," I said.

"Maybe?" He was silent a moment. "You're not mad at me or anything, are you?"

"No. I'm just . . . trying to catch my breath. So much is happening, has happened. I want to think about it all quietly."

"Right. Think about it," he said, his voice sharp with annoyance. "Okay, I'll call you to see if you changed your mind. In the meanwhile, have a good tree thing."

I said good-bye and stared at the phone after I hung up.

What was I doing? There wasn't a girl in my school who wouldn't want Aaron Podwell to be her boyfriend. In my mind, I had committed myself more to him than I had to any boy. Why was I blaming him for trying to do the very thing I had told him I wanted to do? Why was I blaming him for caring?

Or was I doubting now that he really cared? Did I have more reason to suspect that everything he did was for one purpose, to make it with me, to add me to his list of conquests? Was I getting smarter, wiser about all this?

All the girls in my class now believed I was one of the most sophisticated among us, that somehow I had leaped beyond them when it came to romance and sex. Certainly, I wouldn't make any mistakes or be just someone's little conquest. They assumed too much. I wasn't the person to go to with a romance question, but I didn't let them know it, because I was happy that they saw me this way, happy that my ego was being stroked just when I was falling into a deeper and deeper hole of self-pity. It had pushed back the veil of darkness that had threatened to overwhelm and bury me in sorrow.

Everything negative could have followed if Aaron hadn't shown interest in me. I could have given up on my schoolwork, on caring about my looks and my social life, on life itself. No one would have blamed me. I'd have been the primary one seeing a therapist, and my self-image would have dwindled until I was a mere shadow of who I had been. I might as well have crawled into the ground beside Willie. Shouldn't I be thankful that Aaron came along? Why was I so confused about it? The mental turmoil was making me angry.

But this constant questioning wasn't really surprising. At some point when you're growing up, you suddenly realize that life is very complicated. I think that makes us all mad. We realize our childhood faith was an illusion. I had discovered that truth much earlier than other girls my age. My parents' deaths had turned everything inside out and left a hole in our lives so big and deep that it seemed we would never crawl out again, never enjoy anything we ate, anything we were given, anything we used to enjoy. The emptiness inside us threatened to expand until we were two children with vacant eyes who didn't know how or when to laugh or smile again. Our grandparents and Myra and My Faith brought us up for air, and we began to live again. However, like some giant pushing my head back under every time I emerged from the cold darkness, death visited us again and again.

I was coming up for air once more, and now I wondered if I was only bringing the darkness back by forcing Count Piro to face his own horrid memories. As I had unfortunately learned at an age not much older than he was, emotional and psychological wounds could be more painful than physical ones. He, however, was suffering all three kinds. How well did he sleep? What clicked on and off in his mind when he opened his eyes in the morning? A wall separated us, but somewhere in the darkness, we were both screaming.

I shook off these chilling thoughts and joined my grandfather, who I knew was waiting for me to go with him to pick out a Christmas tree. At first, Dorian thought she would come along herself and bring Count Piro, but he had developed some stomach trouble, and she thought it was best that he remain in bed for a while.

"I don't think it's anything serious," she said. She thought a moment and then shook her head and held her tongue. Maybe she didn't say anything because she would be saying it in front of me. It was difficult to navigate through all this mystery. Secrets gave birth to more secrets. They multiplied like rabbits in this house.

"Don't worry. The tree will cheer him up," Grandpa Arnold assured her. "We have all the fixings, and we'll get out the electric trains, right, Clara Sue?"

I looked at him with surprise. I had forgotten about the electric trains and the tiny people and little houses. Putting that all together had been Willie's

prized Christmas assignment. He hated to have anyone, even me, help him. But what good would it do in
boxes left in a closet? Of course we should take them
out. "Right, Grandpa," I said.

He nodded at Dorian. I caught the silent words
they exchanged with their eyes and knew they were all
about me. Were they suspicious about my willingness
to cooperate now? I didn't like not being trusted, but I
couldn't deny that I had earned it.

Moments later, we were off to hunt for the best
darn tree in Virginia, as Grandpa would say. I felt him
looking at me, trying to read my thoughts and feelings, especially now that we were doing this for our
Christmas. The first time he, Willie, and I had done
this after our parents' deaths, he had talked all the way
to the tree farm and back. I knew he didn't want us
to concentrate too long on our memories of decorating the Christmas tree with our mother and father. It
was Willie who remembered that Mommy wanted the
angel put on first. Every Christmas, she would tell us,
"The angel has to look down and approve of what we
do to her tree."

"I don't know how we do it," Grandpa Arnold
suddenly said. It was as if he was thinking aloud. He
kept his attention on the road. I waited for him to continue, but he didn't.

"Do what, Grandpa?"

"Come back to the living. Every time something
terrible happens in our lives, something terrible to
someone we love, we think, *Why bother going on?*"
He turned to me. "Yet we do, don't we? We go on."

"I guess I believe Mommy or Daddy, Grandma, or even Willie would want us to," I said.

"Exactly. That would be like adding insult to injury if they didn't. I mean, who's to say they can't feel guilty about something like that, even in heaven?"

I smiled. "You telling me you believe in heaven now, Grandpa?"

He looked at me, that subdued but loving smile trickling through his face as if the firm, serious face he habitually wore had become a transparent mask through which I could now see the true William Arnold. "I can't think of anyplace else they'd be," he said. "But don't go and tell My Faith I said that, or she'll smother me in Bibles," he quickly added.

He tried to look serious about it, but we both laughed.

This is something we haven't done for a while, I thought, *laugh together at the same thing*.

After we reached the tree farm, we walked among the rows, inspecting. We needed a rather big and tall tree for a living room our size. Grandpa was not only good at picking out a tree that had a perfect shape, but he was also good at negotiating the price for it.

"You always try to negotiate when you're buying things, if you can," he told me after we loaded the tree onto the small pickup he kept for odd jobs. Jimmy used it mostly and would have come with us if it wasn't his day off. "People respect you more. I wish your uncle Bobby understood that. Artistic people are softies when it comes to the real world."

"He's a talented and lovely man, Grandpa. You should be proud of him."

"Lovely, huh? Anyone ever called me lovely, I'd have their two front teeth."

"Growl, growl," I muttered, and he laughed.

Then he turned serious again. "Bobby knows he can go his own way, and I'll still do whatever I can for him. Your grandma Lucy would rise from the grave and give me what for if I didn't."

"You'd do it anyway, Grandpa. You're the softy at heart. That boy wouldn't be in our house if you weren't," I said, thinking of what Aaron had told me.

He glanced at me. His expression revealed that he was caught between arguing and agreeing. Instead, he just drove on. To our surprise, Jimmy had returned on his day off and was there to help unload the tree and help Grandpa set it up in the tree stand in the living room. While they did that, I went to the storage room and began bringing out the Christmas decorations and Willie's electric trains and model village. Before we got started, My Faith announced lunch, and Dorian came down to tell us William was feeling better and she thought he might be up to watching or even helping in a small way to decorate the tree.

"What did he say about it?" I asked.

"Oh, I haven't told him about it yet. I thought I would just get him down here and surprise him with it." She gave Grandpa one of those conspiratorial glances and told me that Dr. Patrick had suggested it and asked her to take note of his reaction. "We're not even sure he ever had a Christmas tree in his home," she pointed out.

"Well, he should believe in Santa Claus," I said, and nodded at my grandfather. "Not Saint Nick but Saint William."

Dorian widened her eyes. They looked at each other, and Grandpa surprised me with a smile. I thought I had sounded sarcastic, but apparently, I didn't know my own thinking anymore.

Grandpa brought in a ladder after lunch so one of us could place the angel at the top of the tree while Dorian went back up to get Count Piro dressed and into the chair to be brought downstairs. I spread all the decorations out carefully, trying to recall how we had each one placed on the tree last Christmas.

I heard the chair coming down, heard Dorian transferring him to the wheelchair waiting at the bottom, and then turned to the doorway to watch as she wheeled him into the living room. Grandpa stood there holding the angel in his hands. I stood up, thinking I would invite the boy over to attach some of the sparkling crystal balls to the lower branches. He could do that easily while in his wheelchair. He looked from me to Grandpa to the tree, and then his face began to tremble as if it was made of putty and he was being shaken.

It was clear that the tree was connected with a strong memory for him, and now the sight of it brought back some horror like a gust of wind slapping him in the face. He screamed what I thought sounded like "Carry!" and then his head jerked back, and the trembling in his face rippled through his body. Dorian looked shocked, actually stunned, and for a moment, I wondered if she could do anything.

"What . . ." Grandpa cried.

Dorian quickly turned Count Piro's wheelchair and pushed him out of the room and back toward the stairway. Grandpa and I followed. Before she reached the stairway with him, his head fell to the side. She paused and felt for his pulse. I knew Grandpa was holding his breath like I was while we watched Dorian examine him.

"He's passed out from the hyperventilating," she said. She started to lift him out of the wheelchair. Grandpa shot forward and scooped him into his arms, and then, like carrying a baby, he started up the stairs, Dorian following.

By now, everyone in the house was aware that something terrible had happened. Myra and My Faith came rushing down the hallway. One of the maids appeared behind them. I stood on the bottom step and watched Grandpa and Dorian move up quickly, rushing the boy to his room.

"What happened?" Myra asked me.

"I don't know. We thought it would be nice for him to see us doing the tree and maybe getting him to participate, but when he saw it, he had some kind of emotional crisis," I said.

"Poor child," My Faith said.

No one moved. We just stared at the top of the stairway.

Grandpa finally appeared. "We're calling Dr. Friedman and Dr. Patrick," he said as he descended.

"He's come to. He's all right for now." Everyone stepped back as he turned and headed for his office.

"Just the sight of a Christmas tree did that," Myra muttered.

"He shouted something, but I didn't really understand it."

"What?" My Faith asked.

"It sounded like 'carry' . . . maybe he meant carry him away. What's for sure, I think, is it reminded him of his last Christmas, maybe, or every Christmas. Whatever, it wasn't something nice," I said.

"That poor child, so tormented. He needs plenty of tender loving care," My Faith said.

"Maybe too much," I muttered, but neither of them heard me. I returned to the living room and just sat looking at the naked tree and the decorations on the floor. Grandpa had put the angel on his chair when he rushed out to follow Dorian. It looked like it was staring at me. *So?* I could hear it asking. *Do you want to trick him into telling you everything so you can get rid of him faster and send him back to whatever horror he came from? It looks easy to do now.*

I barely did anything with the tree. Instead, I spent most of the remainder of the afternoon setting up Willie's electric train set, imagining him beside me as I put the little village together and placed the toy people where I thought he would have liked them to be. While I was working, Dr. Friedman and Dr. Patrick arrived and went upstairs. I heard them all gather in Grandpa's office later. I didn't ask any questions or try to be a part of it. I felt myself trembling a little. Did this mean they were going to send him back to the hospital or to some mental clinic? Had they discovered more, and would the police be called?

I imagined them arriving, followed by an ambulance, perhaps, or some vehicle to take him away. The silence that would follow would be deafening. Dorian Camden would pack her bags and be off. The emptiness in the house that I knew Grandpa feared the most would settle in, and those shadows would deepen and darken and come rushing under doors and through windows and rising through the floors to create cobwebs of sorrow and mourning. Whatever energy had returned to the house—to Myra and My Faith and all the servants—would slip away. What I had wanted from the start would happen.

We would all return to mourning Willie.

We would hate the mornings and resist the evenings and sleep.

We would sob through our days and face the winter with only expectations of cold and dreariness. The jingle of bells, the sound of a child's laughter, and joy with the falling snow would be only painful memories. The protective castle walls that Willie and I had imagined around our grandfather's luxurious home would crumble. It would become more like living in a museum. I would live for the day when I could leave.

I heard them all come out of Grandpa's office. Dr. Patrick stopped at the living room to look in on the tree and me.

"This is going to be very pretty," she said. "I have a younger brother, and he used to look forward to setting up his electric trains. Actually, my father was more excited about it."

I looked up at her. I had been sitting on the floor, struggling to recall where every toy person had stood in Willie's village. "I was doing all this for my brother," I said.

"Were you?" She had that face again, the one with microscope lenses for eyes and that all-knowing smile that at first had annoyed me because it made me feel naked. What was more personal to you than your thoughts and feelings? Having those visible made you vulnerable, even helpless. It was like trusting someone to hold your hands in a trapeze act. You were dangling and totally dependent on your partner's grip.

"Maybe for the boy upstairs, too," I confessed.

She changed her all-knowing smile to a warm one. "I suspected that," she said.

"What's happening with him?"

"We'll keep things as they are for the time being," she said. "Physically, he has made good improvements, although his motor skills, his walking in particular, will take time and, as we feared, might never be what they should be."

"And?"

"Some breakthroughs. Right now, they don't make enough sense to act on, but your grandfather's taken control of that part and will be dealing with the search."

"For his parents?"

"Whatever family can be located. He'll tell you

more about that. I have to go." She started to turn away but stopped. "He's still quite fragile mentally. I know it sounds self-serving, but my working through his trauma and fears takes the same skill employed by a brain surgeon. Don't press him too hard. Your boyfriend did well with him, but make sure he understands, too, okay?"

I nodded. She smiled again and left. Dorian walked by with Dr. Friedman, but they didn't stop to speak with me, too occupied with what they were discussing. I heard Dorian go back up the stairs and Dr. Friedman leave the house. Grandpa remained in his office, so I decided to go up the ladder and place the angel at the top of the tree.

"Perfect," I heard Grandpa say just as I finished. "Be careful on the ladder." I started down, and he came over to hold it.

"Dr. Patrick stopped in," I said. "She said he was all right for now."

"Yes. I'm going to see the police detective who has been on the case," he said.

"What did you learn, exactly?" I asked.

He stepped back and sat on the sofa. "I promised Dr. Patrick that you and I wouldn't pursue him on these clues."

"I told her the same."

"Good. Whatever else he says, of course, we'll relay to the police. So . . . when he shouted that word, 'carry,' it seems it's a name probably spelled C-a-r-r-i-e, because it appears to be a girl's name. That's what Dr. Patrick believes."

"A sister?"

"We believe so. He also mentioned a Cathy, but then he called her Momma, so we're unclear if that's another sister or if that is his mother's name. There's also confusion over a name that seems to be his father's but also might be an older brother's."

"He does have an older brother. I knew it," I said.

"We're not absolutely sure yet, Clara Sue. He referred to a Christopher, but the references would be ones you thought meant a father. It's very cloudy."

"But what about his full name?"

"He seems quite reluctant about saying his name. What he gave us as a last name makes no sense."

"What?"

"Doll."

"Doll? Could anyone have a name like that?"

Grandpa shook his head. "I don't know. I guess anything could be a name. I'll give them what we have and hope more comes from him over time. For now, everything will stay as is."

"But what about the poison? Did he say anything, give you any clues to what might have happened?"

He shook his head.

"Why not?"

"Dr. Patrick believes he won't accept that. He'll only accept being sick."

I thought a moment. "So someone he trusted might have done it?"

"Maybe." He paused and then added, "That's what Dr. Patrick thinks."

"How horrible."

"Yeah, it's a mess." He stood up. "Get started if you want. We'll finish after dinner tonight, unless you had other plans. It *is* Saturday night."

"No, I'm staying home to do this. With you," I added. "And we'll have our usual celebration dinner."

He smiled, and then he came over and kissed me on the cheek. "Sometimes I think I'm looking right at your mother and I'm twenty years younger."

The tears that came to my eyes wouldn't let me speak. I watched him leave, and then I turned back to the tree and to Willie's toy village. How could anything so beautiful cause someone to panic?

Where had he been?

What had happened to him?

Did I want to know? Maybe it was better to leave it all in some sort of limbo. On the other hand, what right did I or any of us have to keep him from his family?

Even if they didn't want him? I asked myself.

How could they possibly not want him? But why weren't they looking for him?

Maybe they were all dead.

These gruesome thoughts were discordant notes rung in the presence of our Christmas tree and the electric trains and tiny village. I plugged everything in and watched the trains start around slowly. Willie's look of joy lit up my mind and pushed those dark thoughts away. My doing what he loved brought him back beside me.

Of course, he faded away again.

After you lost someone you loved, memory was a painful thing, even for the dead.

Thornton Wilder was right in his play *Our Town*. We had read it last year aloud in class, and everyone, even the boys, had tears in their eyes when Emily Webb returned to watch the living. The narrator warned her not to. He said the dead gradually lost interest in the living. They went on to something else, and memory only slowed that down. She would only suffer more.

I had to go on to something else.

And maybe Count Piro also had to.

Maybe he would reach out for my hand and let me help him step out of the darkness.

Would I take hold?

18

"How pretty. There's a phone call for you," Myra said. She had come up behind me without my knowing and stood silently for a few moments taking in the work on and around the tree that I had completed.

"The phone rang?"

Aaron had said he would be calling, pressuring me to do something with him, but I thought he would at least wait until tomorrow.

"I guessed that you might be too involved in the tree to hear someone ringing you up, so I answered."

"Thank you, Myra," I said, and went to the phone in the living room.

It wasn't Aaron; it was Lila, and from the sound of excitement in her voice, it was clear she couldn't wait to get to a phone to call me. "Something happen between you and Aaron?" she asked as soon as I said hello. She was breathless. Maybe she had run to the nearest phone.

"Why are you asking?"

"A bunch of us got together at the Meadows for lunch." The Meadows was one of the half dozen upscale restaurants in Prescott that featured a buffet lunch on Saturdays. They had a few rooms for dining, and Prescott teenagers laid claim to one occasionally.

"No one called me about it, not that I could have gone."

"Well, I just assumed you'd be with Aaron, so I didn't call you. I'm sorry."

"That's all right."

I sensed her hesitation in the pause. "Aaron showed up," she blurted.

"And?" Did he start telling everyone what was going on at my home? Most of my classmates avoided the subject of the poisoned boy and what my grandfather was doing for him. At least, they didn't want to ask me questions directly, but I was sure Aaron was enjoying being a source of information about it all. To be fair, I never said he shouldn't say anything. In fact, I had hoped the attention would give Grandpa Arnold second thoughts. But that was all a while ago. I didn't know what I wanted to happen now.

"And almost immediately, he began flirting with Sandra Roth. Vikki Slater is having an open house tonight. I heard Aaron tell Sandra he'd see her there. He made it sound like she should wait for him. Won't you be going?"

"No. No one told me about that, either, but it doesn't matter. My grandfather and I are doing our Christmas tree. It's a tradition for us to have dinner together the night we finish."

"We did ours already. We usually have it up a week or so before Thanksgiving."

"We had some distractions," I said, my voice dripping with sarcasm.

"So what about Aaron? He's not going to see you tonight if you don't come to the party?"

"He'll live," I said.

"What?"

"We're having some serious problems at my home, Lila. My social life is not at the top of the list at the moment."

"Oh, that boy. Your grandfather still wants to keep him there?"

"Yes. Until more is known, at least. My grandfather's constantly checking with the police," I added. "Thanks for calling to cheer me up."

"I thought you'd like to know what's happening," she whined.

"Sometimes it's better to be stupid," I replied.

"You're really weird sometimes."

"I wonder why," I said.

She giggled nervously.

"I have to go, Lila."

"Do you want me to tell you what happens at the party?" she quickly asked.

"Enjoy yourself, Lila. You don't have to be my little spy."

"I'll call you tomorrow," she said, ignoring everything I was saying.

"Whatever," I replied. "Gotta go."

It wasn't until after I hung up that her phone call

bothered me. Was Aaron trying to show me that if I didn't act more obedient, he would move on to someone else? He probably knew Lila or someone else would call to tell me about his flirting with Sandra Roth, especially if he had made it that obvious. Would he go home and wait for my phone call, expecting me to be hurt? If so, he'd wait a long time.

What I had just told Lila was true. As my grandfather would say, my little romance had to take a backseat to what was going on here. Sometimes something was so unimportant in relation to everything else that he would emphasize it by saying, "Not only does that have to take a backseat, that has to go into the trunk for now."

I returned to decorating the tree. I heard Dorian come down the stairs and go to the kitchen and then hurry by again and head back upstairs. She didn't even look in on me. I hoped nothing more was happening. It was like walking on brittle glass around here now. I couldn't help anticipating cries for help or someone shouting, "Get the doctor quickly!"

Myra returned to keep me company.

"Is everything all right upstairs?" I asked.

"Oh, yes. Mrs. Camden just wanted to get him a nice cup of tea with some honey."

"Your influence, I'm sure," I said.

Myra even made fun of herself and the way the British turned to a cup of tea no matter what the problem. "Our main contribution to the civilized world," she joked. She sat on the sofa watching me. While I worked, she told me more stories about her youth, how her family celebrated the holidays, how important a Christmas pudding was to her mother, who was proud of what she had made. Suddenly, she began talking about her older brother, who had died in the First World War. She rarely spoke of him. I always assumed they weren't that close. I pretended to be concentrating on the tree decorations and barely listening, but the truth was, I was hanging on every word. From the way she described him now, it seemed he was more like a second father to her.

"He had a great sense of humor and was so easygoing that he rarely got angry at anyone. He would just give someone who annoyed him a pitiful look, shake his head, and walk away. I always had trouble imagining him on a World War One battlefield. I could see him trying to reason with the enemy pointing a gun at him. He taught me patience. 'Myra,' he would say when I was annoyed, 'you take a breath, count to ten, and reconsider how important that is.' I refused to accept that he had been killed and simply forced myself to believe he was still away. Until the war ended, that is. Others were coming home. I would stand outside our door and imagine him appearing on the street, limping along, maybe, but there in the flesh, proving the report of his death was just a mistake."

All this time, I never really gave thought to the fact that she had lost her brother, too. Of course, she'd had him longer, and the circumstances were different, but it was still the loss of a sibling. Like me, she had to rely on memories. I wondered if they faded and then, when we were older, returned as vividly as she was relating hers now. She, too, must have been very lonely for a while.

"Didn't you ever meet anyone and fall in love, Myra?" I asked her when she paused, sinking back into her reminiscing.

"Oh, I did," she said. "I was engaged, you know."

"I never knew that." I turned to face her. "What happened?"

"Something called the Spanish flu," she said. "Millions died from it after the war."

"Yes, I know. We read about that in history class. What was his name?"

"Brenden," she said. "Brenden Stormfield. He was tall, with light brown hair. He had a mustache that was more auburn, however. And eyes your color and your mother's. His father was a barrister. He had a sister a year younger than me. She married a man in the import-export business and went off to live in India." She smiled. "Pretty little thing."

"Did she ever write to you or anything?"

"No. People are like that, you know. We pass each other like trains in the night. You see a face in a lit window as the train goes by, and you'll never see it again. Oh, listen to me," she said after a moment. "You have me in a chin wag." She stood up. "I've got to see about that problem My Faith was having with the hot water in the kitchen. No one fixes anything right unless you're hovering over him. You're doing a lovely job on that tree. Your grandfather will be proud."

She hurried off. I knew she was making up the chore. She was just embarrassed at how much personal information she had told me, but she had so much to tell. No matter how well we were taught history, nothing compared to hearing her express how it was to live through two wars, especially when she described the bombings in London during the Second World War. Lately, it seemed, she was more forthcoming about the details. I thought she had decided that I was finally old enough to appreciate and understand what it meant to battle for survival. Maybe she thought that was what I was doing now, what we were all doing, battling for survival, especially my grandfather and me.

How lucky I am to have her in my life, I thought, and turned back to the tree with more enthusiasm. About an hour later, Grandpa returned and, just as Myra had predicted, applauded how much I had gotten done.

"It's coming along beautifully," he said. "Better than ever."

Before I could ask him anything about his visit with the police, Dorian stepped in and asked him how it had gone. I wondered if he would tell her anything in my presence. He glanced at me first and then began.

"They're circulating the new information. A check was done on outstanding police bulletins, but there was nothing meeting William's description or situation. I'm bringing my man back into it," he added. He meant his private detective. I was surprised at how determined he was to find out what he could and perhaps, as a result, have Count Piro returned to his family after all.

"He's doing a lot better," Dorian said. "However, I

think tonight I'll bring his dinner up and sit with him. He's still so fragile emotionally."

"He's lucky to have you, Dorian," Grandpa told her. She smiled, and then, when she turned to leave, he followed her out, and they spoke in whispers in the hallway.

I didn't have all that much left to hang on the tree. I went back at it, and while I worked, I had Willie's electric trains run over the tracks and through the model village. When he and I had worked on the tree together, we were just as silent as I was now, both of us concentrating too hard on what we were doing. But it was in that silence that we tightened our love and dependence on each other. There was always joy in Christmas, but this year, the joy heightened the ache in my heart. It would be a battle to smile and laugh. On Christmas morning, there would be a gaping space under the tree where Willie's presents normally would be. Did Grandpa think he could fill it with presents for Count Piro? I hoped not. Was that mean?

"Sorry I wasn't here to help more," Grandpa said when he returned and interrupted my musing. "Can't believe how much you did and how perfect it looks."

"Kept my mind off things. Holidays bring smiles and tears," I said.

"Yes," Grandpa said. "We'll try for more smiles. Say," he continued, looking around as if someone could be hiding behind the furniture, "where's that young man of yours today? Why wasn't he here to help?"

"He's not my young man, Grandpa. We've just been dating a little."

"Oh?" He lifted his eyebrows. "When I was your age, seeing a girl as many times as he's seen you meant marriage was just around the corner."

"It did not. You could fill a zeppelin," I said, which was how Grandma Arnold used to check him when he exaggerated. He laughed and fiddled with one of the silver balls that had yet to be hung. He looked at me to see if I approved of where he was placing it. I nodded.

"Okay, but don't expect advice to the lovelorn from me," he said. "I know more about trucks than I do about women. Trucks are less moody. Maybe Dorian can help there. I imagine she'd be more helpful about such things than Myra or My Faith."

Since we were being so honest with each other all of a sudden, I grew brave. "You seem to know how to please Dorian," I said, and held my breath. Would he growl back at me?

"She's settled in a groove, just like me. We're two of a kind," he replied instead.

"Yes," I said. I felt how he was studying me. He knew that at the start, I wasn't fond of how quickly she had become part of our lives, but I didn't have those feelings now. "You're right. She's very nice and more than just some private-duty nurse."

"She is," he agreed. I waited to see if he would add anything more, but he decided to change the subject. "I'm going to be really hungry tonight," he said, slapping his hands together. "You're having dinner here, right?"

"It's Christmas tree dinner," I said, and his smile

deepened. Was it possible? Was it possible that happiness and love could return to this house?

"I'll take a picture of this one," he said when we had finished the decorating. "We'll call this Clara Sue's tree."

"It's our tree, Grandpa. You picked it out, didn't you?"

He reached out to put his arm around my shoulders and pulled me closer for one of his William Arnold hugs, practically lifting me off my feet and planting a kiss on the top of my head. Then he started out. "Got to get ready for dinner," he said. "I'll wear that Christmas shirt your grandmother bought me a while back."

I turned off the electric trains and slowly followed him up the stairs. Count Piro's door was open. I looked in, expecting to see Dorian, but instead, I saw only him in his wheelchair, his back to the door as he gazed out the window. I wondered what he was thinking. Was he regretting that he couldn't be out there like Willie often was, maybe wearing his Superman cape and rushing about chasing imaginary villains? Or was he thinking about his lost family? Did he dream of going out our gate and home?

His shoulders were hoisted a little as if he had a cold breeze at the back of his neck. He was clutching the arms of his wheelchair like someone who was about to rise out of it and stand on his own. His arms were tightening, extending.

That's exactly what he's hoping to do, I thought. I watched and held my breath. He had his feet on the floor and was beginning to rise. *Oh, do it*, I thought. *Stand on your own two feet, and begin your journey home.*

He rose higher, his arms extending and tightening further. I heard him groan with the effort. He leaned forward as he rose, and then, when he was just about out of his chair and on his feet, he toppled over to the right and fell to the floor, collapsing as if his bones were only pipe cleaners. He moaned, but he didn't cry. I rushed to him.

"Are you all right?" I asked, kneeling beside him and taking his right hand.

He gazed up at me. I saw no pain in his face, no physical pain. Instead, there was sorrow and loneliness, a look of desperate solitude, the look of someone chained to a wall, shut up in a room without windows, and confined to the sound of only his thoughts. Even his voice had disappeared. His lips moved ever so slightly, and then he whispered. I drew closer to hear him.

"Cathy," I heard him say softly. "Momma."

I put my arms under his and lifted him. It wasn't difficult, because he was so light. As carefully as I could, I got him back into his chair. Should I run for Dorian? I wondered. She was probably in her room, maybe in the bathroom. Instead, I fixed his feet on the footrests of the wheelchair, brushed back his hair, and checked to see if he had bruised himself. He watched me silently. Then he turned to look out the window again.

I sat on the floor with my back to the wall and

looked up at him. He didn't look at me, and he didn't cry. *This is a special moment*, I thought. *Take advantage of it.*

"Where do you want to go?" I asked.

When he looked at me, I thought for sure he was going to answer, but just then, Dorian returned.

"What's happening?" she asked, smiling.

He turned to her as she approached.

"I was walking by, and I saw him try to get up and then fall out of the chair," I said, rising. "I got him back on it and hung around to be sure he was all right."

"Oh. Are you hurt, honey?" she asked him.

He shook his head.

She looked at me. "Very good, Clara Sue."

I considered her and then made an instant decision, turning back to him. "I'm sorry you were upset when you saw my Christmas tree, Count Piro. I've finished it now, and I hope you'll look at it again. It was a lot of work, and the electric trains are set up, too. I can show you how to work them," I added forcefully, looked defiantly at Dorian, and walked out of the room.

Was I in bigger trouble now? Would my grandfather come rushing in to bawl me out? When I entered my room, I closed the door behind me and sprawled on my bed. I had so many different emotions battling to be acknowledged that I felt like I was in a tornado. Should I be ashamed of my relationship with Aaron Podwell? Had I made a fool of myself by believing in him so quickly? Should I be more angry than ashamed? Could I pretend to be indifferent, or would anyone look at me and see hurt in my face?

Was I wrong now not to feel guilty about caring for Count Piro? Was this a betrayal of Willie's memory?

Could I stand having my grandfather be angry at me again? Was I losing everyone's love?

Was it wrong to look forward to the holidays? Should I have refused to work on the tree? Should I have insisted that no one touch Willie's trains and toy village? Was I pushing the memory of him farther and farther away? Would my parents hate me? Grandma Arnold?

Should I be crying or screaming?

I pounded the bed and then folded my arms under my breasts and stared defiantly at the ceiling, gathering up my fury and not only waiting for my grandfather to come to my room but hoping he would. I'd give it back as quickly as he dished it out. Rage seemed to be winning.

There was a knock on my door. I didn't say anything. I pulled myself up against my pillows and waited. The door opened, and Dorian stood there, smiling.

"What now?" I snapped at her.

"You did it," she said. "He wants to go down to see the tree and the trains."

She turned and walked away, and the rage that had been flowing through my veins like boiling water instantly cooled. I rose slowly and went to the doorway. Dorian was wheeling Count Piro out and toward the stair lift. I stood watching until he was securely put into the lift and descending. Then I followed slowly.

Grandpa came out of his room, too, and followed behind me. When we reached the living room, Myra and My Faith came in from the kitchen to watch. Dorian wheeled him closer to the tree. She stopped and waited. Everyone's eyes were on him as he looked at the tree. I think we were all holding our breath. The seconds ticked like a clock set to trigger an explosion. Suddenly, Grandpa shot forward and plugged in the tree lights. Myra and My Faith gasped in appreciation as the tree burst into its beautiful colors.

I stepped up and glanced at Count Piro. His eyes had widened when the tree was lit. I went over to the train control and turned it on. He was fascinated with its movements through the tunnels and up and down the small inclines, past the houses and the train depot to go around again. I nodded at Dorian, and she wheeled him closer. I put the control in his lap.

"Just make it go faster or slower with this little lever," I explained. "You can also make it stop anytime you want."

He touched it gingerly and then gently moved the lever to speed it up. His eyes were dazzling with glee. He slowed it down and then stopped it and looked at me.

"Very good," I said.

He smiled and started the train again. Grandpa watched from behind, nodded at Dorian, and then turned and went back upstairs to finish dressing for dinner.

"Maybe we'll stay downstairs and eat at the table tonight, right, William?" she asked him.

He looked at her and then at me. I nodded, and he nodded. He went back to the train, and Dorian exchanged a look of pleasure with me.

"I'll stay with him for a while," I told her. "Go get ready for dinner."

"You sure?"

"Absolutely," I said.

Myra was beaming, and My Faith was shaking her head with joy.

I sat by the train tracks and shifted some of the toy people about, talking about them and the village the way I used to with Willie, imagining their comments about Christmas and their businesses and families. He looked fascinated with everything, dividing his attention between me and the trains. About twenty minutes later, Dorian and my grandfather came down the stairs. He was in the shirt he had said he would wear, but there was something about the dress Dorian was wearing that looked familiar.

"Your dress," I said to her, standing and looking at Grandpa.

He nodded. He didn't have to say it. It was one of Grandma Arnold's dresses.

I hurried out and up the stairs. It was as if the pages of a book about my family were being turned, and on every new page, a face was changed. I paused at Willie's room and recalled the moment when I saw Grandpa Arnold gazing into it and contemplating bringing Count Piro to our home and into Willie's room. The shock that I had felt seemed to have dwindled. I was thinking more of Count Piro than myself.

After all, his family book's pages were turning as fast as mine were, and all the faces he knew were disappearing, too. Perhaps he and I were more like a brother and a sister than I would like us to be.

There was nothing left to do but wait to see how our stories ended.

19

Our Christmas tree dinner was the happiest dinner we'd had since Willie's death. There wasn't the heavy tension and sadness invading every sentence and battling back every smile. Count Piro ate better than ever, and faster, too, because he wanted to get back to the trains. Grandpa and Dorian talked more about their pasts. They were so into their conversations that sometimes it was as if they were alone at the table. We did talk more about Thanksgiving and Christmas, which started Dorian describing some of her happier holidays. I realized that she, too, was still often mourning the loss of people she had loved in her past.

"Love has a way of making memories sticky," she said, and Grandpa laughed. I began to suspect that what she and Grandpa Arnold were sharing of their pasts was bringing them closer to what might be their future.

After dinner, I returned to the living room and

helped Count Piro work the trains and maneuver some of the toy people that I gave names to, just as I did when I played with Willie. Dorian and Grandpa sat together on the sofa enjoying an after-dinner cordial and watching us, but I sensed that they were really more interested in each other. I was still a little jealous, but I had to admit that Dorian was making Grandpa more mellow.

When Dorian thought it was time to take Count Piro up to bed, I returned to my room and started to do some of my homework just to keep my mind off everything else, but it proved impossible. My eyes drifted from the pages I had to read, and I read and reread the same sentences. Finally, I put it all away and took out my stationery.

Dear Willie,

So much has happened so quickly since I visited you at the cemetery. I didn't want to like the poisoned boy, and as you know, I hated that he was using and enjoying your things. But I keep remembering how happy you were sharing your toys with friends. I'm sure now that if you were here, you would be friends.

He's very sad and helpless, Willie. I think he misses his family as much as you might be missing Grandpa and me. Grandpa is trying to find his family again. I hope for the boy's sake he does. Everyone should be with his or her family, don't you think?

*But until then, don't be angry at me for
pretending at least that I'm like his older sister.
I'm sure now that it will help him get stronger
and better and maybe even walk again. Just
because bad things happen to you, that doesn't
mean you have to be mean. Right?*

*Most of all, Willie, I'm afraid. I'm afraid
of being alone, afraid of not having anyone to
love me.*

*Maybe that's why the boy is the way he is,
Willie. He has the same fear.*

Clara Sue

As before, I folded the letter, stuck it in an envelope,
and put it in the drawer with the others. Then I went
to bed, and somehow, despite the roller coaster of
emotions I rode all day, I fell asleep dreaming of my
family together on a Christmas morning years and
years before even the thought of any sadness was born.

In the morning, My Faith went off to work at her
church, and Myra and I started on breakfast. Dorian,
who had gotten the Count up and dressed, joined us
to help cut up fruit. He watched us from the doorway.
While they made the pancakes and eggs, I set the table.
Grandpa came down and was pleased to see Count
Piro sitting with us again. While we ate, we planned
what we would put out for Christmas decorations.
Although everyone agreed we should have some, there
was the sense that we would be more subdued than
usual. Grandpa said he would take us shopping before

Thanksgiving. He and Dorian planned on speaking to the doctors about Count Piro going along. I wondered, *If Grandpa gives him money to spend, will he think about his lost family and reveal more, or will it make him sadder?*

Afterward, I did work on my term paper, but Lila, who had gotten up late, called to give me her blow-by-blow description of Vikki Slater's party.

"Now, I can't swear to what happened," she said when she got to Aaron, which was her whole purpose for the call, "but he and Sandra disappeared for almost an hour, and she looked like the cat who ate the canary when she and Aaron came back."

"You have it wrong. He was the cat. She was the canary," I said.

"What? Oh," she said, and laughed. "I'm sorry. Are you very upset about it?"

"Only at myself," I told her. She didn't understand, and I didn't feel like going into a long explanation. I changed the topic to our homework, which ended the phone call quicker.

For a while after, I sat thinking about Aaron. Should I be upset only at myself for being innocent and trusting? Should I forgive him? I wasn't very nice to him. Didn't I drive him away after all? Wasn't I the one giving mixed signals, encouraging him to help me get Count Piro out of our lives and then resenting him for planning how to do it?

It wasn't hard to see why he might have thought I liked him much more than I had liked any other boy, why I was promising to be special, too, being more intimate with him than I had been with any other boy. Or was that really something special to a boy like Aaron? If he had done it with Sandra last night, was doing it as special to him as it would be to me? Should I be the same way he was, casual, almost indifferent about sex?

I heard Dorian in the hallway and looked out. She was starting away from the Count's room, her head down. She looked a little tired, but I stepped out impulsively and called to her. She paused and looked back at me.

"Something wrong?" she asked.

I nodded.

She smiled. "C'mon," she said, holding out her hand. "We'll talk in my room."

For some time, I hadn't been in the room my parents always used. It was easy to picture them there. Sometimes when Willie was still just a baby and we were visiting Grandpa and Grandma Arnold, I would rush to them and crawl into the bed to lie between them as soon as I woke up. Those were precious stolen moments before Willie would wake and command my mother's full attention. For those minutes, I was like an only child again.

Wasn't that what I was now?

"So," Dorian said, sitting in the antique gray wing-back chair Grandma Arnold had bought especially for this bedroom. My mother enjoyed sitting in it and reading one of her magazines or a novel, especially on rainy days. "What's troubling you, Clara Sue?" she asked softly.

"At what age were you no longer a virgin?" I asked. The abruptness of my question and my standing there with my arms folded under my breasts, stiff-postured like an attorney cross-examining a witness, stunned her for a moment. I thought she would get angry and order me out or something, but instead, she smiled.

"Things were different when I was your age. You'd never know it from the way women my age behave nowadays, especially when it comes to their own daughters. You'd think they were living in the Victorian age. Anyway, by 1928, I was seventeen. That was what people often refer to as the Roaring Twenties. Yes, hard to believe, I know, but I was a flapper, to my mother's displeasure, I might add. Women had gotten the right to vote, and there had already been something of a sexual revolution going on. We had romances, but for the most part, my girl-friends and I didn't, as you guys say, go the whole way. At least, I didn't until I was in my twenties and it was my first real hot-and-heavy romance. I thought it was inevitable that we'd get married."

"But you didn't?"

"Not to him, no. There were some complications. His family was pressuring him to find someone more suitable from a wealthier family."

"How did you feel? Betrayed? Stupid?"

"Both for a little while, but I got over it when I met my husband."

"Did he care?"

"He wouldn't come out and say it, but he cared. I guess every man wants to be his girl's first, but it wasn't enough to sour our romance. I will tell you I was glad I wasn't totally inexperienced. When I realized that, I regretted my first serious romance less, and then I read somewhere that a romance without sex is only imaginary. And I knew women who saved themselves for marriage and never got married. They weren't nuns, either. I know this is all confusing, but the decision has to be very personal and shouldn't be based on what everyone else is doing or did, Clara Sue."

"How do you know when a boy really likes you, as opposed to just doing it with you?"

"Wow." She thought a moment. "The problem is that for that moment or that time, it could be both. It's not whether he really likes you, I suppose. It's for how long he will before he really likes someone else."

"So you don't believe in Romeo and Juliet?"

"One person out there for everyone? I suppose it happens. It doesn't hurt to believe in it unless you reject everyone because you're waiting for all sorts of bells and whistles that might never come. You have to have confidence in yourself, the confidence that you'll know when someone right for you happens."

"The parents of one of our girlfriends are getting a divorce because her father cheated on her mother. I bet they thought they'd be in love forever."

"That's sad. I feel sorrier for your girlfriend than her parents, though. We don't know what sort of relationship her parents have or had, so it's hard to make conclusions. My Faith likes to say, 'Judge not that you be not judged.' I think she's probably right." She paused, her eyelids narrowing. "This boyfriend of yours, Aaron Podwell, he's pretty sophisticated, huh? He's kind of smooth."

"And proud of it. You realized that, huh?"

She smiled. "You have to be a little suspicious when they're that perfect. Listen to your own voices, Clara Sue, not his and not anyone else's. Whatever decision you make, it will be yours and, I'm sure, right for you." She was silent a moment. "I guess I'm not much help, huh?"

"No. You are," I said. "Thanks."

"Thanks for trusting me enough to ask me," she said, and stood up. "You're quite a girl, Clara Sue. You're stronger than you think."

I gazed into her eyes. Was I? She looked sincere. Before I turned to leave, she embraced me, gave me a hug and a kiss, and stepped back. I didn't say anything. I glanced at the bed my parents used to sleep in, imagining them there listening and agreeing, and then I walked out.

All the remainder of the day, I anticipated Aaron calling. I rehearsed how I would sound and what I would say. I went from total forgiveness to indifference to anger, especially as the day waned and it was becoming clear to me that he expected I would call him and not vice versa. Perhaps my not calling convinced him that I was angry about him being with Sandra and he was sorry and didn't know how to react. Or maybe he had decided to move on. I was tempted to call him to see which way he would go. In the end, I went to sleep thinking it was better to just let things happen.

In the morning, before I went out to get into the

car to be taken to school, I anticipated a phone call or perhaps the bell at the gate to be sounded and to see him coming around to pick me up, but that didn't happen. Grandpa had left for work, and Dorian was busy with a full day for Count Piro: physical examinations, his physical therapy, and then finally perhaps bringing him to the living room to enjoy the trains.

I wouldn't deny that I was very nervous, especially when I entered the building alone and paused for a few seconds to see if Aaron would suddenly appear. He didn't, so I went on to homeroom. Lila was already there, chatting with the other girls. From the looks on their faces when they saw me, I knew I was the hot topic. Sandra wasn't sitting with them. She was talking to Billy Gibson, but she turned to give me a smile of self-satisfaction. I tried to look as indifferent as I could, but with everyone throwing questions my way, it was difficult.

"No, Aaron and I hadn't broken up, because we weren't officially going steady. No, he didn't call to apologize. He had nothing to apologize for if we weren't going steady, right?"

Nothing I could say would satisfy them, but my seeming not to care enough to sound mournful started them on other topics. I had yet to see Aaron. When the bell rang for us to go to our first class, I anticipated him waiting for Sandra in the hall, as he would for me, but he wasn't there for her, either. She walked off with Billy as if they were the two who had been together Saturday night, but then again, she was like that with almost any boy in the school.

I didn't see Aaron until after the second morning class. It was only the two-minute break, but what I noticed was that he wasn't paying any more attention to Sandra than he was to me. He didn't even look my way.

Later, at lunch, however, he stepped up behind me as I entered the cafeteria with Lila and Audrey and hooked my right arm to pull me aside.

"I like how cool you're being," he said. "Makes you sexier."

"I don't feel sexier, but I guess we all see what we want."

"I thought you might call yesterday," he said, now with what, for him, was an uncharacteristically insecure smile.

"Did you?" I asked. I did to him what I had seen Myra do many times to a maid or someone working on the estate who had obviously done something wrong. She would hold her gaze like a spotlight on them without speaking or changing her expression. Any excuse or denial would choke up in their throats.

He kept talking, now nervously. "I thought you said you would be too busy, so I figured you should be the one to call. Because of you, I did all my homework and studied for an English test. You're having a bad influence on me," he added, trying to be funny now. "I had a miserable weekend."

"I heard how heartbroken you were," I said.

He started to laugh but stopped. "A long time ago, I decided no girl was going to turn me into a monk."

"You have nothing to worry about, Aaron. That can't happen to you."

Now he did laugh. "Let's get some lunch," he said. "Smoke the peace pipe or something. You don't want everyone to think you're jealous or really mad at me, do you?"

"They won't."

I could feel all the eyes on us as we stood there talking.

"I like a lot about you, Aaron. I really do. I think you can be a decent person when you finally decide who you want to be and what's really important."

"You're important," he said quickly.

Now I smiled. "You're probably going to be very successful, Aaron, more successful maybe than your father. But you'll always have a problem with something, I'm afraid."

"With what?" he asked, now getting a little annoyed.

"Mirrors," I said, then squeezed his arm gently and walked off to join the girls.

It was odd. I should have been shaking, upset, maybe close to tears, but I felt older, stronger, like someone who had been through a very difficult challenge and now stood straighter. It was as though everything around me was becoming clear and revealing what should be a priority and what shouldn't, what I should take seriously and what I should shrug off. Most everyone else in my school had the same great advantages that I had. Some would do great things because of that, and some wouldn't, also because of that. Their lives were too perfect, too soft. The world would become almost intolerable when they were confronted with the many frustrations and difficulties just everyday living could bring.

I knew that all these thoughts were things that should have been waiting for me later on in life. I shouldn't have been such an adult, but it wasn't years that changed you; it was events, losses and struggles, more significant happiness and contentment, and finally, more responsibility, especially for someone besides yourself. Aaron had a long way to go to reach where I was. Maybe he never would. Right now, he lived for instant pleasure and didn't have the patience that a relationship required. I had been thinking he was more sophisticated than I was, but I was suddenly more mature. There was no doubt in my mind that if he had been closer to what I was now, I would have made love to him many times over. And then if we had parted in the near future and found someone else we could love, we would have been all right with it.

In moments, I was back in the thick of things, and as hard as it was for my girlfriends to comprehend, I was happy. Actually, they seemed in awe of me because of how I was acting. I felt more bounce in my walk. I was more alert in class, volunteering answers more than I had for the past few weeks, and other boys who had been hesitant were talking to me between classes. Even though ten days ago, I didn't think it would be possible, I actually looked forward to Thanksgiving and especially to Christmas, because Uncle Bobby was coming.

The happier, more relaxed atmosphere continued right through the Thanksgiving holiday. Dr. Patrick, however, did not think Count Piro was up to buying presents for anyone, so Grandpa and I went shopping on our own. Since my parents' deaths, he was dependent on me to buy just the right things for Myra and My Faith and something for his personal secretary, Mrs. Mallen. He decided to buy Uncle Bobby a new watch and wanted my opinion on the possibilities.

This time, he wanted my opinion about a gift for Dorian, too. He was looking for practical things. I told him a woman doesn't want a practical thing, she wants a beautiful thing. He laughed, and we went to the jewelry department, where I picked out a pair of earrings and a matching necklace I thought she would appreciate; the rubies would complement her eyes and hair. He didn't hesitate.

After that, we bought some toys for Count Piro. It was painful, because I kept imagining that we were buying them for Willie. Before we left the department store, we split up to buy each other a present. He appeared with three boxes, one from the jewelry department and the other two from clothing.

"I confess," he said, "I had some advice for this."

I knew he meant Dorian. *What will happen*, I wondered, *when Count Piro either is gone or no longer needs her?* I couldn't get up the courage to ask him. Maybe I didn't want to hear the answer.

The days between Thanksgiving and Christmas were always busier than usual. Our teachers seemed in a panic to catch up with their curriculums before the big vacation break. We had more homework, more quizzes and papers due. The school always had a Christmas party traditionally organized by the student government. Every class member had to contribute something for the decorations. Rumors had been swirling about Aaron the week before. Apparently, through some friends of his parents, he had met a girl from Charlottesville and was driving there on weekends to see her. As it turned out, he didn't attend our Christmas party. Although three different senior boys asked me to the party, including the Troy Donahue lookalike, Winston Kettner, I decided to go with Lila and pretend it was like a dance party years ago, when boys had to write their names on a girl's dance card.

On the Saturday before our Christmas break, Grandpa surprised me by asking me to take a ride with him immediately after breakfast. When I asked him where we were going, he just said, "We'll worry about it when we get there." Of course, I was curious, so I went along and soon realized that he was driving us to the cemetery. We parked and started toward Willie's grave. I didn't have to go too far to see why.

Willie's monument had been installed.

I stopped walking, and Grandpa turned to me.

"I wanted you and me to visit it together first, Clara Sue. I hope you approve of what I had done," he said.

I swallowed back the empty but painful feeling that had risen from somewhere inside me, a feeling always there but subdued enough to let me go on with my life. It had to be resurrected now. I nodded, and we approached.

Grandpa had ordered a black marble headstone shaped like a heart. A cherub was resting at the top of it, with a hand reaching down over the stone as if comforting Willie. The cherub's face wasn't sad. It had an angelic smile.

Willie's name was inscribed as "William Sanders," with "Willie" beneath that. The next lines read "Beloved Son, Brother, and Grandson" and then his dates. There was one more line.

"I got advice from My Faith for the inscription," Grandpa said.

It read: "Unless you turn and become like children, you will never enter the Kingdom of Heaven."

"Oh, Grandpa," I said, tears warming my cheeks. "It's beautiful."

He put his arm around my shoulders, and we stood there silently for a few moments. We left in silence and drove home in silence. Myra and My Faith and even Dorian were aware of where we had gone. We all hugged, and then My Faith insisted that I learn how to make the chocolate swirl angel-food cake my grandfather loved.

"Myra's no cook or baker, and I'm gettin' along in years," she claimed. "I could use some assistance once in a while."

I knew why she was trying to keep me busy. Dorian gave me a knowing look and a smile, too. But I didn't have much time to fall back into sadness and mourning, anyway. The second surprise of the day arrived just before dinner: Uncle Bobby. He burst in like a breath of fresh air. He was full of excitement. His Broadway opportunity had been solidified. Even Grandpa uncharacteristically listened to his stories about show business and asked good questions at dinner. The conversation between them was going back and forth so fast that I thought I was watching a Ping-Pong game. Count Piro was intrigued by all the chatter and had to be continually reminded to eat.

The first week of my Christmas holiday was filled with activities and short trips to see Christmas decorations and store windows. Uncle Bobby was working on his choreography, and during the afternoons, he would let Count Piro and me watch him creating new steps and moves. Count Piro looked fascinated with it all, and then, one afternoon, without any prodding, he turned to me and said out of the blue, "Cathy dances, too." It was as if he and I had been talking about his past for days.

Uncle Bobby heard him say it, but he just looked at me cautiously. He had spent time with Dorian and Grandpa and was updated on Count Piro's recuperation, especially how to handle him. Dorian wasn't in the room at the time.

"Is Cathy your sister or your mother?" I asked him.

"Sister," he said.

"Where is she now?"

He looked at me. "With Christopher and Carrie," he said.

Uncle Bobby stopped dancing. "Careful," he whispered.

"Where are they, Count?"

He shook his head. His eyes were starting to tear. I looked helplessly at Uncle Bobby. Any moment, the Count could have an episode.

"Hey," Uncle Bobby said quickly. "What do you think of this?" He did a twist, a kick, and then a split. Count Piro smiled again. "I can do it backward," Uncle Bobby told him, and he did so. His smile widened, and his tears receded. I breathed with relief.

Afterward, I told Dorian everything, and then the three of us met with Grandpa in his office.

"I'll get the information to my guy and to the police," he said. "Maybe we can finally get to the bottom of it all."

However, days passed, and nothing new happened. Dr. Patrick had some more sessions with Count Piro, but she didn't share the results with anyone but Grandpa. When I asked, he merely said, "We're making progress."

We exchanged presents on Christmas morning. Count Piro was there for it all and overjoyed with his gifts. Our Christmas dinner was as wonderful as ever. The following morning, we had our first snow of the year. It was light but enough to create the winter wonderland that Willie had loved. Like Willie, Count Piro was eager to go out and feel the flakes on his face. Dorian bundled him up, and we took him for a short turn down the driveway and back.

Later that day, Uncle Bobby came to my room to say good-bye.

"I think all of this is on the verge of some sort of

resolution, Clara Sue," he began. We were all aware of how Dr. Patrick's sessions with the Count had intensified during the past few days. "I think you've done a terrific job of handling the situation. Dad's been the happiest I've seen him in a long time."

"Might not only be my doing," I said, and he smiled.

"Yes, I know. She's very nice, and she's gotten him almost housebroken."

I laughed. Then I stopped and took his hand. "Everything's changed so much, Uncle Bobby. I miss everyone so much, too."

"I know. All you can do is keep busy and try to make them proud of who you are and who you will be. Now, listen," he said, eager to change the topic. "You'll be coming to New York for sure. My father and I agree on that. Maybe all three of you will be coming."

"I'd like that so much."

"Me, too."

We hugged, and he started out. Then he paused in the doorway. "A good-bye is just the curtain closing for this evening's performance. It will open again," he said, and performed a sweeping bow, threw me a kiss, and went off.

I couldn't help feeling that he was right.

The curtain had come down on Act I.

Now, for Act II.

Epilogue

Perhaps the most magical thing in our lives is time. Sometimes it passes quickly; seconds cascade into minutes, minutes into hours, and hours into days, like a flooded stream tearing its way down a mountain and through a valley. It seems impossible to hold it back. Daily routines help. It's the empty spaces that make hours longer than they are. Waiting for the next thing to do is like waiting for a train or a bus. My Faith liked to say, "A watched pot never boils." The more you anticipate, the longer it takes.

Count Piro's days ironically were fuller than mine, so time passed quickest for him. He went from his homeschooling to his therapy to his meals and playtime. More often now, Dorian took him out, and Grandpa and she took him for rides when I was at school. Grandpa bought him a sled when the snow was heavier, and he enjoyed being pulled around on the property. Jimmy and some of the other employees took a liking to him and pulled him around, too.

He was filling out, growing stronger, and then, one day in early March, with his therapist's help, he began to use crutches. He could stand for a while, but moving forward was still a problem. Dr. Friedman was happy with his progress, but he wasn't confident that he would ever toss away those crutches or not need a wheelchair from time to time. Going up stairs was still a huge problem.

I began to help him with his homework and still read to him occasionally. The same rules applied to how to handle him and his memories. I understood that Dr. Patrick had made some important inroads, and little bits and pieces about his past began to dribble out to me. But there was nothing yet that would bring his ordeal to a conclusion.

At least, that was what I believed for the longest time.

And then I started to notice that Grandpa was in deep thought and spent a lot of time in his office after work. Sometimes I caught him looking at me as if he was about to say something, and when I looked at him, he shook his head and moved off to do something else.

The night before my seventeenth birthday, he came to my room. Myra, Count Piro, and I had eaten dinner together. Grandpa and Dorian had gone out to dinner. They had been doing that more often, but this time, they had been talking about me. I knew it from how quickly he had come to my room when they returned. He knocked on the door and peered in when I said, "Come in."

"Got a few minutes?" he asked.

"I'll try to pull away from this math problem," I replied.

He smiled, came in, and closed the door softly behind him. I was at my desk. He sat on my bed.

"What's up?"

I was expecting him to tell me that he had decided to ask Dorian Camden to marry him. I had already decided to be happy for him, but as it turned out, that wasn't his primary reason for visiting me.

"I'm going to tell you a story," he began, "and then I'm going to ask you what you think we should do about it. If you don't want to answer now, that's fine. You don't have to decide immediately. Okay?"

I closed my book and turned completely around. "Yes, Grandpa."

"Once upon a time, there was a family of four, an older brother somewhere between thirteen and fourteen, an older sister twelve or thirteen, and twins about five or six, let's say. They seemed to be a happy family, but something terrible happened to the father, and not long afterward, they left their home, went on a train somewhere at night, and went to a big house owned by their grandparents. As weird as this sounds, they were shut up in a room and an attic and, from what we can tell, were there like that for years."

"Years?"

"Maybe three or more. Their mother did not live in these rooms with them. She visited them, brought them presents, but never took them out."

"How could any mother do that?"

He nodded. "Yes, how could any mother do that? The older brother and the older sister tried to take care of the twins as best they could, and the twins eventually saw them more as parents."

"But they were so young. How could they act like parents?"

"Maybe they had no choice."

"And the grandparents let this go on, too?"

"It's confusing, but it seems so."

"They weren't proud of them or happy about them?"

"I don't know the reasons, Clara Sue. I know only this much. Whatever was brought for them to eat eventually contained arsenic. Too much over too long a time was consumed for it to be a one-time, accidental thing."

I felt a chill. I had to take a breath. "But who would do that to them? Their own mother, their grandmother?"

"No one else brought them food. I don't know much more. This has taken months to put together from answers William has given to Dr. Patrick. She had to figure out most of it. Besides the trauma of being poisoned, he was undernourished, as you know, and it is coming from a child's memory."

I knew Grandpa wasn't telling me all this to make me feel bad about the way I had treated Count Piro, but I couldn't help it. "Where are the rest of them now?"

"I don't know. So far, there's no trace of such a

family in our immediate area or even the state. The thing is, I was thinking of giving up the search for them, for the answers."

I stared at him. I realized he wanted my approval for no longer trying to find Count Piro's real family. He would be permanently a member of ours.

"I don't think I could send him back to that world, if it's out there."

"What about him, Grandpa, what he wants?"

"I think he's happy here."

"But his brother and sisters?"

"I don't know. Maybe they'll turn up someday, maybe not."

"Maybe they were all poisoned?"

"If not by arsenic, by their horrible imprisonment."

"He doesn't cry for them when he talks to Dr. Patrick?"

"Mostly for his twin sister, but even that is less and less. You've become more of a sister to him these days," he added. "That's very kind of you."

"Who knows about all this?"

"You, me, Dorian, and of course Dr. Patrick."

"Myra doesn't know?"

He shook his head.

"So it's all a big secret?"

"Yes."

"And you want it to always be?"

He pressed his lips together and nodded.

Oh, Willie, I thought, *you really are gone.*

"He can't replace Willie, Grandpa. I can't think of

him as Willie, no matter what he's called and what we give him of Willie's."

"He won't replace Willie. Willie will always be in our hearts and minds. He's his own person and will grow into his own identity. For now, being William helps him adjust to this world, this life. Like I said, you don't have to give me an answer right now. This is a family decision, and I won't make it without you."

"What did Dorian say?"

He smiled. "She said it was time to ask you." He stood up.

"You're going to marry her, aren't you?" I asked.

"Would that bother you?"

"Not if you don't take too much longer to do it," I replied.

He smiled and nodded at my desk. "Sorry to take you away from math," he said, and left laughing.

I didn't return to my math.

I went to my window and looked out at the snow-covered grounds and the trees whose leafless branches glittered in the moonlight. I imagined Willie down there pulling his sled up the drive to take another run. I was at the bottom waiting for him to be sure he was all right. I was always looking after him one way or another.

It didn't surprise me that Count Piro's older sister had become more like a mother to him. She and I were quite alike in that way. From what Grandpa was telling me, it was as if she had lost her parents completely and had no choice but to grow older faster.

Did she miss him as much as I missed Willie?
Wouldn't she want him to be safe and happy?

Please, she would say, if she could call me, *let him be your secret brother now.*

"Yes," I whispered. "I promise he will be."